COLLEEN GLEASON

THREE TOMES BOOKSHOP

D1453337

TOMES SCONES AND CRONES

Published by Oliver-Heber Books

0 9 8 7 6 5 4 3 2 1

 Created with Vellum

PROLOGUE

Three women gathered around a large elliptical mirror that rested on the table in front of them. They were all looking down into its surface.

Wisps of something like fog curled delicately from the mirror's surface, rising in tendrils and then dissipating into the air. The faint, pleasant scent of something floral and pungent filled the room, steaming from a cauldron that hung over a fireplace. Bundles of herbs hung from the ceiling to dry, and there were rows and rows of jars on a set of shelves on one wall. The jars were neatly labeled with things like *Lavender, Butcher's-Broom, Monkwort, Cedar Fronds,* and more. Knives, athames, mortar and pestle sets, bowls, and similar tools cluttered the countertops.

"So that's her," said one of the three women. "Jacqueline Finch." She was slender, with sharp, elfin features and short, spiky hair, currently ink-black tipped with purple. Her skin was golden, and hardly sagged or wrinkled anywhere even though she was pushing eighty.

Or maybe she even *was* eighty; she wasn't telling.

"'That's *she,*' I think it would be, Andi," replied one of her companions. She was shorter, rounder, with a lovely collection of tiny dimples near the corner of her mouth, and about the same age. She wore a bright pink caftan trimmed with cobalt beads that clinked when she moved her arms. "Right, Z?"

The third woman, also the same age as her companions, nodded. She sat at the head of the table simply because it had the lowest stool, for she was over six feet tall and tended to loom if she sat any higher. She had dark brown skin and was not currently wearing a wrap on her shaved head. "Yes, Pietra, if you're going to be a grammar queen about it—"

"Which Jacqueline probably is, don't you think?" the round woman named Pietra replied. "Being a librarian for more than twenty-five years."

"That doesn't necessarily follow," replied Andi, whose full name was Andromeda. "A librarian isn't always a grammarian. And *anyway*," she went on firmly when Pietra tried to argue further, "the point is, that's Jacqueline. She's the one."

"Poor thing," said Pietra, waving away some of the smoke. "She has no idea what's about to happen to her, does she?"

"Not a clue," said Andromeda.

"I hope she can handle it," said the tall, dark-skinned woman, whose name was Zwyla.

"Well, we will find out, won't we?" replied Andromeda. "Are you sure *you* want to do this, Petey? Do you really have it in you to destroy a woman's life so utterly and completely?"

Pietra nodded firmly. "Of course I can. I'm looking forward to it, to be honest." She smiled beatifically. "It's for a good cause."

Zwyla shook her head, looking down through the foggy wisps to see the poor woman whose life was about to be upended. "You sound far too excited about the prospect," she told her friend dryly.

"Well, I don't see any other way of getting her here, do you?" replied Pietra. "And more importantly, *keeping* her here. She's far too settled in her boring, staid life and nothing short of an earthquake—not *literally*," she said when Andromeda cried, "What?"

"Nothing short of a *figurative* earthquake would jar her out of her complacency," said Pietra, giving Andromeda an exasperated look.

"I'm sure you're right," said Zwyla. "And we promised Cuddy."

The other two sobered. Cuddy Stone, their dear friend and neighbor, had died only yesterday. She'd been well over a century old, and the four of them had been close as peas in a pod here on Camellia Court. She'd owned Three Tomes Bookshop for over sixty years, and her dying wish had been for her three friends to make certain the new owner fit in.

"Yes. We promised Cuddy. Nice of her to mention it on her deathbed," said Andromeda with a little laugh. She wiped a tear from her eye.

"I just hope she made the right choice," muttered Zwyla, then ducked as if someone had swatted her.

Pietra giggled, for Cuddy probably *had*.

Andromeda looked up and around the room. "All right, Cuddy, we'll take care of everything. It might take a month or two, but we will. We promise."

And a gentle waft of breeze, scented with cedar, rustled through the room.

1

Two months later

Jacqueline couldn't believe how it happened... how quickly her calm, quiet, predictable life had been destroyed.

One day she was the head reference librarian for the largest branch in the Chicago Public Library, a keep-your-head-down, get-the-work-done kind of gal who went home most every night alone to her neat little rental house and did ten minutes of simple stretches before brushing her teeth, putting on retinol face cream, and going to bed... and the next day, she was out of a job, her reputation had been smeared, and her home of fifteen years had been sold out from under her.

When she woke up that fateful day, Jacqueline had no idea her life was about to become shambles. She was in a fine mood because it was Friday and the start of the weekend—which included her forty-eighth birthday—and she had *plans*.

The latest TJ Mack thriller, *Trip Wire*, had been released on Tuesday, and she was the first name on the reserve list for it at the library (one of the perks of being there for twenty-five years). Although she could have grabbed it the first day, she liked the anticipation, so she was picking up her copy on the way home. That way she could read the whole thing uninterrupted by mundane tasks like going to work.

She'd already put a decent bottle of Pinot Grigio in the fridge, and she intended to order in Thai and enjoy it with the crisp white wine on her little patio, surrounded by the just-blooming daffodils, crocuses, and tulips she'd nurtured over the last ten years, while savoring the latest Sargent Blue adventure.

It was weekends like this that she was glad she hadn't married Josh all those years ago, because then, surely, she wouldn't be able to take a whole weekend to curl up and read. No husband, no boyfriend, no children, no parents, no pets, too early in the season for gardening... nothing to disrupt her plans. She was on her own schedule, with no expectations from anyone, and she *liked* it that way.

Thanks in part to Josh and his philandering, Jacqueline had learned years ago that her favorite people were in the books she devoured, because at the end of the day, they never betrayed you. They never let you down. They always did what they were supposed to do: entertain, amuse, thrill, teach. Sometimes they even frustrated you, but at least you usually understood *why* they did dumb things.

Book characters were always there, and like comfortable socks, the stories she reread ended the same way every time. No surprises, no betrayals, no upsets.

She'd figured all this out after she discovered her fiancé Josh was screwing one of his coworkers. Her life flipped completely topsy-turvy during that time, but once she righted things and put herself back together post-Josh, she'd made certain there was never an opportunity for that sort of painful upside-down again. But when her longtime best friend Stacey died a few years ago, Jacqueline felt another wave of that upside-down grief... and then she dug her heels into her quiet life even more: no connections, no demanding relationships, just her books. And that was just fine.

Jacqueline did have one close girlfriend at work and a smattering of other friends to do things with when she wanted to, plus a sort of friends-with-benefits male friend—no obligation, no attachments, just a companion and sex when she wanted it—and that was the way Jacqueline liked it. Her life was simple and easy (if dried up and staid), and she had only herself to worry about.

And that was exactly what she intended to do to celebrate the weekend—pamper herself.

But despite Jacqueline's best intentions for a fantastic birthday, it didn't matter. The Universe had other plans for her weekend.

The Universe said, "A woman makes plans and we laugh at her."

Shortly after she arrived at work that Friday morning, Jacqueline was summoned into the executive director's office and given a literal pink slip.

"Budget cuts," said Director Ferris with an awkward smile. "You know how it is."

Never mind that Jacqueline Finch had been employed by the CPL for twenty-five years and held seniority over pretty much everyone, including Director Ferris.

Never mind that patrons asked for her by name when calling in with their reference questions—including three very famous writers (one was a Pulitzer nominee and one was an Agatha *and* an Edgar winner) and several professors at the University of Chicago.

Never mind that she'd never missed a day of work for the last ten years.

She was out the door, kicked to the curb, no longer needed... like a sixty-year-old woman's box of tampons.

Just like her outspoken, pragmatic BFF Stacey used to say: "Let's be honest: a woman's usefulness basically ends at forty-five. Everyone knows it, even if it's not PC to admit it. We're done with child-bearing and -rearing, we're too old to change careers, we're all dried up and saggy and not interested in sex anymore... it's downhill from forty-five on. That's just the way it is."

Since Stacey died just after her forty-fourth birthday, she'd never had to feel useless and dried up. She'd never had to experience her warnings coming to fruition.

Unlike Jacqueline, who was feeling exactly that right now.

On her way out of the library, carrying the requisite banker's box of personal items from her desk, Jacqueline saw her closest friend leaving the staff break room.

"You'll never believe what happened," she said breathlessly to Wendy. "I just got *fired*. I can't believe it —Ferris actually gave me a pink piece of paper saying I didn't have a job. You'd think she could have been less—I don't know, *hackneyed*—about the whole thing. She gave me a *literal* pink slip!"

To Jacqueline's surprise, Wendy merely lifted her thick black brows. "Sorry to see you go, but it's probably for the best."

"What do you mean?" Jacqueline replied.

"I wouldn't have thought it of you, Jacqueline. I wouldn't have ever thought you'd have stooped to such a thing. The man is *married*. And in the workplace?"

Jacqueline nearly dropped the box, which would have been a shame, because it held her favorite coffee mug and matching glass-topped desk mug warmer. "What on earth are you talking about?"

Wendy gave her a withering look. "You going after Desmond. Everyone knows about it. Gracie told us she *saw* you. I really thought better of you."

And then she strode past Jacqueline and darted through the door to the stairs without even holding it open for her.

"*Me* going after Desmond?" Jacqueline said, staring at the door as it closed behind her friend. Former friend. "What the...?" She didn't even finish her sentence as fury rushed over her.

The only inappropriate interactions between her and Desmond Triplett had been last week, when he cornered her in Basement Level Two—way in the back of the stacks, where the ceiling was low and the rows were tight and no one ever went unless they were looking for reference materials about medieval weaving techniques—and *he* tried to kiss *her*. While groping her ass!

"Jackie," he muttered as he covered her mouth with his. "You're so hot—"

"It's *Jacqueline*, you ass," she said as she caught her breath, then awkwardly jammed her knee upward while holding on to his jacket for balance. Fortunately, her knee actually landed in his crotch. "And you're *married*."

She could still hear him keening pathetically in the corner when she got to the stairwell. Shaking with fury and mortification, she paused to smooth the French twist she wore nearly every day then climbed the steps on wobbly knees while trying to hold back angry tears. She figured that was the last she'd hear about *that*.

Apparently, she'd been wrong.

And it wasn't only Wendy who seemed to have heard whatever story Gracie Brownfield had told her. As she descended to the main floor of the branch with her box of belongings, Jacqueline passed Betsy Pollack and Tim Manaugh—both of whom gave her their own sneering looks. She heard the sibilant whisper of "her and Desmond," and, gritting her teeth at the injustice of it all—as well as the poor grammar—kept going.

As someone who always tried to do as Monty Python suggested and look on the bright side of life, Jacqueline decided that maybe it was best that she wouldn't have to ever see Desmond Triplett again, now that she was no longer employed by the CPL. At least she'd have a decent separation package (as it was euphemistically called) after being an employee for a quarter of a century.

It wasn't until Jacqueline got onto the commuter train that would take her out to the suburb where she lived that she realized she'd forgotten to stop by the circulation desk for her copy of *Trip Wire*. She was still fuming over that when she actually unfolded the pink slip to read the information from human resources.

She really had no excuse not to have looked at it before leaving Director Ferris's office—or at least leaving the premises—other than her own naivety that twenty-five years of employment would guarantee her a decent severance, the option to continue her own health insurance (at her own expense, of course), and a minuscule but vested pension.

"Are you *freaking* kidding me?"

Jacqueline stared at the bullet points on the memo, uncaring that the few people on an outbound train in the middle of the morning were staring at her as she shrieked at the paper.

Five days' severance?

"That's *it*?" she shrieked again, ignoring the woman with two young children who were staring at her. The toddlers moved their fingers to their mouths and gaped at her, drool spilling everywhere. "Five measly days?"

What the heck did I ever do to deserve this?

Stacey had been right all along.

∽

"THE POOR DEAR HAS A POINT, PETEY," said Zwyla, looking up from the mirror. "The five days of severance is really just a slap in the face after all of the other indignities—"

"And she hasn't even gotten home yet to learn that her house has been sold out from under her," said Andromeda, pushing her electric-blue cheaters up the bridge of her nose. She waved a hand to clear some of the gentle mist that wafted from the glass. "Don't you think that's a bit of overkill? The five days, I mean."

"Do you want her here or not?" demanded Pietra, planting her gnarled hands on cushy hips. "Jacqueline Finch is not the kind of woman who just ups and leaves—"

"No... she just plugs along as she always has for the last thirty years. She never makes a ripple, does her job, and has a pretty staid life. Really boring, actually," said Zwyla, giving a low, gravelly laugh. "And yes, of course she needs to come. She's Cuddy's choice. But we don't want her to be a complete sniveling mess of insecurity when she arrives. After all, she's going to have to deal with Danvers."

"She didn't even stand up for herself when she got fired," said Andromeda sadly. "Or try to talk to her so-called best friend. She just sat there and took it, then sort of slunk away."

"Well, she's definitely got *some* spunk. Did you see the way she nailed Desmond in the crotch when he grabbed her ass?" Pietra looked down at the silvery, smoking mirror. The looking glass, which was two feet long and about a foot wide, nestled in an ornate stand made from brass.

"That? It looked like an accident to me," said Zwyla. "She nearly fell over. It was just an accident she got him in the gonads."

"Exactly. It took her a minute to get it together, but at least she did, kind of, fight back—in an accidental way. So there is hope. You know, a little yoga would go a long way helping her with balance," Andromeda said thoughtfully. "Maybe Nadine will be able to work with her."

"Poor thing only gets laid about nine times a year by that skinny CPA—what's his name? Lester?—and I'm betting it's pretty damned predictable insert Tab A into Slot B sort of stuff," Pietra mused as she waved a beringed hand through the foggy mist so she could see better. "What else would you expect from a guy named Lester? And you know he'd marry her in a heartbeat if she gave him even a hint."

She tsked while she watched in the mirror as Jacqueline crumpled up the pink slip (that detail *had* been a little clichéd, she admitted privately) and shoved it into the box of her belongings. "You didn't do a very good job cleaning this after last time, Andi.

It's giving off too much mist and it's making everything blurry."

"Bitch, bitch, bitch," muttered Zwyla, as she adjusted the two dozen bracelets on her arm and continued watching the mirror.

"We're running low on witch hazel," Andromeda replied as she settled back into her chair, crossing her legs at the ankles. "I have to wait until it's ready for harvest, and that'll be another week unless Z wants to hurry things up a bit. But it'll help with the mist when it comes in. So are you going to fix the five days or not, Petey?"

"Fine. I'll fix it. But you know, this always happens —you ask me to handle something, and I do, and then you complain about how I do it. Next time one of *you* can get someone fired and ruin their life," Pietra grumbled.

Zwyla rolled her eyes. "Sure, I'll take care of it next time—that'll be in about thirty, forty years. At least, I hope she lasts that long." She grimaced as she looked down into the mirror. "Stars... we'll be lucky if she lasts a week."

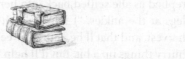

2

It was just so weird—so *very weird*—that on the day her entire life went kaput, Jacqueline learned about Three Tomes Bookshop. Not that it existed, but that she'd *inherited* it.

She'd inherited a bookstore from some distant relative she'd never even heard of.

What could be more trite, more hackneyed, more "on the nose" than a librarian inheriting a bookstore?

A suddenly-out-of-work librarian inheriting a bookstore... in an entirely different state.

It sounded like a freaking Hallmark movie. Not that there was anything wrong with Hallmark movies; she and Stacey used to watch them all the time. And Jacqueline had watched quite a few over the last few weeks in the company of more than one glass of Pinot Grigio or Chardonnay. The flicks were as soothing as a hot bath—which she could no longer enjoy as often because of the hot flashes. Yay.

Either the Universe was rolling on the ground laughing at her, or it was trying to make up for destroying her comfortable, if predictable, life back in Chicago.

She doubted it was the latter. Things just didn't work that way.

It was three weeks since everything had blown up, and Jacqueline was still numb over the nosedive her life had taken. All she could think over and over was: *You were right, Stacey. Dammit, you were right.*

And wish her friend was here to commiserate with her.

Jacqueline didn't feel even a blip of emotion as she angled her car to exit the highway for Button Cove, the town on the northwest coast near the "little finger" of Lower Michigan that was going to be her new home.

She still couldn't believe the owner of the house she'd been renting for *fifteen years* had sold it to someone else, without even a hint of warning to her.

"It was an offer I couldn't refuse," he'd said with a shrug. "Cash."

But worse than that, the rumors about her and Desmond Triplett really took the cake.

Jacqueline was dealing with a *lot*: the elimination of her job, the unexpected loss of her home, and the smearing of her reputation... but the fact that someone—several someones, in fact, including her closest friend—actually thought that Jacqueline Finch would lower herself to go after *Desmond Triplett* was the real problem.

Sure, she was forty-eight years old, needed to lose ten pounds, and sprouted chin hairs regularly—but why would she stoop to chasing a married man? Especially Desmond Triplett of the triple chins and the horrific coffee breath? Especially when she had Les if she really needed sex... which she didn't really want all that often anyway, so what the hell?

She'd thought about calling Wendy to try to explain what really happened with Desmond, but every time she was ready to do it, she chickened out. The one time she actually did push "send," the stupid phone kept dropping the call before it even connected.

Anyway, some friend Wendy was, to believe such a thing without even *asking* Jacqueline about it. Maybe it was a good thing Chicago was several hours behind in the rearview mirror of her trusty Subaru Outback.

Obviously, she and Wendy hadn't been that close after all. Not like Jacqueline and Stacey had been. But Stacey had died from breast cancer five years ago, leaving a serious friendship void in Jacqueline's life. Even though she'd known Wendy for ten years and they'd had lots of fun together, Wendy was a poor substitute for the connection she'd had with her oldest friend.

No one could take Stacey's place, and besides— BFFs were for high school and college girls, and maybe young moms who needed to schedule play dates or arrange car pools for schlepping their kids to school. Not for over-the-hill librarians. Who needed a best friend in their fifties anyway? Nothing in her life was going on that she needed to talk to someone about or commiserate over... at least until now.

It didn't matter. Jacqueline was perfectly fine on her own—she knew who she was, she was set in her ways, and her life was just fine. She had no responsibilities, and therefore no drama, no expectations, and no upsets.

Useless, as Stacey would say. And now, Jacqueline would nod sadly in agreement.

And besides... how did you meet new best friends when you were forty-eight?

She blinked hard at the sting of tears that burned her eyes. Her vision swam a little, and she gripped the steering wheel as she navigated around a long, sweeping curve that followed deep blue Lake Michigan, telling herself to stop being a slushy idiot and to look at where she was. It was beautiful.

On either side were low, rolling hills just starting to turn green from April showers. She saw a few small farms with cattle, goats—even one with ostriches!—sun-dappled, pleasant forests, glimpses and then wide expanses of the beautiful, sparkling Lake Michigan. No one could deny that northwest Lower Michigan was gorgeous land. Instead of feeling sorry for herself, she imagined what it had been like when the Ojibwe and Potawatomi lived here—it must have looked like paradise to them.

Yet... Jacqueline couldn't completely push away her emotions. As optimistic as she tried to be, starting over at forty-eight was *not* her idea of a good time.

Starting over in a brand-new town, with a new job —not to mention currently being homeless because she hadn't even begun to look for a place to live—was even worse.

How was she going to manage it? She didn't know anything about running a business... so now not only did she have to salvage her life, she also had to figure out the whole new world of entrepreneurship.

Stacey was right. I'm over forty-five and I should be done.

Suddenly furious with the whole situation, Jacqueline gritted her teeth and, for the moment, was no longer numb. A rush of heat blasted through her—a hot flash exacerbated by fury, which was *not* a good combination.

She felt the sweat rolling down her back like she was standing under a dripping faucet. When she got out of the car, the entire back of her shirt was going to be soaked. And with her current luck, she'd have sprouted one or two chin hairs over the last hour as well.

Perimenopause was such a joy.

She turned the air conditioning down as low as it would go just as she drove into town.

Button Cove had a population of twenty thousand or so—Jacqueline, being a reference librarian for twenty-five years, had of course done all the research.

Located on the west coast of Michigan near the Great Lake, the town had been established by French Canadian immigrants in 1828, and was currently known for tourism as well as a small but extensive zoo, several nationally renowned wineries and one distillery, and a reputable medical center that served a three-county area. Pictures of what appeared to be a thriving downtown indicated lots of brick structures built around 1900, interspersed with Victorian-style homes, large bungalows, mature trees, and walkways flanked by neat patches of garden.

The town seemed nice enough, both in pictures and in person. There were people walking around even now in the early afternoon on a Friday in mid-April. Jacqueline's palms felt a little sweaty as she turned onto the last block of Camellia Avenue, which actually ended in a small circular court. This was the block where her new job—if one could call it that—was located: at Three Camellia Court. It was the second-to-last building before the circular court, which was dominated by a large robin's-egg-blue Victorian.

Despite the nerves needling her stomach, she allowed herself to look at the bookstore as she drove past. It was adorable—a three-story brick confection of Victoriana, trimmed in electric blue.

Well, there it is, and here I am.

Welcome home, Cupcake.

Speaking of cupcakes, there was a bakery called Sweet Devotion, and it was right across the street from Three Tomes.

Jacqueline didn't know whether that was going to be convenient or simply a detriment to her hips and butt, but at least there was a yoga center right above it. She might even take a class.

She pulled her attention from Sweet Devotion and Yoga4Life as she drove by, then eased around the small, neat circle of the court. The shockingly blue clapboard Victorian home sitting right at the end of the court had an old-fashioned iron-spike fence and a neat, swinging sign that read *Camellia House*. Even without the sign and fence, you couldn't miss noticing the building—it was trimmed with yellow and purple. Jacqueline glanced at it, and the tangled garden that grew behind the wrought-iron gate, and wondered if it was a B&B or something like that.

Having completed the circle, she drove back down the block and barely slowed as she went past Three Tomes a second time. She just wasn't sure she was *ready* to start this new life of hers. As long as she didn't stop the car, get out, and go in, she was still a librarian from Chicago. She could still turn around and go back and find another job and another house and other friends...

She was still in shock over everything that had happened, still mystified at—and terrified by—the possible safety net that had been tossed her way in the form of Three Tomes, and still bewildered. But even through the fog of disbelief, grief, and emotional exhaustion, she nevertheless felt the ping of real fear.

What if it was all a lie, this sudden and miraculous inheritance?

Or what if it wasn't, and the bookstore was a financial or literal mess—another albatross to hang around her neck along with her loss of job, reputation, and home?

Worst of all, she had no idea why a relative she'd never even heard of and had never met would bequeath her such a valuable property.

And that was why she could hardly look at the front of the bookshop as she drove by.

She wasn't ready to find out the truth.

Not yet.

Just... not yet.

~

"THAT'S HER," said Zwyla, peering through a gap in the curtains. "She's here."

"Let me see," Pietra said, shoving her way to the window. She was an entire foot shorter than Zwyla, so she could slip right up next to her without blocking her view. "Why didn't she park in front? We left her that slot right there by the front door."

"Maybe she thinks it's better saved for the customers," said Andromeda, who hadn't risen from the sofa. She was stirring a small infusion of eyebright and couldn't stop until she'd done seven sets of seven rotations. Eyebright for clarity and memory. "What does she look like?"

"Better than I thought, and why does it matter what she looks like, you old crone?" Pietra cackled as she shifted to get a better view.

"That's *wise woman* to you, beeyotch," Andromeda replied mildly. "And I meant does she look normal, smart, kind; you know, the sort of person we actually *want* at Three Crones—I mean, Three Tomes."

"Petey, that was my *toe*," Zwyla growled, "beneath your *foot*. Stop moving aroun—"

"I only got a glance, but she looks like your run-of-the-mill librarian," Pietra replied, ignoring Zwyla. "I can't tell if she wears glasses, but she's got real pretty auburn hair—"

"What does a run-of-the-mill librarian look like, anyway?" Zwyla was still frowning from her foot being trounced. "What does run-of-the-mill *mean*, anyway?"

"Hey, wasn't there a series of books about a red-headed librarian in her forties who solved murders?" Andromeda said, still stirring. "I think her name was Jacqueline too. What're the chances?"

"All things considered, the chances are pretty—"

"We can ask her," Pietra said, interrupting Zwyla, who growled under her breath. "She'll probably know. If she doesn't, she's not a very good librarian."

She shifted again to get a better view as Jacqueline Finch's car slowly eased around the corner of the block then disappeared onto Third Street. Pietra bumped Zwyla, who gave an exasperated sigh and stepped back from the window.

"Maybe we should walk over and introduce ourselves now, before my toe gets completely mangled," Zwyla snapped. "You're not exactly featherlight, Petey."

"If you didn't have such big feet and didn't hog the window, it wouldn't be a problem," Pietra retorted. "*Why* isn't she *parking*? We can't welcome her if she doesn't park."

"Maybe she wants to look at the whole town before she decides whether she's going to stay," replied Andromeda.

"Well, that'll take a while." Pietra was trying in vain to see around the corner, which was impossible due to the glass in the window. "It's not like this is, you know, quaint little Wicks Hollow or anything. We're practically a metropolis in comparison."

"Yes, it might take her a while. You're just going to have to be patient," Andromeda said.

"I haven't been patient since I was in line to buy Commodores tickets in 1978," retorted Pietra.

"Yeah... and even then you were bitching the whole time," Zwyla said.

"It was worth it," replied Pietra, smiling lasciviously. "That Lionel Richie sure had it going on."

"All right, I'm done," Andromeda said, tapping the silver spoon against the side of the small bowl. "Let's go meet Jacqueline Finch."

3

Jacqueline dithered for fifteen minutes, driving up and down Camellia, Dogwood, Tulip, Fourth, and Sixth, before she gave in and parked in the lot behind Three Tomes. She felt like that was a good compromise—instead of coming in the front door, she could slip in through the back. It felt less official that way.

And what're you going to do if you hate it?

Worse... what're you going to do if you love it?

What are you going to do in general? You can't do this running-a-business thing. You're too old and set in your ways.

Besides, everyone knows independent bookstores don't make any money.

Jacqueline told her inner voice to shut up and, with an abrupt snap of her wrist, turned off the Outback's engine. For some reason, she was compelled to glance at herself in the rearview mirror. There was no reason to worry about what she looked like—it wasn't as if anyone was going to be there to see her.

But nonetheless, she freshened her lipstick (a shade of pink that complemented her dark red hair) and smoothed the sides of her French twist, repinning one of the fasteners that had been poking her in the back of the skull since Gary, Indiana. She had to put on her reading glasses in order to do a quick examination of her jaw, which ultimately confirmed that she hadn't, in fact, sprouted any new chin hairs. But holy cow, her pores were huge! And those six little freckles on her cheek that had been fading for years seemed to be more noticeable now. Nothing a little face powder wouldn't do to hide them, though, and her pores too...

She hauled her purse from the passenger seat and extracted the ring of keys she'd been sent by the estate attorney. Then, for some reason feeling as if she were marching to her doom, Jacqueline climbed out of her car and looked at the building that somehow belonged to her.

Located near the end of a block filled with different styles of brick buildings, Three Tomes stood out because it was an old house instead of a flat brick storefront. The only other house on Camellia was the bright blue Victorian, but it was positioned at the end of the court—almost like the bottom dot of an exclamation point—so it didn't seem out of place among the storefronts.

Yet, for some reason, Jacqueline's place didn't look wrong either, despite being surrounded by straight-edged buildings and a few mature trees protected by iron grates at the base of the trunks.

Her new possession and potential albatross was an elegant three-story home with tall, narrow windows, and on the third floor, a collection of gables edged with ornate cobalt trim. There was even a square cupola on top accompanied by a little metal railing around the flat roof from which it jutted. Unlike many of the Victorian homes Jacqueline had seen during her drive through town, instead of clapboard or wooden siding, hers was made from brick—a creamy gray color that looked charming next to the frothy blue trim.

As she stood there, looking up at the three stories of pale gray and blue topped by the charming cupola, Jacqueline's first impression was that the place was *old*. Old and comfortable, but not shabby or worn.

Just... well used, well established, even confident.

Yes, the house seemed to exude confidence—as if it had always been there and always would be, despite what might happen around it: new buildings, fancy office centers with glass walls, trendy cafés with outdoor and rooftop seating, or modern shops with picture windows.

Something niggled in the back of her mind as she stared at the building.

Have I been here before?

She paused, for the sensation of déjà vu was very strong. Had she?

No. Definitely not. She'd been living in the Chicago area since she was five and even gone to school there—all the way through her MLS. She'd never traveled much, and certainly not to Michigan. She and her parents had always gone north into Wisconsin for summer visits instead of east and north into Michigan, or to Florida during the winter. That was why they'd retired down there fifteen years ago and now lived near Tampa.

Still... that niggle wouldn't go away.

There was a familiarity about the place. Maybe that was just from the pictures she'd looked at.

But why would someone I've never met leave this to me?

What's the catch?

Feeling a little as if she were in a dream that could

easily turn into a nightmare, Jacqueline approached the back of the house, where the door was at ground level flanked by a small concrete patch that ran like a sidewalk all along the backs of Three Tomes and its neighbors.

To the right was a tiny step-down courtyard surrounded by a three-foot-high brick wall. A wrought-iron gate, currently locked, offered access to the postage-stamp-sized space. The small garden had a winding flagstone path and was landscaped with azalea, boxwood, roses, and other flora still dormant from the winter. An old cedar with sagging branches sat in one corner near the house, and would offer shade during the summer months.

The sense of familiarity, that niggle of déjà vu, nagged at her even more strongly now. She shook her head, dismissing the thought. *You've seen one urban courtyard, you've seen them all,* she told herself. Indeed, there were any number of little bricked-in patios like this back in Chicago. But Jacqueline looked at the courtyard for a long moment, peering through the bars of the gate, before she turned away, feeling slightly unsettled and more than a little prickly.

The keys were all labeled, so it was easy to find the ones that opened the two locks on the back door. She noticed that someone hadn't swept up the winter de-icing salt that been sprinkled on the walkway, and it had collected all along the base of the doorway and along the edge of the building and patio. That would have to be swept up right away—it was late April now, and snow and ice would be improbable, although not impossible, so near Lake Michigan.

She'd surely find a broom inside, but for now Jacqueline just brushed the grimy salt out of the way with her foot. She didn't want to track it inside on what she believed, from the photos she'd seen, were original hardwood floors.

All right, she told herself. Enough delaying. *Let's go in.*

Another trickle of hormone-induced sweat rolled down her spine as she fitted the keys into the first and then second locks. She pushed the door open and, after a brief hesitation, stepped inside.

Immediately, Jacqueline smelled the familiar, comforting scent of old paper and binding. Mingled with it was dust and the basic staleness that came with a building unused for... well, for how long she wasn't exactly sure; the attorney never told her much about what happened to the previous owner—just that she'd died and that Jacqueline was a distant relative of hers. There was also another more pungent and very unpleasant scent. She wrinkled her nose. *That* would have to be attended to posthaste.

She closed the door behind her and took a few more steps in, looking around.

She'd stepped past the doorway, and now it was dark and gloomy. Feeling for a light switch, she tried not to breathe in the awful smell coming from somewhere.

"Probably a dead mouse or something," she said aloud, grateful to hear a noise other than the heartbeat that was pounding in her ears.

At last she found a switch, and when she flipped it, a sort of grudging illumination spilled from three old lights hanging from the ceiling. "We'll need a lot more light if we're going to have books here," Jacqueline said, looking up at them.

Just then, one of the bulbs—the one right over her head—gave a loud pop as if in agreement, then went dark. Jacqueline barely smothered a shriek as she jerked away, bumping into the wall and sending something rattling.

Then, furious with herself for overreacting, Jacqueline told herself silently and firmly to *buck up*. It was an old house. Who knew when the last time the lights had been used?

Still... now it was darker, and that unpleasant smell had not waned at all, and she still had the rest of the expanse of the dim, shadowy house through which she had to walk.

Get a grip, she told herself. *As strange as it may seem, this is your place now. For better or for worse.*

As she went through, Jacqueline found more light switches and turned them on, hunching a little in case more bulbs blew or sent sparks, but none did. As she did so, the initial creepiness went away and she found herself charmed by the pretty, cozy, organized bookshop.

The main throughway opened off into different rooms of shelves and stacks—each spacious, well lit, and, Jacqueline had to admit, perfect for a bookstore. Two of the rooms had fireplaces that she hoped worked, and others were large enough to have space for a pair of chairs and small table. It seemed that each room was a different genre or category. Most of the chairs had covers on them, and there was a fine layer of dust over everything. There were a few stray cobwebs, and she was pretty sure the pile in the corner of the mystery/thriller room was either a dead rodent or its nest.

It seemed no one had been here for at least a few months, which had Jacqueline wondering when the previous owner actually died. Mr. Nath, the estate attorney who was not much of a chitchatter, hadn't been terribly forthcoming about the details of her inheritance from this distant relative.

He had pushed everything through probate very quickly, however, and since she'd done her research, she knew that the law firm was very reputable. He and his partners had been around for over fifty years, so she wasn't worried that this was a scam, even if it seemed surreal.

She passed by the romance and science fiction/fantasy room, discovered a biography and history room, and wondered where the science section was. And what about a children's room? She tsked to herself, already mentally listing things that should be changed. Strangely, though, the house felt much bigger inside than it appeared from the outside. There were so many more rooms and nooks and crannies than one would expect from the exterior; they just seemed to go on and on and on...

She found the science section—an entire chamber with shelves arranged in a wonderful labyrinth of reference material, all of it somehow fitting into a single room.

Along the main hallway toward the front of the shop were glass cases that displayed and protected old and rare books. One of the cabinets was tucked under a set of stairs leading to the second floor. It contained what could be a first edition of *The Mysterious Affair at Styles*, which made Jacqueline's heart go pitter-patter. Agatha Christie's Hercule Poirot was a personal favorite of hers.

She was using the flashlight on her smartphone to examine another glass-fronted cabinet that contained some vintage Nancy Drew and Hardy Boys books when she saw something move from out of the corner of her eye.

She spun in time to see a dark shadow flit around the corner, and she froze, staring after it. *What was that?*

Her heart was in her throat as she watched the area there uncertainly. Then, marshaling her courage, she called, "Hello? Is someone there?" even as she looked around for something—a broom? a fire poker? —to use for a weapon.

Jacqueline was pleased that her voice came out smooth and firm, belying the fact that her palms had gone damp and she was trying to think whether she had anything in her purse that could be used as a weapon. She hadn't figured she'd need pepper spray here in Button Cove.

No one answered, and the old house was as silent as it had been when she stepped in.

Maybe she'd imagined it.

Jacqueline turned off the flashlight, and gripping her phone tightly—the library had offered a self-defense class where the instructor had told them to use the weight and solidness of their phones as a weapon —she brandished it as she made her way toward the front of the shop, where she'd seen the shadow disappear.

"Hello? Anyone there—" Her words were choked off when she caught another movement from the corner of her eye again and spun once more...

To see two cats sitting there, watching her.

One was lounging on the front desk, sprawled along the counter with its fluffy tail swishing languidly. He (she was guessing at his gender) was a lush, long-haired ginger with darker, tawny stripes and amber eyes that watched her with what could only be described as flirtatious interest.

The other cat sat on a shelf above and behind the

front desk. He (she assumed) was a sleek, inky black with shorter fur and cool gray eyes that watched her with obvious disdain. Instead of lounging, the black feline sat upright with alert ears and that steely gaze, as if prepared to launch himself at her if she made any sort of misstep.

"Well, hello there," she said, uncertain what to make of the situation. Even though she was a librarian and a book lover and a single woman of certain age, she did not fit the stereotype of cat lover. She was more of a dog person—not that she'd ever had a dog either. "I suppose you live here? I wonder who's been feeding you and—Oh, *that* was what I smelled. Litter box. Who's been taking care of you?"

But of course the cats couldn't—or, more likely, didn't choose to—answer. The gingery-amber one gave her a sly, definitely flirtatious look and rolled onto his back as if expecting a tummy rub.

"Sorry, sir—I don't do that on a first date," Jacqueline said... but she couldn't resist one quick pat on his head. He was as lush and soft as he appeared. So she stroked him all along his spine, causing him to arch with pleasure. He was very soft.

The black cat merely eyed them with continued disdain.

"That's fine," Jacqueline told him. "You keep out of my way and I'll keep out of yours. I have no inherent problem with a shop cat—or two—just so long as you don't expect me to cater to you."

She was just about to search out the stinky litter box when something rattled at the front door.

She looked over to see three older women standing there, crowded at the glass entrance, peering in at her. Jacqueline waffled for a minute, then decided since they could clearly see she was in the shop, she had no choice but to simply let them know she wasn't open for business yet.

As she started to the door, she glanced up and noticed a small framed picture mounted right above it. *Double, double, toil and trouble,* its caption said, and the image was, fittingly, of the Witches Three from *Macbeth.*

Jacqueline smirked to herself when she thought how coincidental it was that the three women peering through the door were positioned similarly to the three crones in the image right above them—even though they didn't look anything like the long-haired, round-faced ones in the picture.

"Hello there," she said, opening the door partway so as to indicate she wasn't inviting them in. "I'm not open yet—I've just taken over the shop, and I'm sure it's going to be—"

"We know," said the shortest woman, who'd maneuvered her way as close to the cracked-open door as possible. She looked like she was pushing eighty, and was holding a basket covered by a red-and-white checked cloth. She was very pretty, with round cheeks and sparkling blue eyes in a face lit with enthusiasm and—which Jacqueline found concerning—determination. "We've come to welcome you!" She lifted the basket she was holding, and Jacqueline got a whiff of something that smelled delicious.

"Oh, well, thank you, that's so kind of you, but—"

"Oh, look, there's Sebastian! I'm sure he's pleased to have company again," said the second woman, looking beyond Jacqueline into the shop. She was also about the same age as her shorter, rounder friend, and had pure white hair cut in a stylish pixie cut, shockingly green eyes, and light, rosy-brown skin.

"Sebastian?" Jacqueline turned to look behind her,

and that was her undoing... for the next thing she knew, the trio had swarmed into the shop.

The pixie-cut woman had moved to the front desk and gathered the gingery-amber cat into her arms, hefting him as if he were an infant. Sebastian—as apparently that was his name—gave Jacqueline a look clearly indicating that he expected such affection, and so much more.

"I—"

"I'm Zwyla," said the third woman after she shut the door behind her. "Sorry to barge in on you like this, but we've been taking care of the cats—that's Max up there. He's a little more disagreeable about being handled than Sebastian, who's a little bit of an attention monger."

Zwyla was tall—at least six feet, Jacqueline estimated—and she had smooth, dark brown skin. Her head was wrapped in a cobalt turban patterned with multicolored peace symbols. She was wearing jeans and a cobalt shirt with wide, flowing sleeves, and lots of bracelets. Although her arresting, unlined face made Jacqueline wonder about her age, when she saw Zwyla's hands, she estimated she was eighty-ish like her friends. Hands never lied about age.

"I'm Pietra," said the short woman with the basket. She was wearing a long pink raincoat with bulging pockets, reminding Jacqueline of the old TV detective Columbo (except without the pink). "And that's Andromeda over there practically making out with Sebastian."

Andromeda, who was wearing yoga pants, tank, and an off-the-shoulder gray sweatshirt that revealed gently wrinkled skin, flashed her friend a dark look as she let Sebastian ooze from her arms back onto the counter.

"Oh, all right, then," said Jacqueline. "Well, um, it's nice to meet you. I'm Jacqueline Finch. I'm the new own—"

"We know," said Pietra with a smile. "We've been waiting for you." She thrust the basket at Jacqueline. "Blueberry cream scones."

Jacqueline picked up a corner of the napkin covering the pastries. "Blueberry cream scones are my absolute favorite treat ever," she said, looking up in surprise.

"I kno—"

"Our Petey is quite the baker," Zwyla said, giving her friend a dark glare. For a second, Jacqueline fancied she actually saw a literal spark flash between them, but of course that was silly.

"They look and smell delicious. Um..."

What was the hospitality requirement for people who barged into your closed shop but brought your all-time favorite baked goods? Did Jacqueline have to share the scones? Must she offer tea or coffee—she had no idea whether there was any in the house—sit and chat with them (please, no!)... or could she just thank them and push them back out the door?

The decision was made for her when Andromeda said, "I'm going to feed the cats and attend to the litter box—it's been a few days. Why don't you three sit up in the tearoom, have some tea, and get to know each other? I'll be there in a snap."

"Tea room?" Jacqueline said.

"Oh, it's just lovely! So cozy and inviting, and with a great view of the street. It's on the second floor. People like to just sit there and browse," said Pietra.

"They drink tea while reading books?" Jacqueline said. The librarian in her was horrified. "*Here*? In the store?"

"Oh, yes," Pietra said cheerily. "Three Tomes is known for its array of teas—especially the herbal ones. There are people who come from all over just to buy some of those special blends," she added. "The shop across the street usually provides pastries to be sold for the customers to have with their tea."

Jacqueline gasped at the thought of all those little flaky croissant pieces or cupcake crumbs falling between pages. That practice was definitely *not* going to continue at Three Tomes.

Pietra started up the wide, curving stairway just off to the side in the front of the shop, leaving Jacqueline, feeling strangely out of place in her own store—which she hadn't even fully explored—to follow. In doing so, she had to walk past the bookshelf where Max was still perched, located just above her head. He gave her a sneering glance as she passed by, then turned to look out the front window as if he couldn't be bothered by her presence.

"So what do you think?" asked Zwyla, ducking a little as she walked beneath the low threshold leading to the stairway.

"What do I think about what?" Jacqueline asked as she followed her up the stairs, which creaked a little from age.

"The bookstore," said Zwyla as they reached the top of the landing.

Jacqueline caught her breath—not because she'd been climbing steps, but because of what she saw. The tea room *was* the perfect place for cozy reading and drinking—if one were permitted to have any sort of liquid near a book, which was a big no-no as far as she was concerned.

But if one *were* permitted... this would be the place.

Most of the walls had been removed from the front half of the second floor, turning it into one large, airy space with tall, un-curtained windows and several places to sit: sofas with long, low tables, cozy armchairs, and several bistro-style tables with matching chairs. The floor was dark hardwood—maybe walnut, and it needed a good cleaning—while the plastered white walls boasted bright paintings. She recognized many of them as Michigan landscapes, having just driven four hours along the lakeshore and hilly, forested areas. A small counter also offered three sturdy stools for patrons and the equipment for making tea and, Jacqueline hoped, coffee.

The sofas were currently protected by covers, but Zwyla used a napkin to wipe the dust off one of the bistro tables.

"Well, I've hardly had a chance to look at it"—Jacqueline was careful not to sound accusatory even though she was still a little bewildered at being railroaded by the trio of women—"but it seems nice."

"*Nice?*" Pietra said, sloshing water as she turned from the counter with two steaming mugs. "Just nice?" She was looking at Zwyla with goggling eyes and a pursed mouth.

"Well, I mean... it's *very* nice?" Jacqueline suggested. "There's a lot of work that needs to be done to get things organized. And cleaned up."

She felt as if she were in some sort of surreal dream with everything that was going on—inheriting a bookstore where people felt free to not only drink beverages that stained, but also bring in baked goods, being invaded by three women who weirdly reminded her of the *Macbeth* witches, and seemingly being the benefactor of two cats.

"So you don't like it?" asked Andromeda, whose

spiky platinum hair had just appeared at the top of the stairs. She sounded as if she were personally affronted by the thought.

"I didn't say that," Jacqueline replied. "I've only just arrived. I haven't looked at the entire place yet, and—and I don't even drink tea." She looked down at the steaming mug that Pietra had placed in front of her on the clean table.

Pietra froze in the process of removing the luscious blueberry scones from her basket and putting them on a plate that had come from who knew where. "What do you mean you don't drink tea?" she asked, somehow making it sound as if Jacqueline had announced she didn't wash her hands.

"I don't like tea," Jacqueline replied, wondering how she had ever gotten herself in this pickle—and how she could get herself extricated from the three old ladies who'd hijacked her day.

"But—"

Zwyla spoke quickly, interrupting Pietra. "It's a shame you don't like tea," she said, then picked up her own mug and sipped. Whatever it was, Jacqueline had to admit, it smelled heavenly. "This is a particularly excellent herbal brew."

Mostly out of self-defense, Jacqueline picked up her own cup. Maybe if she drank the bloody tea, the three ladies would *leave*. Besides, those blueberry cream scones were definitely calling to her...

They looked delicious, filled with large berries looking like they were ready to burst, and each pastry had a shiny glaze on top. Pietra had finished placing them on the plate and was distributing napkins.

"So," Jacqueline said, looking at Andromeda, "you've been taking care of Max and Sebastian?" She might as well make conversation. "Did they belong to the previous owner?"

That was a good segue—maybe she could learn more about the woman who'd owned the shop before. At least get something out of this little coffee-klatch-without-the-coffee.

"Insofar as they belong to anyone," replied Andromeda, swooping in and taking the first scone. "Oh, Petey, I think you've outdone yourself with these! I'd say Max and Sebastian belong to the house."

"What happened to the previous owner?" Jacqueline asked, lifting her mug reluctantly. The tea did smell wonderful. Sort of floral, with a little nip of something bright and pungent at the end. "I wonder if there's any cream," she said, rising to go look behind the counter. Even the little plastic cups of non-refrigerated creamer substitute would work—anything to mask the taste of the tea. "And sugar."

"Oh, no, no, no, you don't want cream," Pietra said quickly. "Not in this tea. Or sugar, either. Right, Andromeda?"

Jacqueline hesitated, then sat back down. Then she silently berated herself: *Why am I letting these ladies tell me what to do?*

Because that's what you've always done. Been the people-pleaser. The rule-follower. The non-wave-maker. The amiable but distant friend, the good employee—and look where that got you: out the door on your butt after twenty-five years of hard work, and everyone believing the worst of you.

Besides, these ladies might be patrons—no, she corrected her thoughts: customers. And the customer was always right.

"All right, then." Jacqueline reluctantly raised the mug, realizing it was probably the only way to get rid of these busybodies. The scent assailed her once more. She took a sip and was pleasantly surprised. "This is *good*," she said, unable to hide her shock. "Like, really good."

"Of course it is. It's Andi's special brew," Pietra said, glancing at her friend. "One of them, anyway."

Jacqueline took another taste of the tea—a larger sip this time—and was treated to a warm, comfortable feeling... and yet she felt a spark of energy shuttle through her. "Is there a lot of caffeine in this?" she asked, realizing her last coffee had been several hours ago. She could use a boost of energy.

"None at all," replied Andromeda. "It's herbal, so no caffeine, and no added sugar. Just beautiful, pure ingredients from nature. I grow most of my own, and the hint of honey is from my bees."

Huh.

Having done her duty and tasted the tea, Jacqueline felt it was permissible for her to move on to the scones. She broke one of them open over the small plate that had materialized through Pietra's rummaging behind the counter. The blueberries oozed their juices without making a mess and staining everything, and the pastry itself was the perfect combination of crumbly and moist. She managed to contain a moan of delight as she took her first bite. It was heaven.

"You asked about the previous owner," said Zwyla, setting down her cup. The woman's presence, along with her height and the steady, serious regard in her dark, dark eyes, made her a little intimidating to Jacqueline. But there was also something about her that put Jacqueline at ease.

"Yes. I've never met Cuddy Stone or heard of her—apparently I'm—was—a distant relative of hers, but I can't figure out why she would have bequeathed this place to me. Surely she had other, closer relatives," Jacqueline said—then felt strange for having shared her private misgivings.

Zwyla didn't seem surprised or put off by her honesty. She gave Jacqueline a smile. "Cuddy had her own way of doing things," she said with a little shrug. "Her family has owned the house—or lived on its land—for centuries. All the way back to when indigenous people lived here, before the Europeans came in.

"Cuddy was a good friend of ours, so naturally we were curious about the new owner of Three Tomes. I hope you don't mind us barging in on you like this," Zwyla continued. "I realize we can be a little overwhelming."

"Oh, no, not at all," Jacqueline heard herself saying. *People-pleaser.* "It's only that I'd just arrived only minutes before you showed up, and I haven't even seen the place yet. It seems to go on forever..."

"Of course you haven't. And you should definitely take your time, get a feel for the shop. It's a very special place. Settle in," Andromeda said kindly. "Drink your tea, love."

Jacqueline obediently lifted the mug and sipped again. It really was *quite* good for tea. She wasn't able to identify the floral scent: not rose, but maybe lily— but lilies were poisonous, so she didn't think anyone would make tea with lilies... *or would they?*

Drink your tea, love, Andromeda had said.

Jacqueline set down the mug.

What if these ladies had come in here to poison her because they didn't want anyone new to take over the bookstore? What if they were addled with grief over the loss of this Cuddy Stone person and were doing what crazy old ladies did and taking matters into their own hands? After all, it seemed as if they'd had access to the building in order to take care of the cats...

"So what exactly is in this tea?" The warmth that spread through her from the brew abated a little. "Do I smell lilies?"

"*Lilies?* Of course not. I would never put them in a tea—they'll make you sick as a dog," Andromeda replied, clearly affronted. "It has lavender, elderflower, eyebright, and a few other things."

"Oh, I see," Jacqueline replied a little uncertainly. *Eyebright?*

Suddenly, Zwyla stood. Her bracelets jangled as she beckoned to her friends. "I think we'd best let Jacqueline get settled in a little more. She's had a long drive, and we're keeping her from getting herself settled."

"Oh, yes, of course," said Andromeda. "I'll leave some of that tea for you if you like. It's really soothing, and it will help to open your sixth chakra."

"Yes, of course, thank you," Jacqueline said obediently, relieved that the ladies had taken the hint. She had no intention of drinking any more of that tea, but she wasn't going to say that. It was fine, but it sure wasn't coffee.

"And I'll leave the rest of the scones for you," said Pietra with a smile. "I know how much you love them. There are some catnip biscuits under the napkin on the bottom of the basket for Max and Sebastian. It'll help you make friends with them."

"She won't need help making friends with Sebastian," Zwyla said dryly. "Max, however, is another issue." To Jacqueline's relief, Zwyla started for the stairs.

They really were leaving!

"It was just lovely meeting you, Jacqueline," said

Pietra as she followed her friends. "Do you ever go by Jackie?"

"No," Jacqueline replied firmly.

"Very well, then—Jacqueline it is. All three lovely, lyrical syllables of it." Pietra beamed at her, and that warm, sparkling smile in her round pink cheeks was the last thing Jacqueline saw as Pietra descended the stairs and disappeared.

Jacqueline didn't relax until she heard the front door open and the ladies chattering as they walked out.

Whew.

That had been a little much. Hopefully they wouldn't be back for a while.

At least they'd left the rest of the scones... and the tea. Jacqueline frowned at her half-filled cup, then picked it up and took another drink. Before she knew it, she'd finished it and a second scone.

Thus fortified, she decided it was time to finish looking at the rest of the house. But just as she rose from the bistro table, there was a dull thud from downstairs.

4

What now? Jacqueline thought as she started down the stairs. Admittedly, her palms were a little damp and her insides a squiggling mess of nerves, but she had no choice but to find out what made the loud noise.

When she got to the first floor, she saw both of the cats sitting on the same bookshelf. Sebastian was innocently cleaning one of his paws, and Max was eyeing Jacqueline as if she were interloping on his territory.

It took her a moment to discover the source of the noise. Her keen librarian ears had already assessed the thudding sounds and categorized them as books tumbling to the floor—an event that, alone, made her wince at the thought of old bindings and fragile endpapers tearing, pages bending, and covers being crushed—and she was correct.

There were three books that had somehow fallen off the shelves and were lying innocently (and unharmed, as far as she could see) on the floor. Interestingly, two had fallen open and lay upright with their pages splayed wide. Even more interestingly, none of the three were from the same shelf.

"I don't know how you did it," Jacqueline said, casting a suspicious look at the cats, "but at least you didn't ruin the books. But let's not make this a habit or there'll be no catnip treats for you."

She stooped to pick up the books, one by one, pausing to admire each of them. All were very old—vintage, one might call them—and had obviously been well read over the years.

Great Expectations lay neatly closed on the floor in the corner of the room with the classics section—a shelving choice that Jacqueline had already decided was going to have to change. Fiction was fiction, and genre categorization was all right, but who was to say what was a classic and what wasn't? Jacqueline was of the mind to just mix the "classics" in with all the other fiction by genre.

A collection of Sherlock Holmes works was also on the floor, open to "A Study in Scarlet."

"*Rebecca*," she said with a fond smile as she bent to pick up the third book, which had landed open to chapter three. "'Last night I dreamt I went to Manderley again.' One of the best first lines ever. There's no argument that this is a classic gothic novel. Not as good as du Maurier's *Jamaica Inn*, in my opinion," she told Sebastian, who'd wandered into the room with his bottlebrush tail bopping at the tip. She paused to pet him, then rose. "But definitely goosebump-inducing—"

"I'm certainly pleased you think so."

Jacqueline dropped the three books she was holding and barely stifled a scream as she saw the figure standing there.

"Who are you?" she managed to say, afraid that her racing heart was going to pound from her chest.

The woman in front of her looked to be in her forties. She was wearing a plain, mid-calf-length blue-black dress cinched at the waist with the type of skinny belt that was fashionable in the late 1930s. Her jet-black hair was pulled back into a severe figure-eight knot at the back of her head, leaving her pale face with nothing to soften its attractive, angular features. She'd spoken in a smooth British accent, and stood ramrod straight with her hands clasped neatly in front of her waist. A large ring of old-fashioned keys hung from a clip on her belt.

"I'm Mrs. Danvers, of course," replied the woman.

Mrs. Danvers, as in the creepy-as-hell, obsessive, and controlling housekeeper from *Rebecca*?

Jacqueline stared at the woman. Wild thoughts rioted through her mind, but none of them settled into anything that made any sense.

"Um..." Jacqueline couldn't form words. She simply didn't know what to say. She couldn't believe her eyes. Or her ears. She simply stared.

Mrs. Danvers gave a disdainful sniff. "You're no better than she was," she said, giving Jacqueline a once-over with cold eyes. "The second Mrs. de Winter. She had no idea what she was doing at Manderley, and she certainly could never fill the shoes of my lovely Rebecca. Apparently, I shall have to attend to everything. As usual."

"I..." Jacqueline still couldn't make the words come. She surreptitiously pinched herself in the wrist, and, *ouch*, she was definitely awake.

The woman standing in front of her seemed as substantial as Jacqueline herself was, but she certainly wasn't going to reach out and touch her.

She was quite familiar with Mrs. Danvers and her ways.

Before she could respond, the woman gave another derisive sniff and walked out of the room.

Jacqueline's knees gave out. Fortunately, she was standing in front of a chair, and her butt more or less managed to hit the seat. She stared at the empty doorway.

What in the hell?

Surely she'd imagined all of that.

Of course she had.

It wouldn't be a surprise if she were suffering from some sort of posttraumatic stress disorder after everything that had happened in the last few weeks. Not to mention hormones.

And if she *were* going to have hallucinations, it sort of made sense that it would be of a literary character... especially from a book she'd just picked up from the floor.

"But why couldn't I have been imagining M. Poirot?" she said, giving an unsteady chuckle as she reached to pick up Sebastian. She needed to feel something alive and warm next to her, and he was more than willing to oblige. "That would have been far less unsettling."

Whew. It had been a long day, and an even longer three weeks. She was emotionally, mentally, and physically exhausted.

And she could really use a cup of coffee.

"All right, shall we see whether there's any coffee left in the tea room?" Jacqueline said when she felt as if her knees wouldn't buckle on her again. She let the soft, fluffy Sebastian—who'd been purring like a gingery machine—ooze from her arms to the floor and decided *he* was worthy of a catnip treat. "There's lots of work to do here, and time's a-wasting."

She wanted to at least start putting things in order so she could open the shop for business as soon as possible. Not that she knew what she was doing in that regard; unfortunately, Mrs. Danvers had been right about that.

Jacqueline had booked herself a room at Chance's Inn, a small bed-and-breakfast in Button Cove, for the time being, but she needed to find a permanent place to live as soon as possible. The estate attorney had told her there was an apartment on the third floor of Three Tomes, but Jacqueline was quite certain she wouldn't want to live above where she worked. She didn't like the idea of her business taking over her life that much. Aside from that, she was used to living in a house with a backyard and patio, not a third-floor flat. She could rent out the place, however, and make some extra money.

As she came out of the classics room, she saw Max, who'd moved to the top of the highest bookshelf in the front of the store and lay there looking like a small black panther watching for prey. He sneered at Jacqueline, who still carried Sebastian, as they climbed the stairs to the tea room, then returned to surveying his domain.

As Jacqueline neared the top of the steps, she heard quiet clinking sounds coming from up ahead. She hesitated, then forced herself to keep climbing. What now?

When she reached the top and most of the café area was visible, Jacqueline saw a woman behind the counter. At first she thought it was Pietra having returned to clean up the dishes from their tea, but she immediately dismissed that because this woman wasn't quite as short and round.

"Well, now, hello there, dearie," said the woman when she caught sight of Jacqueline. She was wearing an old-fashioned blouse with a high, ruffled collar that looked Victorian. A bibbed apron covered the blouse and the long, dark skirt that made up the rest of her attire. Her graying hair was pulled back in a bun far less severe than Mrs. Danvers's but just as practical. She looked as if she were in her mid-fifties, and she spoke with a British accent.

"Hello," Jacqueline said faintly, and pinched herself again. It hurt and she didn't wake up.

Where are all these people coming from?

"You look like you could use a nice, hot cup of tea, dearie," said the woman. She was bustling around behind the counter as if she worked there. "Have a seat now, and I'll be taking right care of you—but don't get too accustomed to me waiting on you, luv, because I've far too many other things to do."

Jacqueline found herself walking over to one of stools at the counter where the woman had already placed a delicate china teacup on its saucer.

She was almost afraid to ask, but she had to. "Wh-who are you?"

"Why, I'm Mrs. Hudson, of course," replied the woman, as she set a small metal strainer over the top of the cup, then poured a stream of steaming tea from a pretty china teapot. The strainer caught a few random tea leaves from landing in the cup and sinking to the bottom. "Now drink up, dearie. There's nothing a nice cuppa can't solve, is what me mum used to say."

Jacqueline picked up the cup, and for the second time that day reluctantly sampled the tea. This brew was strong and black and very hot, and she frowned at the taste.

"You'll be wanting some milk, then, dearie, will you?" Mrs. Hudson offered a small pitcher.

"Yes, and some sugar," Jacqueline replied, wondering how long this vision was going to last. No one had ever mentioned hallucinations as a symptom of perimenopause.

"Mr. Holmes never took sugar, but that Dr. Watson liked his sweets well enough," said Mrs. Hudson, producing a sugar bowl that matched the teapot and cup. "Although Mr. Holmes had *other* habits, didn't he now." She frowned. "I warned him about the heroin, didn't I, but he just told me, 'Hush now, Mrs. Hudson, it helps my mental capacity,' and then he'd go on about playing that screeching violin at all hours. A body couldn't ever get a good night's sleep when he was on a case." She tsked and began to wipe up a few drops of tea from the counter. "It was even worse when he *wasn't* on a case, with all the pacing and experimentation and horrendous *smells* coming from up there."

By now, Jacqueline had discovered that Mrs. Hudson was right about one thing—a cup of tea certainly was bracing. Jacqueline felt better already. So much so that she was emboldened to say, "I just met a —a—another one of your—uh—type downstairs."

Mrs. Hudson scoffed. "And isn't that why I'm giving you a nice, hot cuppa? Nothing better for a body than good, strong English tea—especially after having to speak to that Danvers woman."

"You know her?"

"Unfortunately," replied Mrs. Hudson. "All she ever does is yammer on about that Rebecca. Lands, if I talked about Mr. Holmes as much as she blathers about how perfect Rebecca was—and we all know she *wasn't*, now, was she?—nothing would ever get done around here." She set down the small tea tin she was holding with such force that it banged the counter.

Jacqueline tried not to think too hard about the fact that she was having a conversation with... what? What exactly *was* this—this *entity* standing in front of her, serving her tea, and giving her advice?

A hallucination. Or maybe just a dream. No, she'd pinched herself twice, and both times it had hurt. Jacqueline didn't think she was dreaming.

Definitely hallucinating.

But if she was hallucinating, how was she drinking tea?

Or was she imagining that part too?

Speaking of tea... could the tea Andromeda had insisted she drink be the cause of these weird visions? The thought struck her as a viable one. The kindly woman had seemed very insistent that Jacqueline drink the tea... but then the other three ladies had had some as well.

And eyebright seemed a possible culprit for causing hallucinations. Jacqueline knew that early healers looked at the way plants appeared for clues as to how they might be used to heal the body—a practice called the doctrine of signature. Eyebright's little white flowers resembled eyes, so it became used for treating eye concerns. Maybe it worked in the opposite way as well—causing your eyes to see things that weren't there.

Jacqueline closed her eyes, then opened them. Yes, Mrs. Hudson was still there, bustling about behind the counter.

Jacqueline decided she should just leave the bookstore, go and check in to her hotel, and get a good night's sleep. She nodded to herself and took another sip of Mrs. Hudson's tea, then slid off the stool. Yes. That was a good plan.

She would come back tomorrow morning refreshed and ready to start her new life... and hallucination-free.

5

Jacqueline arrived at Three Tomes just before nine o'clock the next morning. She carried a coffee-filled go-cup, considerately provided by the proprietress of Chance's Inn, and was pleasantly full from a delicious breakfast of a savory mushroom crepe and scrambled eggs, along with assorted pastries and fruit.

She'd slept fairly well, despite some very lucid dreams with elements that lingered even after she woke. They weren't frightening as much as unsettling —in one, she remembered, her hand was covered with red... blood or paint, she didn't know. She opted to believe it was paint, telling herself that she'd surely be painting at least somewhere in the bookshop in preparation for opening it and that her subconscious was aware of that. In another, she was in a dark place with a dirt floor—in the dream she didn't feel trapped or frightened, but it was odd nonetheless.

Now, having arrived at Three Tomes, she was ready to face the day—which included cleaning and organizing the bookstore and trying to determine how soon she could open for business. It would take at least a week of cleaning and learning her way around the place—including the computer system. And then there was the fact that she'd have to do inventory and —the most exciting part—decide what new books to order in! Jacqueline couldn't wait to do that.

But business before pleasure—and that meant the cleaning and organizing bit had to take priority. She could save the poring over publisher catalogs for her breaks or evenings.

Before bed, Jacqueline had spent last night *not* thinking about her crazy, hormonal visions of literary characters come to life, and instead closely reviewing the financials provided by Mr. Nath, the attorney. She had resisted giving them more than a cursory glance before now, telling herself she wanted to see the place before having any preconceived notions about its via- bility—and her feelings about it.

To her astonishment, everything seemed to be in order. The bookstore not only made a small profit from its walk-in business, but there was an online arm that sold vintage and out-of-print books on eBay and other websites with an even tidier profit margin. All together, that meant she could pay herself a reason- able salary. She'd also been surprised to see that the tea room did a fair amount of business both in the café and online, selling tea blends—just as Pietra had said. Any rent she might make from the flat above the shop would just be gravy.

The other thing that put Jacqueline in a good mood was that she'd happened to look again at her pink slip from the library. It must have fallen out of her purse, because it was sitting on the passenger seat in her car. She'd picked it up, prepared to be angry all over again about the insulting five days of severance... but when she read it, Jacqueline saw that it said five *months* of severance, not five *days*.

"How could I have made that mistake?" she asked herself, staring at the paper. She frowned, looked at it for another several minutes, and concluded that she must have read it wrong the first time—which was not terribly surprising, considering the state of her mind at the time.

Not that the state of her mind was any better yesterday, what with hallucinating about two different literary housekeepers!

But last night she'd come up with an explanation for that. The illusions had been a combination of stress, anxiety, hormones—and the fact that the two knocked-over books open on the floor were ones that featured those particular characters, so they'd been at the top of her mind. It made sense in a warped sort of way.

Thus when she arrived at the shop, Jacqueline was feeling full—of a tasty breakfast, a shot of caffeine in the form of her beloved hazelnut-flavored coffee, and bald optimism. With a lot of hard work over the next week or two, she just might be able to pull off this running-a-business thing.

Maybe you *could* teach an old dog new tricks.

The first thing Jacqueline noticed when she opened the back door of the bookshop was that it smelled different inside.

Yes, the litter box had been cleaned yesterday by Andromeda, so that nasty smell was gone... but when she stepped across the threshold into the house, Jacqueline caught the distinct aroma of lemon. And the place smelled far less stale. In fact, it smelled *fresh*.

She reached for the light switch, reminding herself that she'd need to look around for bulbs—or add the purchase of them to her list—and flipped it. To her bewilderment, all three of the lights illuminated... including the one that had sparked at her and gone out yesterday.

There was probably a short in the wire.

Jacqueline had taken two steps into the shop when she heard voices. They seemed to be coming from the front of the store, and they sounded agitated.

Maybe there were people outside on the street in front. Or maybe there was a radio, and the cats had turned it on somehow. Or the radio was on an alarm clock that came on automatically for company for the cats.

She hurried through the house and came to a stumbling halt when she reached the front room of the shop.

Mrs. Danvers and Mrs. Hudson were standing there facing each other, clearly in the middle of some sort of altercation.

"—take yourself right back to Manderley if you're so unhappy here," Mrs. Hudson said, her hands fisted on her hips. Her chin jutted forward and her cheeks were flushed pink.

"Pah!" Mrs. Danvers scoffed. "This place would be in shambles in a fortnight if I did. I—"

They both caught sight of Jacqueline at the same time and turned to face her.

"Good morning, ma'am," said Mrs. Danvers. Her words were polite and correct, but there wasn't even a hint of deference in them. Instead, her blade-like nose was lifted as if she smelled something bad—or low class—and her mouth was flat and devoid of any hint of smile.

"Good morning, dearie," said Mrs. Hudson. The pink flush of emotion still colored her cheeks, but she'd removed her hands from her hips, and she was smiling at Jacqueline. "We didn't know when to expect you, so I haven't heated the water for your tea yet."

Mrs. Danvers sniffed and lifted her nose a trifle higher as Jacqueline stared at them. She was feeling dizzy and as if someone had punched her in the stomach.

"Wh-what are you doing here?" she asked at last. *Am I going crazy?* "Who are you?"

"Why, I told you, dearie, I'm Mrs. Hudson, and *that*"—Mrs. Hudson pursed her lips—"is Mrs. Danvers. We're here to help you. At least, *I* am."

How could this be happening? Jacqueline took two more steps into the front room of the shop, and that was when she noticed the broom, mop, and dust rag... and the much stronger scent of lemon. Then she saw that the covers had been removed from the two chairs by the street-side window, and that the front counter gleamed as if it had been polished. So did the floor.

"I was about to unlock the front door and turn the sign to *Open*," said Mrs. Danvers in an accusing tone. "But *she* told me not to."

"*I* said it would be best to wait until you arrived before we opened the store, dearie. Don't you agree?" said Mrs. Hudson.

"Um..." Jacqueline really wanted to sit down, but the nearest chair was across the room, and she didn't think her legs would carry her that far. Instead, she leaned against the bookshelf and tried to assimilate what was happening.

She'd heard perimenopause could be ugly, but she'd never imagined it could be this bad.

"Well?" Mrs. Danvers demanded.

"I-I think there's a lot of cleaning to be done before we—*I*, I mean—open the store," Jacqueline said. "And

I need to figure out the cash register system and the inventory, and—"

"Oh, no, dearie," said Mrs. Hudson with a gentle laugh. "We've finished all of that already, of course. I was just about to put that broom and mop away when *she* told me she wanted to open the store. I told her how we should be waiting for you to arrive, but now that you're here, I see no reason we shouldn't unlock the door and turn the sign."

"It *is* after nine o'clock," said Mrs. Danvers. "That's when the store opens."

Before Jacqueline could speak, the dour woman strode to the front door and flipped open the lock, then turned the hanging sign from *Closed* to *Open.*

"When it's a nice day, we leave the front door propped open," said Mrs. Hudson with a pleasant smile. "Gives a lovely breeze and encourages people to walk inside. And don't worry about the cats, luv," she went on as if Jacqueline wasn't gaping at her wordlessly. "Max and Sebastian won't go anywhere." She gestured to the pair of felines, who were watching the proceedings with mildly interested expressions. "They're literary cats."

"That's good," Jacqueline said faintly.

"I'll put these away and open up the tea room," Mrs. Hudson said.

"I suppose you'll want me to finish upstairs on the third floor flat," Mrs. Danvers said acidly. "The place is uninhabitable at the moment." She looked at Jacqueline as if it were her fault the apartment was a mess.

"Yes, I suppose that would be in order," Jacqueline replied, trying to sound as commanding as Rebecca de Winter would have been.

If you can't beat 'em, join 'em...?

Mrs. Hudson had disappeared up the stairs to the

tea room before Jacqueline realized she hadn't told her there would be no drinking of tea or eating of pastries in *her* bookstore. And Mrs. Danvers, after one more disdainful sniff, took herself off to who knew where—presumably the third-floor flat, where, Jacqueline decided, the bloody woman could stay as long as she wanted.

Fortunately, no one would expect Three Tomes to be open today, so Jacqueline figured she'd have plenty of time to check out the computer system. It couldn't be that difficult, could it?

She had just stepped behind the counter and was logging in to the computer—thanks to the password information given her by the estate attorney—when the front door opened. She looked up as a woman fairly burst into the shop.

She was about Jacqueline's age—maybe a little younger—and her shoulder-length walnut-brown hair was cut with long layers in a sort of updated Rachel Green look. She wore no makeup on her light skin, but her dark eyes didn't need anything to enhance them—they were large and bright and filled with enthusiasm. The stretchy athletic clothes she wore showed every bulge and curve of her stocky figure, and Jacqueline realized she was a little envious of a woman who didn't seem to mind showing off her shape in close-fitting clothing.

"Oh, I'm *so* glad you're open," the newcomer said breathlessly as she hurried across the room. "I came in for some of that tea." As she surged toward the counter, she seemed to recognize Jacqueline's disconcertion, and she slowed down, nearly coming to a halt.

"I'm sorry," the woman said with a friendly smile and a little laugh. "That was a little much, wasn't it? Let me try that again. I'm from right across the street, and I've been waiting for the shop to open again because I've been out of my favorite tea for over two months. My name is Nadine Bachmoto, and it's a pleasure to meet another businesswoman on the block! Welcome to Camellia Court." She began to extend a ringless, dimpled hand, then hesitated. "Um... you are the new owner, right? Andromeda said you'd arrived yesterday."

"Yes, I'm the new owner. Jacqueline Finch," Jacqueline said, shaking Nadine's hand. She must be the owner of Sweet Devotion. "I must admit, the minute I saw the sign across the street, I thought it was going to be very convenient to have you right there." She decided not to mention her rule about no food in the shop right away; it wasn't a good idea to get off on the wrong foot with another business owner.

"Well, you're welcome to come on over and join a class any time you want," Nadine said. "We've even got mats if you don't have your own."

"Mats?"

"Yoga mats—for loan, if you need one. I like to entice people to try out a class by letting them use one of the center's mats, and then after they take a few classes, they get sucked right in and buy their own." She grinned and leaned one elbow on the counter. "Once people get into yoga, they tend to stick with it."

"You own Yoga4Life?" Jacqueline said. Well, she'd certainly had that wrong—and shame on her for making assumptions.

"Going on two years now," replied Nadine. "Having Sweet Devotion right beneath us has really helped—she's new here too, by the way. Less than a year. I'm sure you'll meet her soon—Suzette's her name. Anyway, people come to the bakery then feel guilty, so they sign up for a yoga class. And people come to the yoga class and are hungry afterward or want to bring a treat home to their children—also feeling guilty—so they go to the bakery after. It's a win-win. We do particularly well with the guilt sales on Saturdays." Her eyes danced. "So, I came for some tea. Did I mention that?"

Jacqueline laughed. "You did. I'm afraid, though, that I literally just opened, and I don't have—"

"It's all right, dearie," said Mrs. Hudson, her long skirt coming into view as she descended the stairs. "I've got it all taken care of."

Jacqueline froze. She kept her attention off the housekeeper and on Nadine. If she ignored Mrs. Hudson, maybe she'd go away. The last thing Jacqueline needed was her customer watching the shop's new owner talk to people who weren't there. "So, anyway, I don't—"

"Oh, hello there," said Nadine, turning to greet Mrs. Hudson.

"Now which tea is it that you're liking now, luv?" asked the older woman as Jacqueline stared.

Could Nadine *see* Mrs. Hudson? And hear her?

"It's the Calendula Chamomile Rooibos," replied Nadine... as if there was nothing strange about talking to the living, breathing embodiment of a fictional character. "It's just perfect to help me relax at bedtime."

"Oh, yes, of course," Mrs. Hudson replied. "I just checked the tin, and we've got plenty. How much do you want?"

Jacqueline barely heard the ensuing conversation about the benefits of loose tea versus bagged tea and how many ounces Nadine was looking for, because she was realizing she *wasn't crazy*.

If Nadine Bachmoto could see and hear Mrs. Hudson, then... then...

How could that be?

Jacqueline mentally shook her head. There was no explanation for it. None whatsoever.

And so she wasn't even going to try to come up with one—at least, not now.

"I'll be showing you how to ring it up, then, dearie," said Mrs. Hudson to Jacqueline as she came around behind the counter with her.

Jacqueline was fully aware of the irony of a fictional Victorian landlady teaching her how to use a computer, but it was the only option at hand. Surprisingly, the process wasn't difficult at all, and was far simpler than the clunky computer system for fines and library cards she'd used for fifteen years before the CPL finally upgraded.

"Thank you again," said Nadine as she sailed toward the door with a sunny smile and a small paper shopping bag. "Gotta run—I have a class in five minutes. I hope to see you at one soon, Jacqueline!"

No sooner had the door jangled closed behind Nadine than Mrs. Danvers appeared. The housekeeper looked even more forbidding than usual.

"There is a situation, ma'am," she said, as though every syllable cost her extreme effort.

"What is it?" Jacqueline asked, still focused on the computer screen.

"You'll need to come with me," replied Mrs. Danvers. "If you'll be so kind. Ma'am." The last was clearly a reluctant, politically correct add-on.

"Very well," said Jacqueline with a sigh. She glanced at Mrs. Hudson. "I... um... If anyone else comes in, if you could please tell them I'll return shortly?"

"Oh, no, dearie," said Mrs. Hudson as she walked to the door and flipped the sign to *Closed*. The *snick* sound of the bolt locking followed. "If there's a situation Mrs. Danvers can't handle, it behooves me to offer me advice and guidance." She cast an arch look at her counterpart, who gave her an icy glare.

Mrs. Danvers silently—and with obvious reluctance—led the way to the third floor.

Instead of being accessed from the tea room, whose steps led only to that level from the front of the shop, the third-floor flat seemed to only be reached by a flight of stairs from the rear foyer of the house. Jacqueline approved of that for privacy purposes, but would make certain there was a fire escape in the event she decided to live there or rent it out.

Though it had never been her intention to reside above the place she worked, the moment Jacqueline stepped over the threshold of the third floor, her decision wavered. The stairs opened near the rear of the east-side wall of the third floor. To the left was the back of the house with some storage, a lavatory, and a small bedroom or office. To the right was a short corridor that led to another bedroom and ended in what appeared to be the living room and kitchen area.

Even from here, Jacqueline could see that the front room was light and airy, with those tall, slender Victorian windows—most of which were open at the moment—and rooms so spacious that she knew walls had to have been removed from the original design. There were bookshelves all along the hallway and into the living room. She caught a glimpse of a fireplace edged with ornate wood trim and green marble. Jacqueline had no idea whether it was wood-burning or gas, but she already imagined her favorite reading chair and lamp situated in front of it. Above the fireplace was a large, round mirror with a wide silver frame.

Since the hardwood floor of the corridor gleamed and there was the faint smell of lemon and vinegar, along with the open windows, it was obvious Mrs. Danvers had been hard at work. But the furnishings in the front room were still concealed with dust covers.

Jacqueline, who had seen nothing thus far that could be described as a "situation," followed Mrs. Danvers without comment. The woman strode down the hall past the larger bedroom to the living room, her heels thumping as purposefully as a marching soldier.

"There," said the housekeeper, pointing to the floor as Jacqueline came into the living room.

Jacqueline came to an abrupt halt, and Mrs. Hudson bumped into her from behind. (At least now Jacqueline knew the woman was corporeal and not an amorphous spirit.)

But that was the last of her coherent thoughts, because the "situation," as Mrs. Danvers had so mildly put it, was the *body of a man.*

The body of a man—who was clearly dead—was on the floor of Jacqueline's living room.

6

"Z! Andy! Get over here!" Pietra was standing at the window again.

Andromeda sighed. "I can't right now, I've—"

"There are *cops* at Three Tomes!" Pietra went on. She was so agitated that she pulled the curtain rod from its moorings and it nearly bonked her on the head. She tossed away the mass of curtains, glad for an unobstructed view.

"What?" Zwyla was there in a heartbeat, bracelets jangling, as she looked out over Pietra's head. "Is that Detective Massermey walking in?"

"What's *he* doing there?" Andromeda said, swishing over to the window in a colorful muumuu.

"I doubt he's buying an Agatha Christie novel," said Zwyla.

"No, but I could see him getting the new Michael Connelly," Andromeda replied thoughtfully.

"That can't be good," said Pietra, straining on her tiptoes as if being taller would help her see better. Which it didn't because the front of the bookshop was fully visible from their window. "Why is there a detective there?"

"Either someone died suspiciously," said Zwyla carefully, "or there's some other investigation."

All three of them pulled away from the window and looked at each other. "Crones' bones," breathed Andromeda. "I put the salt barrier all around the house, and every day when I feed the cats, I've been checking to make sure it's not been broken."

Zwyla's expression relaxed a little. "Then it's probably nothing."

"We should go over and find out," said Pietra, her nose pressed to the window in another vain attempt to see more. "Andi, did you get more witch hazel to clean the mirror? Maybe we can take a peek—"

"No, we're not going to *take a peek*," her friend replied. "That's an invasion of privacy."

"And it wasn't an invasion of privacy to peek at Jacqueline three weeks ago, on the worst day of her life?" Pietra fired back. A stray spark snapped between them, but Andromeda just waved it away.

"I don't actually think that was the worst day of her life," said Andromeda. "I'm pretty sure the actual worst day of Jacqueline Finch's life was the day she found out her fiancé was cheating on her—what, three days before their wedding?—and she decided to dump him. But then Stacey dying too... that had to have been an awful day for Jacqueline as well." She looked at her friends. If anything happened to one of the three of them, the other two would be devastated. It would feel as if one of their limbs had been cut off.

"Anyway, that day three weeks ago couldn't have been Jacqueline's worst day ever, because she learned about Three Tomes that day. She inherited a big, beautiful, very special house and a viable business," Andromeda went on. "How could it be her worst day?"

"Josh cheating on her was awful, and her losing

her best friend was even worse, but I'm pretty sure losing her job, her home, and her reputation all in one day was even worse than that," Pietra argued. "Even with the inheritance."

"I'm not so sure," Zwyla said, still looking out the window. "Think about it this way—since Josh Wenczel broke her heart and destroyed her trust, Jacqueline has never let anyone—particularly any man—get that close to her again. She clung to Stacey as her best friend and otherwise closed herself off, went through the motions of life, and has been sort of half living for the last twenty years. And once Stacey passed on... well, I think Josh's betrayal had already changed Jacqueline at the core, deep inside. And not for the better."

"And then she came to Button Cove," said Pietra in a singsongy voice. "And began to live again."

"That remains to be seen," said Zwyla. "We don't know whether she's the right one or not."

"Cuddy said—"

"Cuddy made plenty of mistakes over the years. Need I remind you of Chloe Brownley?" Zwyla replied, looking meaningfully at Andromeda. "And Federica Rozinsky?"

"Right. I still think we should go over there and offer some support," said Pietra, reaching for her pink trench coat.

"You mean find out what's going on," said Andromeda.

"Well, of course." Pietra rolled her eyes. "Get some of your abundance tea, won't you, Andy? It's as good excuse as any."

"Not that you need an excuse," muttered Zwyla. But she followed them to the door.

~

"I JUST ARRIVED HERE YESTERDAY," Jacqueline said. "Like I said, it was the first time I'd been up here, so I don't know how long h-he's been there."

She sounded calm, she thought, but inside, her nerves were jumping around in fits and starts, and her stomach was joining them in frenetic hula circles. The mushroom crepe was no longer sitting very well either.

How could there be a dead body in her house?

The Universe really did hate her.

"All right, ma'am," said the police officer whose name she'd already forgotten. Or maybe she hadn't been listening through the roaring in her ears. He seemed nice enough, but he'd asked her the same questions several times already. At least he'd put one of the furniture covers over the body, even though there was no blood or signs of trauma. "Oh, here's the detective."

Jacqueline turned, wondering how many more times she was going to have to answer the same questions.

When she saw the man striding down the corridor toward them, her first thought was: Leif Erickson in the twenty-first century. He was broad-shouldered and with a muscular build that was just starting to soften a little with age. His footsteps were solid and confident.

His hair was not Nordic-explorer long, but cut so that it was just a little spiky on top—or maybe he'd just ruffled his hair so it was messy. It looked like it was going from strawberry blond to silvery white, but his beard and mustache were still vibrant Nancy-Drew-titian. As he drew closer, Jacqueline could see the freckles all over his fair skin that gave him a sort of sandy-brown, outdoorsman cast. Unlike the uniformed cop, he wore street clothes of dark dress pants, a pale blue button-down shirt open one button at the throat (no tie), and a jacket.

"Hello, ma'am," he said. His eyes were a mild blue-gray, and the crinkles at their corners suggested he was in his early fifties. "I understand we have a situation here. I'm Detective Miles Massermey of the Button Cove Police Department." He showed her his badge.

"Miles Massermey? Who's the James Bond fan?" Jacqueline blurted out without thinking, then she felt her face heat up.

The detective looked at her, his heavy red-blond brows lifting. "My mother," he said slowly. "Not many people know the literary reference."

She spread her hands. "Librarian for twenty-five years. Hazard of the trade."

"Still, he's Miles Messervy in the books," the detective said. "I'm surprised you made the connection, and so quickly."

"Messervy is Cornish and there are many variations of the surname," Jacqueline said, unable to stop herself. She could pull out factoids faster than Ken Jennings. "I just assumed Massermey was one of them." She wondered if the detective was trying to relax her by talking about something *other* than the dead body lying on the floor. If so, she appreciated it.

"That's right," he replied. "Now, how about you tell me what happened here?"

"Nothing really happened," Jacqueline responded, suddenly getting nervous. His demeanor had changed into something sharp and intimidating. "I mean, I w-was downstairs with a customer, and then I came up here"—she absolutely couldn't tell him that a person who didn't exist had first discovered the body—"and there he was. I-I didn't touch anything. I just called 911."

And when she'd hung up from the call, she realized Mrs. Danvers and Mrs. Hudson had disappeared. She wasn't certain whether their escape was permanent or temporary. Either way, that had to be a good thing. A policeman interrogating two fictional characters would have just been the icing on the cake. What would they have said when he asked where they came from or where they lived? Jacqueline shuddered at the thought.

"All right." Massermey nodded at the officer. "Lift the sheet, Officer Whitt, and let me take a look."

He squatted next to the body as Jacqueline watched with morbid fascination. She'd read countless murder mysteries and thrillers over the years, of course, and being the sort of person who was always interested in new information, she found the situation both upsetting and compelling. And since the man wasn't known to her, and there was no sign of trauma or injury, she figured he—whoever he was—had died of a heart attack or stroke or something.

But what he was doing upstairs at Three Tomes was anyone's guess.

After he checked the man's pockets and gave him a brief examination, Detective Massermey rose, and she heard the soft cracking of his knees.

"Getting old sucks," he said with a wry smile, gesturing to his knees. "But it's better than the alternative. Like this poor man here. Now, I understand you arrived here in Button Cove only yesterday. Is that correct?"

"Yes. I got here about three o'clock."

"Was anyone with you? Husband, children... anyone?"

Jacqueline felt her cheeks warm. "No, neither. I am —was—alone. I hadn't ever been here before, and there was-was so much work that had to be done downstairs—mopping and dusting and getting things ready to open—that I didn't even come up here until this morning." Even though everything she said was absolutely, strictly true, she felt nervous.

"So you got some cleaning done up here, then?"

Crap. She couldn't exactly explain that Mrs. Danvers had done the work. "A-a little," she replied. Then she smiled ruefully. "I'm sorry if I sound scattered. I've never been interrogated about a dead body before."

Massermey gave her an understanding smile. "Not many people have, despite what Hollywood might have us think. So you were cleaning up here and then you got to this room and what happened?"

"Well... there he was," Jacqueline said, guessing that was how it had happened for Mrs. Danvers. "Just lying there. It-it was obvious he was dead."

"Do you know this man, Ms.... Finch, is it?"

"I don't know anyone here in Button Cove, Detective. I only just met a few people yesterday and this morning. And I didn't want to—uh—contaminate a crime scene, so I didn't get close enough to look. But I'm certain I don't know him."

"Crime scene? What makes you think this is a crime scene?" Massermey's eyes locked on hers, and Jacqueline felt a jolt of nerves.

"Well, I don't know," she replied. "I just... He doesn't *live* here and he wasn't *invited* here, and he's dead, and so there's at least *some* kind of crime—breaking and entering at the very least." She lifted her chin, delighted she'd pulled that last bit out of thin air.

"I need to file a report that someone broke into my property, Detective. And that someone had the temerity to *die* here. Either with help or without. Which I assume you'll be investigating."

She could have sworn the corner of his mouth twitched a little, but it was hard to tell with the beard. "You will definitely need to file a report," he said agreeably. "But I do think you should take a look at him so we have an official answer on the record as to whether you know him or not."

"Very well," she replied, suppressing a shudder. At least the man wasn't covered in blood or anything.

Jacqueline had only seen one dead body outside of a funeral visitation, and that was when a woman literally dropped dead of a heart attack at the library about eight years ago. This was a similar situation, she told herself as she went over to look at the man.

She noticed the dead man's clothing, which was nothing remarkable: a pair of slacks and a long-sleeved t-shirt of light material. His feet were shod in athletic shoes, and he wore neither ring nor watch from what she could tell.

Officer Whitt lifted the covering away, and Jacqueline gave the dead man's face a good look. He appeared to be about her age, clean-shaven and with a very short graying haircut. The side of his face was pressed into the rug, causing it to be distorted, but she was confident in her statement.

"No, Detective, I don't know who this man is. And I have no idea why he was here or how he got inside."

"No evidence of breaking and entering? Anything missing?"

Besides her sanity? Jacqueline choked off a laugh. "It's difficult for me to say, Detective Massermey. As I mentioned, I only arrived yesterday and had never been here before. I wouldn't know if anything was missing."

"When you were here yesterday, you didn't come up here at all?" When she shook her head, he continued, "Did you hear any noises from up here, either today or yesterday?"

"No, Detective. And I don't think he was a squatter, if that's where you're going with that line of questioning. There's no evidence anyone was living here—the place was dusty and dirty and all of the furniture is still covered." At least, that was what Mrs. Danvers had given her to believe.

He nodded and pursed his lips. "All right, then, Ms. Finch. I don't have any further questions for you right now." He dug into his pocket and withdrew a card. "If you think of anything else, please contact me here—my cell phone is on there as well as my e-mail."

Jacqueline took his card, but before she could speak, she heard the sound of voices coming from the hallway.

"Now don't you worry, Officer, we won't get in anyone's way," trilled a voice that Jacqueline recognized. It was Pietra.

"We can't imagine what Jacqueline is going through," said Andromeda. "But we're here to help."

Detective Massermey stifled a groan. "Oh no," he muttered. "Not those three."

But it was, indeed, those three.

7

"**O**h, dear Jacqueline!" cried Pietra as soon as they came into view. "We heard all about it. How are you holding up, my dear?" She was carrying a basket covered by a pink-checked cloth, and Jacqueline couldn't help but hope that it contained more blueberry scones.

"What an awful shock it must have been," said Andromeda, whose platinum hair had acquired blue at the tips since yesterday. And her green eyes looked bluer for some reason. She held a round metal tin that reminded Jacqueline of the little lunchbox Laura Ingalls Wilder used when she was teaching school on the prairie... and then as soon as she had that thought, she banished it.

The last thing she wanted was Laura Ingalls showing up here too, with her prairie locusts and horrific blizzards.

Zwyla, who was two inches taller than Detective Massermey, didn't have anything in her hands, but her eyes were compassionate as they met Jacqueline's. "We're very sorry to hear about what happened. If there's anything we can do..."

Jacqueline was about to reply, but Pietra interrupted. "Oh my word, is this him?"

Before Massermey could stop them, the three women surged toward the dead man.

"Ladies, I'm going to have to ask you to step away," the detective said, sounding harassed. "This is a potential crime scene."

"Crime scene?" Zwyla turned with a jangle of bracelets. Today she was wearing a lime-green turban and tangerine lipstick. She gave off such a regal air that Jacqueline almost felt bad for the detective when Zwyla fixed him with those dark, steady eyes. From two inches higher.

"Potential crime scene," Massermey replied. "Now, ladies, I know you want to help, but—"

"Who're you calling a lady?" said Andromeda, batting her eyelashes teasingly. "I haven't been a lady since I was fifteen."

Massermey's beard and mustache twitched and the corners of his eyes crinkled a bit, then the flicker of humor was gone. "Come on now, you three. Downstairs. No one needs to be up here until we finish our work."

"Will CSI be coming?" asked Pietra, her eyes dancing. "I want to watch them dust for fingerprints."

Massermey sighed. "You know very well we're a small department and don't have a full CSI crew. But yes, of course there will be someone here taking all of the trace evidence."

"Sounds like a murder investigation," said Zwyla, looking at the detective.

"Suspicious death," retorted Massermey. "Now, let's go." He began to herd the trio and Jaqueline toward the hall that led to the back set of stairs.

No sooner had the four of them reached the ground floor than Pietra said, "Let's have some tea and talk about all of this. Poor Jacqueline."

Before Jacqueline could reroute them, the ladies led their way from the rear of the house to a tiny, well-hidden elevator that took them up to the tea room. It took two trips because it was so small. The elevator opened in the back of the second floor, taking them through the area behind the café that Jacqueline hadn't yet seen—a children's reading room with a comfy rocking chair and loads of picture books, and another room that was filled with a variety of non-book sorts of objects. She only caught a glimpse as she was whisked past, but there were crystals, incense sticks, statues of Buddha, earth mothers, angels, fairies, and other figures, candles, and hammered metal bowls. She was enchanted while also being astonished. How could the house hold all of these rooms —these comfy, interesting spaces!—with rooms that opened into more rooms and nooks and little hallway crannies?

When they reached the tea room, Jacqueline was startled to find Mrs. Hudson hard at work behind the counter. Apparently even knowing there was a dead body in the house wasn't enough to scare off the woman.

"Oh, and there you are, dearie," Mrs. Hudson said by way of greeting. "I've got some water heating for your tea, now, haven't I? Take a seat, all of you, there, and I'll bring it right over."

What *was* it with these old ladies and tea?

When the three women greeted Mrs. Hudson familiarly, Jacqueline relaxed a little. It seemed Zwyla, Pietra, and Andromeda could not only see the Englishwoman, but had met her before. Jacqueline wasn't certain what that meant, but it was another check in the column of *I'm Not Crazy*.

"I've brought some of my violet and dandelion abundance tea," said Andromeda, holding up the metal tin so it dangled from its handle. "It's got bergamot and birch in it."

"Land sakes, dearie, I think a Situation Like This deserves a good, strong cup of black English tea." Jacqueline could actually hear the capital letters in Mrs. Hudson's speech. "Now you just let me take care of it—but don't you be getting used to this sort of service," she warned Jacqueline. "I'm a landlady, not a housekeeper, mind."

"Right," Jacqueline replied faintly.

What would happen if she just got in her car and drove away and never came back? She could find another job in Chicago. Another cute house with a tiny yard she could plant flowers in. And Lester the CPA was still there to hang out with. Maybe having sex (mediocre as it was) would help clear her mind...

But no. Despite all of the craziness (and Jacqueline thought *craziness* was a feeble word to describe what had occurred in the last twenty-four hours), she felt the house continuing to pull at her.

It was a beautiful, comfortable, cozy place, and if she'd ever imagined the perfect bookstore, Three Tomes was pretty close to being just that. Except for the idea of eating and drinking with abandon near printed material. She was really going to have to say something to Mrs. Hudson—and the three other ladies—soon.

"... salt was disturbed at the back entrance," Andromeda was saying in a low voice as Jacqueline's attention returned to the conversation. "That must be how he got inside."

"I don't like Massermey being involved," Zwyla said. "There will be lots of questions." When she realized Jacqueline was listening, she smoothed out her frown and smiled. "Must have been quite the shock for you, finding him."

"It was," Jacqueline replied, eyeing them thoughtfully.

"Now here we go," said Mrs. Hudson, bustling over with a steaming teapot. "Nothing like a nice, good, strong English breakfast tea to brace yourselves up during a Time of Trauma." More capital letters. As she poured, she said, "I knew it was something awful when that Danvers woman came down to tell us." She tsked. "Of course, I was going to be needed, having had the likes of Mr. Holmes living upstairs. He and that Dr. Watson were always getting themselves embroiled in problems and mysteries—and then there were the *smells*! Lands, I don't know what he was doing up there all those times—he wouldn't let me inside to see."

Jacqueline watched her companions for their reactions as Mrs. Hudson prattled on. The fact that none of the three older women seemed surprised or confused by her words mollified Jacqueline a little. It appeared that not only could Pietra, Andromeda, and Zwyla see, hear, and interact with Mrs. Hudson, but they weren't shocked by the fact that she was Sherlock Holmes's landlady.

"Yes, yes, we know all about it," Andromeda said with a wave of her hand. "Mr. Holmes was a terrible tenant. You don't know why you put up with him. Yada, yada."

"But he paid me a princely sum every month to be

putting up with him." Mrs. Hudson was quick to defend the famous fictional detective. Jacqueline had to keep reminding herself that Sherlock Holmes, John Watson, and Mrs. Hudson never actually existed.

And yet, once again, here she was, drinking tea poured by the landlady of 221B Baker Street.

When Mrs. Hudson went back to her business behind the counter, taking Andromeda's tea tin with her, Jacqueline decided it was time to ask some questions —and get some answers.

"You've met Mrs. Hudson before," she said, looking at all three of the women in turn.

"Yes, of course," replied Pietra. "She's always here. She and Da—"

Zwyla interrupted. "I'm certain it was a shock for you to meet her."

"Not to put too fine of a point on it, but *yes,*" Jacqueline retorted. "I mean... you're making it seem like it's all so *normal* to have fictional characters wandering about and—and doing things."

"You've seen more than one?" asked Zwyla cautiously.

"Well, yes, Mrs. Danvers is here too. Or she was," Jacqueline replied. "Maybe she's gone now that she found the body."

"No chance of that," replied Zwyla with a grimace. "Now that she's back, she won't leave again. I was hoping she hadn't returned."

"Back from *where*?" asked Jacqueline.

"Well, they came out of the books, didn't they?" said Pietra with a comforting smile. "That's how they always come."

"Is there a way to put them back?" Jacqueline said desperately.

The three women shook their heads.

"Why? Can't I just... keep the books closed? Tie them shut? Or sell them?"

"If you can find them," replied Andromeda with a wry smile.

"You mean to say their books are gone? Is that what that man was doing here? Stealing books?"

Zwyla shook her head again. "No, he wasn't after books. And Danvers and Mrs. Hudson have—if the past is any indication, which I'm certain it is—removed their respective books and put them somewhere where they can't be found."

"But why?"

"Neither of them will leave while the other one is here," said Pietra with a smile that rounded her already round cheeks even more. "It's like a mutual destruction society contract."

"Mutual destruction is a damned good description," muttered Zwyla.

"You mean I'm stuck with them?" Jacqueline didn't care that her voice pitched higher than library level.

"It's not that bad," Andromeda said, patting her hand. "After all, they do all the work—each one is always trying to outdo the other. Cuddy actually liked having them around."

"Speaking of Cuddy Stone," Jacqueline said, "do you have any idea why a distant relation I've never met —never even heard of—would have bequeathed this place to me?"

The three women exchanged glances, which seemed to result in Andromeda being the one chosen to respond. "It doesn't matter how *distantly* you're related. You're the right person, Jacqueline. Who else would understand this whole arrangement—and embrace it—or, rather, *learn* to embrace it, which we hope you will do?"

"If you like this place so much, why didn't one of *you* inherit it?" Jacqueline shot back. "If you were such good friends with Cuddy Stone, why didn't she leave it to one of you?"

"Oh, we've got other things to do besides run a bookstore," Pietra told her with a wave of her hand. "Plenty of other things. Like keeping the likes of Hen—"

Zwyla moved sharply, and Jacqueline heard a definite thump beneath the table. Pietra jolted and made an "*ow*" face.

But Jacqueline was done with being talked over and around. "You knew that man, didn't you?" she said. "The dead man."

The trio looked at each other, and for a minute, she thought they were going to deny it.

Pietra caved. "Yes. That was Henbert Stone upstairs. Oh, get off it, Zwyla. She's got to know," she added, giving her friend a look.

"Henbert Stone, as in some relation to Cuddy Stone?" Jacqueline felt a strange prickling over her shoulders. "Why was he here? Was he stealing something? Did he think he should have inherited this place?" To her surprise, she felt a pang of worry that there might be someone who'd fight her over the bequest... which had somehow turned from a potential albatross to a treasure in less than a day.

Once again, Andromeda seemed to be the one elected to speak. "Distant cousin of Cuddy, yes, and he did think he should have inherited the store when she died. But Cuddy was never going to let him get his hands on this place."

"So now that I'm here, he decided to break in? It seems counterintuitive for him to wait until someone

takes possession of the place before he breaks in—
why didn't he break in while it was vacant?"

Andromeda glanced at Zwyla, whose face was as still
as carved walnut, then looked back at Jacqueline. "We
did everything we could to make sure he didn't get inside. It worked until—well, when you arrived yesterday."

"I certainly didn't leave the doors unlocked—Wait,
did Mrs. Hudson or Mrs. Danvers let him in?" Jacqueline was outraged.

"No, no, no," said Pietra quickly. "They wouldn't do
that. In fact, I would guess they didn't even know he
was there. It was the salt line. You must have
broken it."

Jacqueline stared at her, prickles erupting all over
her body. "Salt line." She'd read *A Discovery of Witches*
and *Jonathan Strange and Mr. Norrell*, among many
other novels about witchcraft and sorcery. "You're
telling me you put a salt line around Three Tomes to...
protect it from... evil?"

"Yes," said Zwyla, breaking her forbidding silence
at last. "You must have broken it somehow."

Things were starting to make a little bit of sense—
crazy as they were—for Jacqueline remembered how
she'd seen what she thought was snow- and ice-
melting salt at the back door, and how she brushed it
out of the way when she came inside.

"I did," she replied slowly. "I didn't know."

Of course she didn't know. *How* could she know?

"It's all right, Jacqueline," said Pietra, patting her
hand. "Although now we have this entire problem
with Henbert to deal with."

"Why do you have to deal with it?" asked Jacqueline. "It's Detective Massermey's problem, not yours."

Once again, the three ladies looked at each other.

Pietra sighed and her shoulders slumped a little. "Well, because—"

"Because now that Henbert is dead, his sister Egala is going to show up," said Zwyla. "And she's going to be *pissed*."

8

Later that afternoon, Jacqueline was reshelving some of the so-called classics, cataloguing them into their proper fiction genres like mystery or romance, when she heard the front door of the shop open.

Hoping it was a patron—er, customer—and not the three older ladies returning with more dire predictions and other unasked-for advice, she hurried out to the front room.

"Good afternoon," she said, looking around to make sure Mrs. Danvers wasn't lurking about. The last time Jacqueline had seen her was shortly after Detective Massermey and his team left, when the dour housekeeper complained bitterly about being unable to get back to cleaning the upstairs apartment. She clearly didn't understand the concept of a crime scene.

Jacqueline was not looking forward to what Mrs. Danvers was going to say about the fingerprint dust.

The woman who'd entered the shop gave Jacqueline a shy but warm smile. "Hi," she said, ducking a little as she waved. "I'm Suzette Whalley from across the street—Sweet Devotion. I just wanted to introduce myself and welcome you to the neighborhood, so to speak."

She looked to be in her mid-forties and had smooth olive skin, with a pointed chin and sharp cheekbones. Her curly jet-black hair was liberally interspersed with strands of silver, and there was one streak of white in the front. She wore jeans, a casual long-sleeved tee, and thick-soled black clogs, and there was a smudge of flour at the edge of her jaw.

"Very nice to meet you," said Jacqueline. "I'm sorry I haven't had the chance to come over and say hi—things have been a little crazy here." *You have no idea.*

"Oh, I completely understand. I saw the cops—I mean, the police—were here. I hope everything is all right, and honestly, I didn't come over trying to be nosy and find out! I really, truly just came over to introduce myself... and to let you know that Nadine and I usually get together on Sunday evenings after her last class for a little, you know, girl time—and to gear up for the week here on Camellia Court. Neither of us are married, my kids are busy with their dad this weekend, and Nadine's daughters are off at college..." She spread her hands. "The bakery is closed on Mondays, so Sunday—gosh, is that tomorrow already?—is the only evening I can stay up late and not have to worry about getting up at four a.m. to knead dough and drop cookies onto baking sheets." She grinned a little shyly. "If you want to join us, we get together around seven thirty. We meet upstairs at Nadine's."

At first, Jacqueline didn't know how to respond. She wasn't one for social gatherings—especially with people she didn't know well—and she had so much to do here at the shop that she didn't think she could spare any time.

But somehow, she found herself responding, "That

would be really nice. I don't know anyone here in Button Cove—except, um, well, there are these three older ladies who have been by a few times."

Suzette chuckled. "Oh, I know Petey and Andromeda and Zwyla—everyone does. They're... a lot to take in, aren't they?"

Jacqueline gave a little laugh and shook her head. "I'll say. They seem nice, though."

And strange.

"Nice as can be," Suzette assured her. "Nosy as hell, but sweet as pie. They have quite the garden in the courtyard behind their house—based on its yield, you could almost call it a small farm, but a lot of it is vertical, so it doesn't have a large footprint. Honestly, it's almost magical, the volume they can harvest from that small plot.

"Theirs is that blue Victorian at the end of the court—I'm sure you've seen it; it's hard to miss. I get my rhubarb from them and some of the herbs I use in breads and rolls." She seemed to hesitate, then went on, "I know you're just getting settled, but when you have time, maybe we could talk about whether you want Sweet Devotion to continue supplying some of the treats for the tea room upstairs."

Jacqueline's smile remained fixed, but inside, her stomach dropped. *Crap.* Here she was, just getting to know this woman, and now she was going to have to tell her she wasn't really interested in having baked goods inside her shop. "Oh, right, yes, we should talk —after I get settled and everything," she said, wondering how long she could put off that conversation.

"No pressure," said Suzette with a smile. "Honestly. I just wanted to let you know Sweet Devotion is happy to continue the relationship we previously had with Three Tomes. And I mainly popped over here to invite you to come on Sunday. We usually drink wine and have a pizza—I make sure to have some dough on hand."

"That sounds wonderful," Jacqueline said, and meant it. Now that she was a business owner, she was probably going to have to schmooze a little with other business owners, and this sounded like a good way to do it. "I can bring a bottle of wine and a salad if you want."

"Nadine's got the salad this time, but wine is always, *always* welcome," Suzette replied with dancing eyes. "We'll see you tomorrow night, then! And once again, welcome to the neighborhood!"

Jacqueline waved her out the door and was just about to return to the reshelving of the classics when the bell at the back of the shop jingled.

To her surprise and delight, it was a pair of young women who turned out to be actual customers.

"We're so glad you've reopened the place," said one of them as she browsed through the new releases that Jacqueline had arranged on a front table.

"Yes, we really missed Three Tomes when it was closed," said the other, bringing the new thriller by TJ Mack up to the counter. "Oh, hello, there, Sebastian," she crooned, stooping to pet the ginger cat. Even from behind the counter, Jacqueline could hear him purring his approval.

Meanwhile, Max sat on a high shelf, watching the display of affection with cool gray eyes. The end of his tail snapped and twitched, indicating his mood.

Jacqueline spent some time chatting about books with and waiting on the two young women, along with a steady stream of customers who meandered in. It was Saturday in Button Cove, and the late spring weather had brought everyone out to the downtown area—and they apparently were in the mood to spend money. By the time she had the chance to catch her breath, Jacqueline realized several hours had passed —and she'd sold plenty of books, both new and vintage, without even trying.

Some of the customers had made their way up to the tea room, and Jacqueline could hear Mrs. Hudson serving and chattering with them. Jacqueline hoped the woman wasn't rambling on about Mr. Holmes.

She'd caught sight of Mrs. Danvers, who was dusting some of the shelves, and, apparently having at some point learned how to operate one, was using a vacuum cleaner on the floors. While Mrs. Hudson seemed to enjoy interacting with the customers, Mrs. Danvers remained as aloof and disdainful as Max, going about her business with cold efficiency while ignoring everyone.

Jacqueline remembered what Pietra said about the two women "doing everything" for Cuddy Stone, and it dawned on her that she'd somehow acquired free labor by two helpful and determined characters who knew more about Three Tomes than she did.

Maybe it wasn't such a bad deal, she thought— unless Danvers and Hudson decided to pull a Phantom of the Opera and demand their twenty thousand francs or whatever the equivalent was in today's dollars... and then she was shocked at herself. How easily she'd come to accept the idea of fictional people becoming instrumental to her business!

It was six o'clock and Jacqueline was just about to flip the front door sign to Closed when a woman appeared at the window.

Suppressing a sigh—for she'd had a long day, what with a dead body up in her apartment and the police in and out—Jacqueline stepped back to open the door and gave her a pleasant smile.

The woman pushed through and swept into the shop. "Sorry if I'm keeping you," she said in an unapologetic tone, and looked around. Her expression was one of expectation and undisguised curiosity.

Jaqueline stood at the counter, waiting to see if the woman was going to buy anything or just browse, and fervently hoped it wasn't going to last too long. She needed a big glass of wine—maybe even a cocktail—and to sit down and put her feet up.

What a day.

But at least she had some new potential friends *and*, she thought with a smile, the new TJ Mack book she'd planned to read three weeks ago. One of the perks of owning a bookstore.

"So you're the new owner," the woman said, lingering by the counter.

Jacqueline estimated the customer was older than she was—maybe early sixties—and that was only because of her hands. The pale white skin of the woman's face, however, was smooth and taut. She had sharp, bony features, with very thin brow arches drawn on with dark pencil, and what Jacqueline thought of as "shampoo and set" hair: the type of style that older women went to the salon for on a weekly basis. Her short, curled hair was a faded blond mixed with iron gray, styled in the same manner as the movie version of Professor Umbridge. She wore casual dun-colored pants and a loose tunic with spirally designs that looked like hyperactive rainbows. Her sandals revealed toenails painted bright pink.

"That's right. I'm the owner," Jacqueline said.

"How did you come to get this place? Didn't the previous owner die?" The woman picked up one of the brand-new business cards Jacqueline had optimistically ordered before coming to Button Cove. "Jacqueline Finch, is it?"

Jacqueline was beginning to feel a little strange. The woman seemed more interested in her than in any of the books. Although she supposed that wasn't a surprise; the customer seemed familiar enough with the store to be a regular.

Nor was she certain how to respond to the pointed questions. It would feel strange to explain that a woman she'd never met had bequeathed the place to her. "Yes, the previous owner passed away. Is there something in particular you're looking for?"

"Yes," replied the woman, settling a very hard gaze onto Jacqueline. "I'm looking for my brother. Henbert Stone."

Jacqueline couldn't speak for a moment. Then, somehow, she managed to pull herself together. "You must be Egala Stone," she replied. "I'm very sorry for your—"

"And you must be the bitch who killed my brother."

9

Oh shit.
Oh shit, oh shit, oh shit.

Zwyla had been right—the dead man's sister had shown up, and she was *pissed.*

"I most certainly did not kill your brother," Jacqueline said in her firm keep-your-voices-down librarian's tone, even though her insides felt like a mess of dancing snakes. "It was an accident, I think—"

"You *think?*" Egala's dark eyes flashed with fury and—no way!—literal sparks seemed to be snapping from her hands.

Jacqueline felt a little faint, then she shook her head to clear it. Yes, really freaking strange things were happening here, but there was no way this woman was shooting off sparks into the air just by standing here.

But then one landed on the counter and Jacqueline saw the little flare of ember before she smacked her hand down on it.

Well, Toto, it looks like we're not in Kansas anymore.

The thought popped into Jacqueline's mind and she frantically dismissed it. *No, no, no...*

Egala had placed her hands on the counter, and

she leaned forward into Jacqueline's space. "An *accident*?" Her voice was hardly more than a low growl. "I'll show you an accident, you murderous *thief*."

Before Jacqueline could respond, every book on the front display table rose in a wild cyclone, then scattered, tumbling all over the floor.

Jacqueline cried out in shock and pain—not for herself, but for those fragile bindings and delicate endpapers and all of those beautiful pages and the tender dust jackets. She scrambled out from behind the counter to rescue them as Egala watched.

"I'm not a thief, and you're not welcome here," Jacqueline said furiously as she grabbed up the books, holding them protectively to her chest with one arm. "You can leave—"

"This place belongs to me and my brother," snarled Egala, her eyes lit with rage. "You have no right to be here. You *stole* it—"

"I did nothing of the sort," Jacqueline retorted, gently setting an armful of books on the table. She'd reorganize them later; right now, she was furious with this interloper. Even the sparks in Egala's eyes weren't enough to frighten Jacqueline. "And anyone who'd do what you just did to a bunch of innocent books doesn't *deserve* to be here, let alone *own* a bookstore. Now, I think we're done here." She pointed sharply toward the door, mildly surprised at her own vehemence. "The store is closed."

"Why, you little—"

The door opened. When Jacqueline turned to see who was there, she had another shock. "Detective Massermey," she said. Now her stomach and the rest of her insides were *really* doing the tango, and her spike of fury evaporated and became anxiety. What did he want?

What was the homicide detective doing back here?

"Hello again, Ms. Finch," he replied, looking at the disordered mess of books on the table, then back at Jacqueline. She resisted the urge to reach up and check her French twist to see how disordered *she* was. "I'm sorry to bother you—please, don't let me interrupt you with your customer."

"Oh, that's all right," Jacqueline said in what she hoped was a breezy voice. "We've finished here." Despite her words, she was not at all certain whether Egala would leave, or whether she'd do something else.

But apparently, the presence of a lawman, or perhaps just another person, regardless of their occupation, was enough incentive for Egala Stone to surrender—for the moment, anyway. "Yes, we've finished for now," replied the other woman. She didn't have to say the words "*But I'll be back,*" because Jacqueline read them in her hard, angry eyes.

Great. Just great.

When Egala left, Jacqueline flipped the sign to *Closed* this time, then locked the door. She didn't want anyone else strolling in while the detective was here.

"Everything all right here?" asked Massermey, his attention straying to the jumble of books once again.

"Yes," she replied, resisting the compulsion to begin straightening them up. "What can I do for you, Detective?"

"I just wanted to come by and let you know that preliminary tests indicate the man died from indeterminate causes." He scratched his strawberry-blond beard with long, freckled fingers. "They're doing a full PM—uh, postmortem—so we should know more soon."

"I see," Jacqueline replied. "I'm surprised you'd make a personal visit to deliver the news."

He gave a short laugh and rubbed a hand over his bearded chin. "Truth is, I was getting a pie from across the street when I saw that you were still here. Thought I'd just stop by and let you know in person. And then I got the impression that there might be something... uh... going on... when I looked in the window."

"Oh? What kind of pie?" Jacqueline purposely deflected from his implied question.

"Cherry with ginger ale," he replied with a grin. "My daughter's a big fan. She's home from college this week—just finished her exams. Junior year." He sounded like a proud papa.

"That sounds very unique," replied Jacqueline uncertainly. "The pie flavor. And congrats to your daughter."

"It's the best. And so is she. She's going to be a veterinarian." Massermey looked at the books she'd been unable to keep from straightening up on the front table. "So, everything's all right?"

"Other than someone breaking into my shop and then deciding to drop dead for some reason, everything is just peachy." She did give him a look then. "I still want to know why he broke in here. When will I be able to have access to the apartment upstairs? Maybe—maybe I'll find something that helps explain." Or maybe she'd get the three old ladies to give up some tea—meaning some scoop or gossip, not the beverage. Obviously, Zwyla, Petey, and Andromeda knew something about it all. Maybe even Mrs. Danvers or Mrs. Hudson would have a clue.

"Probably tomorrow," he replied. "Afternoon. Sorry about that, but I've got to cross all the T's and dot all the I's on a suspicious death."

"Yes, I suppose you'd better. All right, then, thanks for stopping by with the info. Where's the pie?" she said, suddenly realizing his hands were empty.

"Oh," he said, and his cheeks got a little red. "I put it in my car."

"Well, I hope you and your wife enjoy your daughter's visit," she said, unlocking the door in a not-so-subtle hint that she wanted him to leave.

"Just me," he replied. "Divorced ten years ago."

"Oh." Jacqueline was startled at how satisfied she was to learn that tidbit, then realized her own cheeks felt a little warm. For pity's sake. She was a forty-eight-year-old woman, not a blushing schoolgirl. The only time her face was supposed to get flushed was from hot flashes. But the guy gave off some serious Leif Erikson-meets-Wyatt Earp vibes.

"And despite what happened earlier today," Massermey went on, "I want to welcome you to Button Cove. We really don't have that many suspicious deaths here. It's a nice little town—even when the tourists descend." He smiled.

"Thank you," she replied, opening the door. "Enjoy your evening."

Finally alone, she locked the door again. Her attention fell on the jumble of books Egala had spun off the table, and she began to rearrange them. It was a familiar, soothing task—and one that kept her mind focused on visual display rather than what had just happened.

Mrs. Danvers and Mrs. Hudson were nowhere to be found, and the shop was very quiet. It felt homey. Comfortable.

She realized she liked it. A lot.

Jacqueline picked up Sebastian, and before she thought about what she was doing, she'd cuddled his warm, fluffy body to her chest as she murmured silly things into his fur. Hm. Maybe she was a cat lover after all.

"I'm not even going to try to do this to you," she said to Max, who'd leaped up on the counter and was judging them with his eyes. "But by the way, where the heck were you two when that crazy woman was throwing books around? You'd think you could have done something to help. You know, defuse the situation, yowl, hiss—something." Weren't animals—cats and dogs—particularly sensitive to otherworldly things?

Maybe living in this weird bookstore had made them immune to otherworldly things.

She reached over to pet Max. He looked away, but he allowed her to give him a quick scratch behind the ears. "If you're going to be on staff, you're going to have to pull your own weight. Vittles and catnip treats aren't free, you know. And neither is litter... which reminds me, I haven't checked your box in a while."

After confirming that the front door was definitely locked, Jacqueline let Sebastian pour from her arms onto the counter. Max gave him an irritated look and arched a little. Sebastian responded with a hiss, then jumped over to a different shelf and decided to wash his front paw.

Max turned away from his frenemy and looked out over the shop. His sleek black tail was curled around him as if he couldn't be bothered with the effort to twitch it.

Jacqueline patted him one more time, then started to the back of the store to take care of the litter box. When she discovered it had already been cleaned out, she grinned. There were definite benefits to having fictional housekeepers attending to such matters. She wondered if they scrubbed toilets.

Feeling a little more optimistic, she decided she had no reason to stay any longer, and the reality of that glass of wine—or cocktail—and her new book was getting closer by the minute. She was just shutting down the computer in preparation for leaving when she heard a thud from one of the fiction rooms.

This time, although her heart didn't jump with trepidation, Jacqueline had a very different sort of apprehension as she headed to where a book had fallen —or been knocked off the shelf.

She'd already turned off the overhead light in the sci-fi/fantasy and romance room, but since it wasn't even seven p.m., there was enough natural light for her to see a single book lying in the center of the room. It was wide open.

There were multiple explanations for such occurrence, and Jacqueline didn't like any of them.

First, she was pretty certain the cats hadn't done the deed—Max was too proud to be bothered with such activities, and Sebastian too lazy. Not to mention the fact that they'd both been in the front room only moments ago.

Second, since she hadn't heard a peep from either of the housekeepers, she didn't think that either of them had dropped the book. And if they had, surely they'd have picked it up.

Third... well, the third and fourth options were no more attractive than the first and second were viable.

The third was that Egala Stone had somehow enchanted the book to fall as a sort of last word to her hasty exit, which was obviously not an idea Jacqueline wanted to entertain very closely.

But most of all, Jacqueline was reminded of the

last time a book—or three—had been chucked randomly from the shelves. *Rebecca* and *The Tales of Sherlock Holmes* had been open on the floor, just like this book was now. And look what had happened then!

She hadn't moved close enough to see which book was lying there. The tome looked innocent enough.

What would happen if she just closed it and put it back on the shelf? Well, that was what she'd done last time, wasn't it? So that didn't seem to work.

Maybe if she didn't even look at it or register in her mind what the title was, nothing weird would happen. It couldn't if she didn't know about it, right...? A sort of if-a-tree-fell-in-the-woods-did-anyone-hear-it type of thing.

Or what if she just left the book there? Maybe the action of closing the book caused whatever was going to happen.

Neither of those things made any sense, and, being eminently sensible herself, Jacqueline sighed and decided to end the suspense. It was probably nothing, really. After all, none of the three old ladies—nor Mrs. Hudson nor Mrs. Danvers—had ever suggested there were other characters who came out of books.

But when Jacqueline got closer and looked down at the book, her insides turned quavery.

The Wizard of Oz.

10

J acqueline considered herself quite fortunate that she made it back to Chance's Inn without encountering any of the three old ladies who lived down the street.

Despite the fact that she wanted to talk to them about Egala, Jacqueline was more interested in a drink. A *strong* drink.

After all, it was Saturday night. And she'd had one hell of a week. One hell of a twenty-four hours, to be accurate.

Laura Clemson, who owned and managed Chance's Inn with her husband, provided Jacqueline with a generous gin and diet tonic. It was in a tall, slender glass and was garnished with a paper-thin slice of lemon and a small sprig of rosemary, the latter to look like spruce, Jacqueline supposed.

"How was your first day at the store?" asked the innkeeper. She was much younger than Jacqueline, probably in her late twenties, and wore her straight black hair in a no-nonsense bun at the nape of her neck. Two ornate wooden chopsticks held the knot in place. She was standing behind a small bar counter of polished mahogany that looked like it might have been an original part of the old Victorian home that had been turned into a bed-and-breakfast. A row of cut-glass decanters lined a mirrored wall behind her. Mismatched vintage glasses of crystal and cut glass were stored in a glass-fronted cabinet on one side of the mirror, and on the other side was a large wine rack.

"It was surprisingly busy," Jacqueline replied as she settled on one of the barstools. She took a healthy sip of the G&T and sighed with gusto. "Oh, I really needed that. Thank you!"

"We're so glad the bookstore has opened back up," said Laura as she wiped off the spotless counter. "It's such a quaint shop, with all those cozy rooms and the tea café upstairs. Everyone in Button Cove was sad when Cuddy died. And I'm not gonna lie, there was a lot of gossip about who might come in and take over— you know, big corporations or chain stores—and whether they'd even keep the store open." She gave Jacqueline a friendly smile. "So needless to say, when word got out that a distant relative who was a librarian was coming in, there was a big sigh of relief from a lot of us."

"Thank you," Jacqueline replied with a burst of pleasure that had little to do with her second taste of the drink. It was nice to feel wanted—especially after being summarily dismissed by the library system and her so-called friend. "I appreciate the sentiment. I understand that Cuddy Stone had a cousin or some other relations who might have wanted the store. Do you know anything about them?" She decided not to mention that said brother was currently in the morgue. If word hadn't yet gotten out that he'd been found dead at Three Tomes, that was fine with her.

Laura's smile faltered, but she recovered quickly.

"They stayed here once—a brother and sister. I think they were Cuddy's cousins. Egala was her name, and what was his... Hedwig or something like that."

"That was Harry Potter's owl," Jacqueline said with a smile. "I think it was Henbert, wasn't it? Henbert Stone."

"Right, yes, thank you." Laura began to slice more of the lemon. "How's the G&T?"

"It's very refreshing. I love that there's more of a spruce essence than a juniper one in this gin," Jacqueline replied.

"It's a popular vintage here," Laura replied. "This particular gin is from a small distillery in Detroit. We like to keep things local as much as possible."

"So I get the impression the Stone siblings weren't particularly pleasant guests," Jacqueline said, steering the conversation back to where she wanted it.

She might not have been so blunt if she hadn't already downed half the drink on an empty stomach. But she was also forty-eight, had had *a lot* of shit happen today, and was pretty much past caring about being tactful. She knew that lack of tact probably had just about as much to do with the decrease in her estrogen, now that she was perimenopausal, than the drink, but it didn't matter.

Laura's hand jerked, making one of the delicate lemon slices not quite as uniform as the others, and she looked around as if to see whether someone—like Egala?—was lurking. That told Jacqueline more than anything Laura might say—an opinion that became stronger when the innkeeper replied, "They were only here for two nights. It was high season, and things were very busy." She gestured to Jacqueline's glass. "Ready for another?"

"Oh, I'd best not," Jacqueline replied. "I haven't eaten since breakfast—which was stellar, by the way."

"Well, if you're looking for a place to have dinner and you're in the mood for Tex-Mex, I highly recommend Lupe's. Just around the block. They have cactus tacos that are to die for."

Although Jacqueline wasn't sure about a cactus taco, she did like the idea of a margarita and being within walking distance of her temporary home. "Thanks, Laura," she said, sliding the now-empty cocktail glass toward her. She hesitated, then thought, *What the hell?* and went on, "Egala came into the bookshop tonight."

"She's in town?" The glass in Laura's hand clinked against the bar.

"It seems so." The G&T had done its job relaxing her, and Jacqueline saw no reason to hold back. "Something really weird happened when she was in the bookstore. I swear I saw sparks coming out of her fingertips—and I wasn't even drinking!" Jacqueline laughed, but she watched Laura's reaction and wasn't disappointed.

The innkeeper looked more than a little uncomfortable. "That's strange," she said.

At that moment, two other guests came into the small lounge and Laura turned to greet them with obvious relief.

But Jacqueline had learned what she wanted to know—another confirmation that she wasn't, in fact, crazy—and decided it was time to have a taco and a margarita and to finally start reading the new TJ Mack.

After all, she deserved it.

～

DESPITE A DEEPLY SATISFYING meal of shrimp tacos served with tortilla chips and three different salsas, along with a frozen passionfruit margarita, Jacqueline couldn't keep her mind off what had happened at Three Tomes—especially later in the day. It probably had to do with the fact that right on the wall across from her table at Lupe's was a sign that read "There's No Place Like Home."

The Wizard of Oz, *huh?* she thought, unable to keep from thinking of the open book she'd found.

Did that mean Dorothy Gale was going to show up in her blue-and-white checked dress?

Jacqueline shuddered at the thought—the last thing she needed was anything resembling flying monkeys dive-bombing her or her shop.

Then she laughed and looked repressively at her empty margarita glass. She was getting a little loopy.

As she strolled back to the inn, however, Jacqueline couldn't help think about what had happened earlier this evening. Egala Stone showing up and accusing Jacqueline of killing her brother *and* stealing the bookshop from them—and then shooting sparks from her fingertips and sending a table of books flying —definitely put Jacqueline in mind of the Wicked Witch of the West accusing Dorothy of similar crimes when the house landed on the Witch of the East and Dorothy acquired the ruby slippers...

Except that was not how it happened in the book.

That was how it happened in the movie, but that wasn't how Frank Baum had originally told the story. In the book, the Wicked Witch of the West didn't even come on the scene until Dorothy showed up at her castle trying to get her broomstick, and she never accused Dorothy of killing her sister, either. And in the book, the slippers were silver and not ruby. *And* in the book, Oz wasn't a dream.

Therefore, Jacqueline decided she shouldn't worry at all about life imitating art—or in this case, literature.

Because Dorothy Gale was definitely not going to be showing up at Three Tomes.

11

Since it was Sunday morning and the bookshop didn't open until ten, Jacqueline saw no reason to rush over to the store.

Besides, she was moving a little slowly this morning, due to fitful sleep thanks to some more weird dreams, in which Egala Stone featured, no surprise, along with that dark place with the dirt floor and her hand dripping with red goop—likely prompted by a gin and tonic and two margaritas.

Jacqueline ate a leisurely breakfast of a ham-and-cheese omelet, pineapple slices, and a bran muffin in the small, Art Deco-style dining room at the inn (while noticing that, although the innkeeper was very friendly and attentive, Laura made certain she was too busy to stop and chat) and read two chapters of *Trip Wire*.

She was getting to a really good part—well, the whole book was nonstop good parts, but this was leading up to the big climactic scene where Sargent Blue had to save the world—but she found she couldn't concentrate because she kept thinking about (that is, worrying) what she was going to find at the store this morning.

Jacqueline finally gave up and got on her way. Camellia Court was a twenty-minute walk from the inn, the latter of which was situated with a nice view of the cove from across the street, so she decided to leave her car. The walk would give Jacqueline a chance to check out some of the other businesses in town.

Her peers and colleagues.

She smiled to herself and realized there was a spring in her step. Despite the strangeness of the last two days, she was actually feeling semi-optimistic about the situation of owning a small bookstore.

Sure, if she were still in Chicago, the only fictional characters she'd have to deal with would be the ones on the page (or screen, as the case may be), and she'd only have to show up for work, complete her shift, and then go home and enjoy a good book or fun movie instead of trying to keep three older ladies from forcing tea down her throat. And there weren't generally any dead bodies at her place of work (although there had been that one heart attack victim). Life as she'd known it would be far less complicated, and with no responsibility.

But tonight she was going to eat homemade pizza and drink wine—she'd have to find a good wine shop later today to pick out a bottle to bring—and maybe get to know her business neighbors.

She hoped they were as nice as they seemed. And normal.

Her step faltered a little. She didn't really know either Nadine or Suzette... what if they were boring? Or weird? Or really nosy? Or they talked too much—or made *her* talk too much?

Well, she could always make an excuse to leave.

Spring was in the air as well as in her step, and

Jacqueline inhaled the fresh essence tinged with the lake as she turned onto Camellia Avenue. April in the Midwest meant tulips, azalea, and daffodils were starting to bloom, soon followed by heady-scented lilacs—and that she wasn't going to be sweating from the humidity. These next few weeks of early spring were her favorite time of year besides autumn, which she liked because it was sweater weather.

The hanging sign for Three Tomes was just in front of her, swaying gently overhead as if welcoming her home. It was what people would call "vintage"— an engraved wooden sign like one might see in small English villages. Jacqueline liked the shop's logo, which was pictured on the sign—a stack of three old-looking books with a cup of tea on top—even though she was leery about the whole tea-room-with-pastries business.

Maybe she could just be honest with Suzette tonight. Surely she would understand that books, frosting, and crumbs just didn't get along.

Jacqueline's palms were a little damp when she unlocked the door and let herself into the building. She considered it fortunate that not only was the door still locked, but that Mrs. Danvers or Mrs. Hudson had refrained from turning the sign to Open. Even though it was only nine thirty, Jacqueline wouldn't put it past them to change the shop's hours—especially since there were several people going in and out of Sweet Devotion with coffee cups and pastry bags.

Hmm. Maybe she should open at nine on Sundays.

The books on the front table were just as she'd left them last night—mostly rearranged but not yet perfect after Egala Stone's mischief. Neither Max nor Sebastian was in sight, but Jacqueline could hear the soft clinks from upstairs and assumed that Mrs. Hudson was on the job.

Mrs. Danvers suddenly appeared, silent as a wraith, and Jacqueline's heart jumped a little at the unexpected sight of the black-garbed figure.

"Good morning, ma'am," said the housekeeper. "You should go upstairs."

Something like terror jolted through Jacqueline at the flat statement, which sounded more like a warning than a suggestion, and which was accompanied by a forbidding expression.

Surely there wasn't another body in the flat.

"Upstairs... to the tea room?" she asked hopefully. If Mrs. Danvers meant for her to go to the café, surely whatever the problem was, it was between the two housekeepers—er, housekeeper and landlady.

"Certainly not. That Hudson woman is in the tea room," replied Mrs. Danvers with a condescending sniff, then after a pointed delay added, "ma'am."

"You want me to go up to the apartment?" Jacqueline asked, her heart sinking.

Surely, *surely* there wasn't another body up there.

"Yes, ma'am."

Then she remembered what Detective Massermey had said—the authorities would still need access to the death scene for at least part of the day. Maybe Mrs. Danvers thought she should be up there overseeing it all.

Since Jacqueline didn't feel like arguing with the creepy housekeeper, and it wasn't yet time for the shop to open (although she suspected it wouldn't matter to her so-called employees if she were even present when ten o'clock came), she decided to comply.

Her feet dragged a little as she made her way to

the rear of the house, but she climbed the stairs resolutely. She was just about to the top when she heard voices—and immediately recognized them.

"What are you doing here?" Jacqueline said, as she hurried to the front room of the apartment.

Zwyla, Pietra, and Andromeda all looked up guiltily. They were sitting in a circle on the rug around the area where Henbert Stone's body had been found.

"The police have this place closed off," Jacqueline told them, gesturing a little wildly toward the yellow crime scene tape that she, too, had ignored when approaching the living room. "Detective Massermey's not going to be very happy about this." She didn't want to get blamed for letting three old biddies contaminate a crime scene; it would be a not-so-great way to become notorious in her new hometown where she was trying to run a business.

"I don't know about you, but that man can burn *my* buns anytime he wants to," said Pietra with what was probably supposed to be a leer, but looked more like she was trying out for a creepy clown show. "He's got that whole silver-fox Viking thing going on, and I'll bet he's pretty handy with a whip. Plus, have you seen the size of his *hands*?"

Jacqueline nearly choked on her own tongue as Andromeda giggled. "Vikings aren't really known for their whips, Petey," said Andromeda—whose spiky hair had lost yesterday's blue tips and now sported bright gold-colored ends. The look gave her a sort of halo effect, which Jacqueline immediately dismissed, since none of these three women were anywhere near being saintly.

And how did they get in here, anyway? They must have a key, she realized, because Andromeda had been feeding the cats. Argh.

"I'll bet Detective Put-Your-Massive-Hands-on-Me does," retorted Pietra with another leer.

"What are the three of you doing here?" Jacqueline asked again. Her voice was, understandably, more strident this time, for she'd just noticed that there was a small metal bowl in the center of the small circle that the three women had formed... and it was *smoking*. More precisely, its contents were smoking, and there was a definite sweet-pungent scent wafting through the room.

"Are you smoking *pot* in my apartment?" shrieked Jacqueline, forgetting that she had no intention of living there. "In the middle of a—a crime scene?"

"It's not marijuana, it's sage," replied Zwyla, rising swiftly and gracefully to her feet with a soft jangle of bracelets. Today she was wearing black skinny jeans on legs that seemed to go on forever, and a drapey, long-sleeved t-shirt the color of almonds. The fact that her shoes were espadrilles and had three-inch platform heels was a little bit of overkill, Jacqueline thought. Zwyla's head wrap was a shiny black material with a beige pattern, and two long chains of earrings dangled from beneath. She glanced at Andromeda, who shrugged and looked supremely innocent. "Among other things."

"What other—Never mind. I don't want to know." Jacqueline really *didn't* want to know. "But you can't be here. The police aren't finished with the—uh —area."

"Didn't you say *crime* scene?" said Zwyla, fixing her dark eyes on Jacqueline. "That's what Massermey said yesterday too."

"Well, yes, but I don't—"

"I *told* you it was murder," said Pietra, hauling herself to her feet. The beaded fringe on the long, flowy shirt she was wearing made soft, anxious clicking noises.

"So you did," said Andromeda thoughtfully.

"I didn't say it was murder," replied Jacqueline, feeling the urge to grab handfuls of her hair and yank them free from their twist. "But Detective Massermey said that the cause of death wasn't obvious. So they have to treat it like a potential crime scene."

"Murder," said Pietra. "Cuddy must have known her cousins—I mean, her *other* cousins—were going to try to take over the place. She must have arranged for some sort of cur—"

Zwyla began coughing violently and made a show of waving away the smoke (which smelled just like pot to Jacqueline, no matter what they said) from her face.

Andromeda picked up the bowl—which was still smoking—and then rose to her feet as well. "What exactly did Detective Massive—er, Massermey say, Jacqueline?"

"He said that the cause of death was unknown and that they were going to do a full postmortem," Jacqueline replied. "And I think you need to come clean and tell me *exactly* what is going on here." She leveled her best Bitchy Librarian stare at each of them in turn—although, to be fair, her glare wavered a little when she looked up to meet Zwyla's eyes.

The tall woman grimaced then nodded. "I suppose we ought to," she said. "It's only fair, since you're right in the thick of it all."

"I'm *what*?" Jacqueline did not like the sound of that.

"Through no fault of your own, you're smack in the middle of everything," replied Pietra kindly. She even reached over to pat Jacqueline on the arm.

"In the middle of *what*?" demanded Jacqueline.

"In the middle of the Stone family feud," replied Andromeda. She was still holding the smoking bowl, and Jacqueline swore she was trying not to be obvious about inhaling the sage-not-pot essence wafting from it.

"Feud is such a kind, gentle way to put it," Pietra said with a dimpled smile.

"Massermey's here," Zwyla said in a tight voice as she stepped away from the window.

"Crud. Let's get out of here, quick." Pietra was already starting toward a door in the little corner kitchen that Jacqueline hadn't noticed yesterday... because there'd been a *dead body* on the floor.

The door opened to a pantry that also included a descending stairway. The steps led to what was nothing more than another pantry, obviously for storage, in the hall behind the tea room. Well, that was handy, thought Jacqueline. One could never have too much storage.

Before she could suggest that they have a seat in the tea room, Andromeda took her arm in a gentle but firm grip. "Let's go back to our place," she told Jacqueline, steering her toward the stairs. "Where we can talk."

She paused at the top of the steps, and when it was obvious the police were heading to the back of the house to climb the stairs to the third floor, she gave Jacqueline a little prompt to start downstairs.

"But the store opens in—well, it should have opened five minutes ago," Jacqueline said as they started down. Nonetheless, she was pleased at how quickly and easily they'd managed to evade the detective and his team. She just hoped he didn't smell the supposedly-not-pot scent that probably still lingered.

Upon arriving at the bottom of the stairs, Jacqueline found that the sign had been flipped to *Open* and Mrs. Hudson was assisting a customer (already? excellent!) in the biography section, while Mrs. Danvers stood like a black scarecrow behind the counter.

Scarecrow. At the thought, Jacqueline gave a mental sigh of relief. No sign of anyone without a heart, brain, or courage had made an appearance. Hopefully, she'd dodged that bullet—especially now that it seemed she was in the middle of some weird family feud... with members of her own family she'd never heard of.

Maybe it was time to call her parents down in Tampa and find out what they knew about the Stones and their family feud. She'd hesitated to do so simply because it was just so difficult to talk to them over the phone—neither could hear well, and they constantly talked over each other as well as herself... She loved her parents very much; she just preferred to communicate with them in person. She supposed she could try e-mail.

It occurred to Jacqueline that she'd never even learned which *side* of her family Cuddy Stone belonged to. Had either of her parents told her when she originally told them about the bookstore? Had she even asked?

"Let's go," said Pietra, darting out the front door.

Andromeda ushered Jacqueline out, and Zwyla brought up the rear. Jacqueline felt a little foolish about sneaking out of her own store, but she wanted some answers—and she didn't want to answer any questions about what had happened upstairs. At least recreational marijuana was legal in Michigan, so Massermey couldn't arrest anyone for possession.

"Should we stop into Sweet Devotion for something?" asked Pietra as they walked across the street.

The smells from the shop made Jacqueline's mouth water even though she was still full from breakfast.

"No, we should not," said Zwyla, giving her friend a little push when she stalled in front of the bakery.

Jacqueline looked in the windows as they walked by, then immediately regretted doing so. How was she going to resist the place now that she'd seen the fancy cupcakes, glistening cinnamon rolls, and chunky loaves of bread lining the display?

She turned her thoughts from baked goodies to the problem at hand—even though she'd rather think about a chocolate fudge brownie than dead bodies and family feuds.

"Oh, look! An eagle," Andromeda exclaimed, pointing. "I love it when they visit."

Jacqueline, who'd never seen an eagle in the wild in her life, squinted up into the bright blue sky just in time to see the powerful bald eagle swoop down to settle gracefully onto the spire atop the bright blue Victorian called Camellia House at the end of the court. He sat there, regal and elegant, sharply eyeing the environment as if he owned the land and lake that spread for miles in every direction.

Awed by the bird of prey's majesty and proximity, Jacqueline kept her eyes trained up and on him as she walked down the street. She tripped on the sidewalk (of course) and nearly took a header, catching herself just in time. When she looked up again, the bird was gone, and she was about to enter the gate of the house where the three old ladies lived.

Camellia House was a quintessential Victorian, with gables and fancy trim, and a single, tower-like projection in the front whose bottom rim nudged the top of the covered porch. Painted robin's-egg blue with cheery lavender shutters and lemon-yellow trim, the house had a front yard that was enclosed by a four-foot wrought-iron fence—complete with swinging gate—and a pea-gravel path that led to the front door. The front yard was completely landscaped with sprawling gardens that were just beginning to show buds, leaves, blooms, and of course, early flowers. Only the tiniest strip of grass grew on either side of the walk to the front door.

Jacqueline understood what Suzette meant when she said the yield from their garden was far larger than an urban yard would suggest. What she could see of the grounds was a wild tangle of clumps, mounds, vines, pots, stalks, and trellises—and that was just flowers. She couldn't imagine what the backyard was like, although she could see hints of its tumbling bounty from behind the house.

Until now, she'd considered herself a decent gardener—planning, planting, and nurturing flowers, bushes, and trees in her small backyard back in Libertyville. She'd even been thinking about how to improve the plantings in the cute little courtyard at the back of Three Tomes. But upon seeing the amazing array of color and variety growing at Camellia House, she decided she was actually little more than rank amateur.

Inside, the ladies' residence was just as colorful and eclectic as its grounds. No one stinted on brights or jewel tones here. There was a variety of throw rugs underfoot (none of which matched); silky, batik, and woven wall hangings depicting everything from organic patterns to mythological and medieval scenes; pots of plants exploding on the window sills and tables; and low, cushiony furnishings—some of which were rattan, others obviously courtesy of IKEA.

The place reminded her of the pad of a flower

child of the sixties—there were even two lava lamps and a macrame plant hanger with an English ivy bursting from it.

"Wow" was all Jacqueline said as she was ushered through the living room and its explosion of vibrant color and comfort into what she expected would be the kitchen but turned out to be a small... well, "herbary" was the only word she could think of. It looked like the place Brother Cadfael would have worked in his medieval village in between solving mysteries. There were bunches of herbs, both dried and fresh, hanging from the ceiling at irregular heights. Zwyla had to duck in order to pass beneath several bundles of lavender and another herb Jacqueline couldn't identify. Chamomile, maybe?

There were mortars and pestles of all sizes as well as several coffee bean grinders on a long worktable, along with glass jars, clay pots (with and without lids and drain holes), and numerous vials. There were scissors, knives, spoons, strainers, and measuring cups. She saw pots, pans, an electric dehydrator, and—

"Is that a cauldron?" Jacqueline stopped in front of a large black iron vessel with three stubby legs. It hung by its arcing handle over a small fireplace built into the side of the outside wall. The pot looked exactly like the cauldron in the picture of the Witches Three that hung above the door of Three Tomes, and exactly like every other witch's cauldron she'd ever seen or imagined in her life.

"What else would it be?" said Zwyla, settling gracefully onto the lowest stool of six that surrounded a trestle table in the center of the room. This lower seat would put her at just above the same height as everyone else when they sat, which Jacqueline realized she was expected to do.

She sat, noticing how smooth the wooden top of the table was. It was slippery from wear, but nicked from cuts and scorched from burns. The table had to be old. Very old. She felt a little prickle of awareness as she thought about where this table had been, what it had been used for, and who had worked at it over the decades.

She felt certain it had been in use for centuries.

Jacqueline looked up when she realized that the other three women had become unnaturally quiet. They'd seated themselves across from her—whether by design or by accident, she didn't know—and they seemed to be waiting for something. Something from her? She didn't know.

"Well, are you going to tell me what's going on or not?" Jacqueline asked a little acerbically. Though she looked at each of them in turn, it was Andromeda—who seemed to always be the one nominated to explain—at whom she finished and settled her gaze.

"Yes, well, you should be told," Andromeda said with a flicker of a glance at Zwyla.

"*I* thought we should tell you right away," interrupted Pietra, who obviously couldn't maintain silence for more than a few charged seconds. "But—"

"It doesn't matter now," Jacqueline said in a firm voice. "But if someone doesn't tell me about this family feud between the Stones, I'm going to scream."

"How about some tea?" asked Pietra, bolting to her feet. "It'll calm everyone down a little."

Jacqueline mustn't have managed to completely stifle the little scream in the back of her throat, because Petey gave Zwyla and Andromeda a "sorry!" look as she darted from the room.

"Right. All right. Where do I begin?" said Andromeda. As the older woman looked completely serious about the question, Jacqueline opened her mouth to demand that she *just begin*, but, thankfully, Andromeda started talking. "Cuddy Stone never wanted the bookshop to get into the wrong hands—meaning the hands of either of her cousins Egala or Henbert—or any of the other Ranfield Stone branch of the family."

"Especially Crusilla," said Pietra, coming back into the room with a tray of tea ware that clinked gently.

"Correct," replied Zwyla in her dusky voice.

"Crusilla?" Jacqueline couldn't ignore the similarity of the name to the villainess in *The Hundred and One Dalmatians,* the book by Dodie Smith—which was so much better than the Disney movies. Even as an adult, she'd very much enjoyed a reread.

"Her hair isn't half black and half white, in case you're wondering," said Pietra with a smile as she set a cup of tea in front of Jacqueline. "But she doesn't care for dogs, so there's that."

Jacqueline gave the tea a disgruntled look, but she supposed she'd have to drink it. "All right, you've delayed long enough. Tell me about this crazy family of mine..." Her voice trailed off as she stared out the window.

A woman was bicycling past, hunched over the handlebars, looking as if she was going somewhere in a hurry. She was bony and slender, and her entire persona screamed drab and disgruntled: scraped-back dark hair, buttoned-up-to-the-chin ruffled Victorian blouse, ankle-length skirt, dark hat, hooked nose, and grimacing mouth. A covered basket was mounted at the back of her bike, and the woman—the very stereotype of a pinch-faced spinster—looked incredibly annoyed with the world as she pedaled energetically down the street.

Jacqueline stared. That woman really reminded her of—

She shook her head. No. She wasn't even going to entertain the thought.

"Jacqueline? Is something the matter?" asked Andromeda.

"No," Jacqueline replied slowly, and automatically lifted the teacup to drink. It wasn't so bad. The temperature was perfect, and the floral scent was different today.

"All right," Andromeda said. Her voice was brisk as she went on, "The feud between two of the branches of the Stone family is centuries old. No one is even certain how it started or why it's still going on, but suffice to say, the members of both sides of the family detest each other and don't want any of their kin on the opposing side to have anything like success or happiness or anything pleasant in their lives."

"It's very sad," Pietra said. "To wish such misfortune on your family, no matter how distant they are."

"Yes," said Andromeda a little impatiently. "So Cuddy inherited the house where Three Tomes is, and from the beginning, her cousins from a different branch of the Stone family thought it should have been left to them. They claimed Cuddy—uh—bewitched Mystera Stone so she would leave the place to her."

"Bewitched. You do mean..." Jacqueline hesitated, then plunged on. "You do mean *literally* bewitched her, don't you?" she said, giving them all the stink-eye.

"Yes," replied Zwyla.

Jacqueline sighed. That simple acknowledgment was what she had expected, but not at all what she'd hoped for. It merely raised more questions, more anxiety, and more confusion.

What sort of crazy mess had she gotten herself into here in Button Cove?

"Well, did she? Bewitch her?" Jacqueline demanded.

She just wasn't going to think too hard about maybe, possibly somehow being related—however distantly—to people who *bewitched* and *cursed* each other. Later, she could go back to the hotel and drink heavily—oh, crap, no, she couldn't do that. She was having wine and pizza tonight with two other women she didn't know.

She could drink heavily there.

But then, wine tended to loosen one's lips, and who knew *what* would come out of hers?

Maybe she should cancel.

"I have no idea whether she bewitched Mystera or not," Andromeda replied. "And I don't really care. Cuddy loved Three Tomes, and as far as I'm concerned—and I think Petey and Z will agree with me—she was the perfect person to own the place. Mystera had the house built, locating it on a site where her Anishinaabek mother and French-Canadian father had lived, and where her mother's tribe had settled before that. It was Cuddy who turned Mystera's house into the bookshop we know today. She lived there for eighty-seven years."

Jacqueline's eyes bulged. "How old was Cuddy when she died?"

"Well over a hundred," replied Pietra. "She took really good care of herself, if you know what I mean." She gave Jacqueline a sly wink.

"There's a lot of history around the house," Andromeda said. "A lot of... tradition. Family tradition."

Jacqueline nodded, the hair on her arms prickling a little. The house she'd inherited was built on a spot that had been lived on by the same family and bloodline for centuries, including by Native Americans.

Her family. It seemed so very strange to think about this part of her ancestry she'd never heard about before.

And yet... she remembered that sense of familiarity that had struck her the very first moment she approached Three Tomes from the back door. The courtyard, the back entrance... Had she been here as a child, and simply didn't remember? But how, or when? Her mother finally remembered that the Stones were from her side, but she confessed she didn't know much about that branch of the family, and she had never heard about the bookshop.

And even if Jacqueline had somehow been here before, that still didn't explain why Cuddy Stone had left such a special piece of property to her.

She realized the three old women were looking at her. "So... what were you doing up there in the apartment this morning?" Jacqueline said. She focused her attention on Pietra, guessing she'd be the first one to actually spill the truth.

But it was Andromeda who spoke. "We were simply cleansing the area. A sage smudge does wonders to banish negative energy—"

"And curses," said Jacqueline. "You think there was a curse up there in *my* apartment—which, by the way, apparently you have keys to, and I'm not certain how I feel about that—and you were checking it out, weren't you? Is that what killed Henbert Stone? A curse?"

"Most likely," said Zwyla.

"And you're qualified to check all that out because...?" Jacqueline said, sweeping the three of them with a hard look.

"We—"

But Andromeda was cut off by Pietra's low cry. "Massermey alert! Massermey alert! He's coming through the gate now!" She bolted to her feet and began to usher Jacqueline out of the herbary. The other two women followed.

They were in the living room by the time Detective Massermey knocked on the front door. As she went to answer it, Pietra gave Jacqueline a gentle shove toward the sofa and hissed, "Sit."

Mystified, Jacqueline did as she was told. Somehow, their tea service had also made its way to the living room and was arranged on the coffee table in front of the firm, low IKEA sofa. As if they'd been sitting there the entire time.

"Why, Detective Massermey, what a pleasant surprise," said Pietra as she opened the door. "Why don't you come on in? We were just having tea."

Massermey's broad shoulders seemed to fill the doorway as he stepped just inside, blocking most of the light from behind. Despite his suit coat and button-down shirt, it was easy to imagine his fading-to-silver strawberry-blond hair in long, Thor-like braids, and his more vibrant beard and mustache braided with leather thongs.

Wait, that was Johnny Depp in *Pirates*, not Thor. Either way, Jacqueline didn't mind the image.

Then Massermey's attention went directly to Jacqueline, and all of those fanciful thoughts evaporated. When he fixed those ice-blue eyes on her, for some reason she suddenly felt like a rodent under a spotlight, even though she hadn't done anything wrong.

Seriously. She'd done nothing wrong. So why was he giving her that suspicious look?

"No thank you, Pietra," he said. "Much as I enjoy

your tea, I don't have time to visit. But I do need to speak with Ms. Finch." That gaze remained fastened on Jacqueline, and she couldn't deny it made her stomach flip... but whether it was from attraction (certainly not!) or nerves, she wasn't certain.

"Of course, Detective," she said, rising from the sofa. As she started to leave, Jacqueline glanced back toward the little hall that led to the herbary and noticed that the entrance was now hidden by a large wall hanging that she was certain hadn't been there a moment earlier.

Slanting a knowing side-eye at Zwyla, Jacqueline bade the three old crones—she couldn't help but think of them that way, especially now—goodbye.

"What can I do for you?" Jacqueline said smoothly as she and Massermey walked down the pea-gravel path out to the sidewalk. She couldn't help but glance behind to see whether the bald eagle had returned to its perch atop Camellia House.

It hadn't.

"I just wanted to tell you that we're finished upstairs at your place," Massermey replied. "You can proceed with whatever you were doing up there."

"Cleaning it up," she reminded him, for she'd heard the tinge of suspicion in his voice.

"Right," he replied. Still with that tinge.

"Is the postmortem complete? Did you find out how Mr. Stone died?" Jacqueline asked.

Massermey opened the gate then followed her through. "I don't remember mentioning his name," the detective said, snapping the gate closed with an ominous clang. "How did you know his name was Stone?" Those cool blue eyes settled on her once again, and this time the squiggle in her belly was definitely *not* from attraction.

"I don't know. I must have heard it from someone." She shrugged and mentally cursed the three ladies. "I guess he's some relation to Cuddy Stone, who used to own the place." Which also made him a relation to her, she supposed, but decided not to mention it at the moment. She wasn't certain she wanted to acknowledge the relationship. "What was his first name again?"

"Henbert Stone," replied Massermey. The corners of his eyes weren't crinkling with those attractive laugh lines at the moment. In fact, he looked far too serious for Jacqueline's comfort. "And yes, it appears he might be related to the former owner of the shop."

"That was his sister in the store when you came in last night," Jacqueline said, suddenly remembering she actually did have a valid reason for knowing the man's name—and not because the three busybody old ladies had told her. "She told me his name."

"I see." Massermey gestured for her to walk along the sidewalk and he strolled next to her. "One of the officers tracked her down and told her about her brother. She must have arrived in town soon after."

"She was pretty upset about him dying," Jacqueline said. "Did the pathologist figure out what happened?"

"Still inconclusive," replied Massermey, somehow managing to walk in tandem with her down the sidewalk while still keeping his eyes on her. "He seemed to have expired from some sudden event that stopped his heart, but he had no apparent history of heart problems and no toxins in his blood or organs. Very strange." He took an extra-long step and stopped slightly in front of her, blocking most of the sidewalk.

"How awful," Jacqueline replied, stopping as well. She was pretty sure she sounded sincere, because that was exactly how she was feeling: it—meaning the whole situation—was indeed awful.

"It is," he said, still obstructing her way. "Ms. Finch, if you know anything about Henbert Stone and what he might have been doing in your place, it would behoove you to tell me."

"Behoove me?" She couldn't control a little gurgle of delight. Who used words like that outside of books? "Oh, yes, of course, Detective. It's just that I really only did just get to Button Cove, and I don't know anyone here. It's all just as confusing—and a little nerve-racking—to me as it must be to you. Not the nerve-racking part, but the confusing part." She gave a nervous laugh, realizing she probably wasn't doing herself any favors with the suspicious detective. Then she straightened herself out with a firm mental reprimand. "The only thing I know is that Cuddy Stone did not like her cousin Henbert, which is why she didn't leave the bookshop to him—or his sister, for that matter—and I have no idea why he would have been in the apartment unless he was looking for something. I can assure you," she went on, deciding for the moment to leave out *her* relationship to all of the Stones, since it simply wasn't relevant, "that I will be having the locks changed immediately."

"I was going to suggest just that," replied the detective in a relatively mild voice. "In fact, I was going to give you the name of a reputable locksmith who would even come out on a Sunday to get that taken care of for you—just mention my name."

"Why, thank you so much," Jacqueline replied as he handed her a business card. "That's very kind of you."

"Maybe. Or maybe I just don't want my Sunday afternoon interrupted by another call to a scene," he replied. But his beard and mustache twitched a little, and she caught a hint of those lines at the corners of his eyes.

Jacqueline thanked him again, and just as they parted ways and she turned to open the door to Three Tomes, she heard the sound of wheels rolling along the sidewalk.

She looked up just in time to see the drab, spinsterish woman brake her bicycle right in front of her.

"I've been looking for you," she said.

Jacqueline ducked into the bookshop even though she knew it was an effort in futility. She couldn't lock the door and keep out customers.

So, drawing in a cleansing breath—she remembered that, at least, from the two yoga classes she'd fumbled through several years ago—she held the door open for the spinsterish woman.

"What can I do to help you?" Jacqueline said, keeping her voice modulated while inside her guts were churning.

The disgruntled-looking woman, who was of an indeterminate age and who precisely fit the description of Miss Gulch, a.k.a. the Wicked Witch of the West, from *The Wizard of Oz* movie, not the book (which Jacqueline found really annoying; couldn't these things be a little more consistent?) leaned her old-fashioned bike against the outside of the store and then walked, with a definite limp, through the entrance.

"I don't know," replied Miss Gulch in a snappish voice. "You own this place?" She looked around with a frown.

"Yes, I do. Is there a book you're looking for? Some

tea, perhaps?" Oh, that was an idea—send her up to Mrs. Hudson! "We have a lovely little café upstairs for tea—"

"You talk a lot," said the woman, still frowning. "And much too fast. I'm exhausted just listening to you."

Jacqueline closed her mouth and ground her teeth. Just then, Mrs. Danvers appeared from one of the genre rooms. She was accompanied by a customer who looked like a normal, modern-day person, and who was carrying three new hardcover books and a charming set of wooden bookends that Jacqueline had never seen before but were apparently for sale. She really should work on that inventory.

To her delight, the customer—who didn't seem at all put off by her interaction with the dour house-keeper, thank goodness—placed her items on the counter. Mrs. Danvers moved around behind it to ring her up.

Miss Gulch eyed the transaction, still with that displeased expression—but now there was a bit of fascination in it too as she watched the computer. Jacqueline stood there uncertainly. What exactly was she supposed to do now?

She could call the locksmith. And she proceeded to pull out her mobile phone and do so.

As promised, the mention of Miles Massermey's name worked like magic—ugh, maybe she shouldn't think in those terms—and the locksmith, whose name was Jerry, said he'd be there in less than an hour. On a Sunday. *Wow.*

As she disconnected the call, Jacqueline was able to thank the customer for her purchase and wish her a good day.

And then she turned back to Miss Gulch, who'd

stood there the whole time, silent and drab, wearing an expression of distaste. Jacqueline wondered if Mrs. Danvers would recognize Miss Gulch as a sort of kindred spirit—meaning, a book character (or in Miss Gulch's case, a movie character), not a broody, perpetually annoyed personality. Though in this case, both were true.

All of these thoughts—which were both pragmatic and crazy—made Jacqueline want to take her head between her hands and scream. Instead, she said, "Miss Gulch, I presume? What is it you need me to help you with?"

"So you know my name, do you?" Miss Gulch gave a sneering sort of sniff. And then, all at once, her expression changed. Her eyes lit up, her thin, downturned lips curved, and her shoulders went back as her insubstantial bosom lifted. "And who is *this*?"

Jacqueline turned to see Sebastian strolling into the front room in all of his fluffy, golden-amber glory. He seemed to realize that he was the object of flattering attention, for he sauntered to Miss Gulch's dark, hose-clad legs and began to twine himself around and between them, easily stepping over her large, clunky shoes.

His purring was loud enough that Jacqueline could hear him, and she watched in amazement as Miss Gulch cooed and oohed and bent to stroke the cat's thick, silky fur.

When Sebastian permitted her to pick him up, Miss Gulch's eyes actually glistened with delight. "You are such a handsome fellow," she said in a voice that sounded nothing like her previous tone. "And look at you, you naughty boy, getting your hair all over my dress! Why, I'm going to have a time getting it all off now, ain't I?" she said in sweet, girlish tones as she nuzzled Sebastian's fur.

Apparently Miss Gulch had as much adoration for cats as she had dislike for dogs named Toto.

"His name is Sebastian," said Jacqueline. She was still feeling frustrated and impatient, but she spoke calmly. "Now, Miss Gulch, what is it that brings you to Three Tomes?"

This time when the spinster looked at her, there was an entirely different expression on her face. "I don't know. I simply don't know." She shrugged her bony shoulders, all the while continuing to cuddle Sebastian close to her. "I don't even know how I got here. I was looking for that horrible *dog*, and the next thing I know, I'm here."

Jacqueline looked at Mrs. Danvers. "Do you know how she got here?"

The housekeeper sniffed. "I certainly do not."

"Well, do you know how to help her get back to... wherever?"

Mrs. Danvers merely lifted her chin and sneered. "Possibly," she said after a moment. "Now that those policemen have left the upstairs, I've work to do up there. Ma'am," she added in a clear afterthought.

And without another word, she walked off, leaving Jacqueline, Miss Gulch, and Sebastian—who was purring like a saw as he lolled in the spinster's arms.

Jacqueline looked over and saw that Max was now perched on top of the tallest bookshelf. He was watching the lovefest with his own Danvers-like sneer, and his black tail dangled and twitched with irritation.

Very well, then, Jacqueline thought. She would have to take charge. And rightly so, as it was her bookstore. "All right, Miss Gulch, suppose we go up to the tea room and get you a nice cup of something to brace you up, and you can tell me what you know."

"Tea?" said Miss Gulch as she started up the stairs. Jacqueline noticed she seemed to be favoring her left leg as she ascended. "No one drinks tea in Kansas. I'll have coffee, if you please."

Jacqueline held her tongue, deciding she would let Mrs. Hudson and Miss Gulch battle out the choice of beverage.

"And there you are, dearie," said Mrs. Hudson when she saw Jacqueline. "It's been a busy morning here already! But people are asking for the scones and those French things, whatever they're called—croysaints? From across the way. Of course, I couldn't leave to go over and get some, could I, with all the customers here and that Danvers creature nowhere to be seen—as usual. Well, then, hello," she said when she saw Miss Gulch. "You look as if you could use a nice, bracing cuppa—let's say Earl Grey, shall we? And a good, healthy dollop of cream and several lumps would do you well too," she said, already bustling about behind the counter.

To her pleasant surprise, Jacqueline saw a middle-aged couple sitting at one of the tables near the large front window with a small teapot and matching cups. But when she noticed the books on the table next to them, her entire body seized up.

Oh no, no, *no*! Tea stains on the books simply would not do! Unless they had been paid for...

"Mrs. Hudson, did they pay for those books?" she asked, sidling up to the counter in order to keep her voice low enough not to travel, but loud enough for the older woman to hear as she banged and clanged around.

"What is it you said?" Mrs. Hudson asked, turning

around and plopping a china teapot onto the counter with such verve that Jacqueline winced. Miraculously, it didn't break.

"Those people over there, drinking tea with those books—did they pay for them? Because I simply can't allow them to drink *and* look at books. What if they spill on the pages? And that's exactly why there will be no more scones or cupcakes or cinnamon rolls here," Jacqueline went on in a firm but low voice. "We cannot have the merchandise be soiled or abused in that way."

Mrs. Hudson stared at her, then she began to laugh. "Oh, dear, of course you wouldn't know, would you, luv? Is that why you've been all pinched-up and dour-faced whenever you come up here?"

Dour-faced? Pinched-up? Jacqueline slanted a look at Miss Gulch, who'd obediently taken a seat where Mrs. Hudson had directed her—with Sebastian still gathered in her arms. (Was that a health violation?)

Jacqueline hoped she didn't look like the old, dour-faced, pinched-up spinster! Why, she only had a few little creases at the corners of her eyes, and some faint furrows in her forehead. *Pinched-up?* She smoothed out her lips just in case.

Before she could respond to this shocking state-ment, Mrs. Hudson leaned forward over the counter, and Jacqueline caught a whiff of lemon scent and dish soap. "The books here, they're protected. They dust off clean as new, they do, no matter what gets spilled or crumbled over them." She nodded sagely. "That was one of the best things Cuddy did when she opened this place up. Put that protection on them. Any book that comes in across the threshold has it."

Jacqueline stared at her. "Do you mean that if

someone spilled a cup of tea on one of the books here... that it would just... what? Go away?"

"Beads up like water on oilskin, it does," said Mrs. Hudson. "Just shake it off a little, and Bob's your uncle."

"And the buttery crumbs from croissants? The glaze from cinnamon buns? They leave grease spots on the pages! And what about those obnoxious cupcake crumbs that creep deep into the bindings? *And the frosting?*" Astonishment, disbelief, and wild hope were warring within Jacqueline.

"I told you, it doesn't stick or stain or collect. Just falls away. Leaves a bloody mess on the tables, it does, all those crumbles and flakes, but the books aren't affected at all."

For the first time in two days, Jacqueline actually beamed with delight. She felt lighthearted and excited, and it was as if a great weight had been lifted off her shoulders. "Are you certain about this?" she asked.

"I been working here longer than you been born now, haven't I?" replied Mrs. Hudson, planting her hands on her hips and glowering. "Now don't you be questioning me about what I know. Even Mr. Holmes never did *that*."

"Right," said Jacqueline, but at her earliest opportunity, she would be testing it out on something.

Maybe she'd test the edition of *The Wizard of Oz* that had fallen off the shelf last night... that way, if it got destroyed after all, she might be rid of Miss Gulch.

Or... she might not. What if destroying the book left the character here forever? Jacqueline shuddered at the thought.

She'd pick another book to test out. *Moby-Dick*. She sure as hell didn't want Captain Ahab showing up here. Or worse... the damned white whale.

"I want some coffee," said Miss Gulch, having finally looked up from Sebastian. The cat lay sprawled in her arms, his head tipped back, his legs flopped open so as to allow his admirer easy access for tummy rubbing. "None of that early gray stuff for me. It sounds horrible."

"Well, now, maybe you should try a bit before you say that," said Mrs. Hudson, who was already pouring the bergamot-scented tea into a pretty cup painted with large sunflowers. Jacqueline silently applauded her choice; sunflowers probably grew all over Kansas in those expansive prairies. Though she didn't remember reading about sunflowers in the Laura Ingalls Wilder books—

She stopped herself right there. She wasn't going to think about any other books or characters. Not right now.

"Earl Grey with a bit of cream is one of Master Sebastian's favorites," Mrs. Hudson went on as she set the teacup firmly in front of Miss Gulch. "If you don't like it, himself certainly will drink it."

"Oh, well, that smells nice," said the spinster, sniffing the cup. "Well, I suppose I'll try it. After all, if Sebastian likes it, maybe I will too."

Jacqueline left Miss Gulch to her tea and edged away down the length of the counter. She gestured for Mrs. Hudson to join her, hoping they could have a conversation without the other woman hearing them.

"I don't know what to do about her," Jacqueline said in a low voice, nodding toward Miss Gulch. "She says she doesn't know what she's doing here. But she obviously wants my help. Or something."

Mrs. Hudson nodded and pursed her lips. "That's how it always goes, then, isn't it? They never do know what they're doing here or how they got here or any of it. Best just to let things work out on their own."

That was easy for *her* to say, Jacqueline thought. Miss Gulch had sought out Jacqueline here at the store, so obviously Jacqueline was somehow caught up in the situation.

Then she realized what Mrs. Hudson had said. *They.*

They never do know what they're doing here.

Did that mean there could be more?

"I'll keep a watch on her, dearie," said Mrs. Hudson. "You've got work to do, don't you?"

"Well, yes," Jacqueline replied, startled by the reminder that she actually did have a bookstore to run, despite the assistance from Mrs. Danvers and Mrs. Hudson.

Part of her wanted to go upstairs to the little apartment and see what condition it was in now that the police were finished, but a bigger part of her decided she'd rather deal with customers and inventory instead of Mrs. Danvers, who was surely still up there cleaning.

Jacqueline spent the next several hours in a gentle blur of activity on the main floor of the shop. She was never any happier than when she was talking about books with people, and she so enjoyed interacting with the range of customers who came in and out of Three Tomes that she couldn't believe it was nearly six o'clock by the time she finally had a moment to notice. She hadn't even realized she'd missed lunch, and the locksmith had come and gone, presenting her with a set of shiny new keys for all the doors.

The best part of all was that she'd overheard two customers talking to each other as they descended from the tea room. One of them had said, "I just love how some of the employees here pretend to be literary characters. It's really fun, and they never seem to break character."

"That woman who pretends to be Sherlock's housekeeper is absolutely perfect, isn't she?" replied the other customer as she reached the ground floor.

"I know. I just wish I could figure out who that other woman is supposed to be. The kind of scary one who dresses in dark blue," said her friend. "I'm afraid to ask!"

The other woman giggled, and they headed to the counter to pay for the small stacks of books they each had. Their conversation left Jacqueline smiling to herself, more relaxed now that she understood how the customers reacted to her employees.

Speaking of the scary one... Mrs. Danvers hadn't made an appearance in hours, and Jacqueline had heard the constant clatter, clinking, and footsteps above that indicated Mrs. Hudson was still at her post. This meant that Jacqueline had been uninterrupted for the first time as a bookseller, and she'd *loved* it. Even when one customer came in to return a book she didn't like, but had a creased binding, which meant it couldn't be resold as new, Jacqueline had been able to sell the woman two other books she'd surely like better, along with a fancy tangerine-scented candle.

It was a good day. She couldn't wait to get some quiet time and relax so she could finish *Trip Wire*. Talking about books all day just made her crave reading her own all the more.

And then she remembered that she wasn't going to be able to go back to her hotel room and do her own reading... she had to go across the street and hang out with two women she didn't know.

Jacqueline considered making an excuse and cancelling—after all, she had plenty of reasons to be tired and distracted, and some of those reasons were even public knowledge—but in the end decided not to bag out on Nadine and Suzette.

She could always leave early—claim a headache or exhaustion. But it was a good idea, a savvy business decision to make friends with some of her fellow shop owners, and besides, now she could enthusiastically place an order with Suzette for baked goods. She'd make sure there were extra scones in every order.

Jacqueline turned the sign to *Closed* at six o'clock then took care of the last customer. Mrs. Danvers still hadn't appeared, and the sounds from upstairs in the café had quieted some time ago. When Jacqueline peeked up there from the top of the steps, she saw the tables and counter were sparkling clean, everything was put away, and there was no sign of either Mrs. Hudson or Miss Gulch.

Thanking heaven for very large favors, Jacqueline quickly shut down the computer and locked up, then made her escape. She had just enough time to dash back to the hotel, freshen up, grab a bottle of wine, and get back to Nadine's place by seven thirty.

Although Jacqueline looked longingly at her book when she got back to her room, she didn't even allow herself to read one page—because she knew it would lead to one chapter, and then she'd get sucked into the rest of the book. Instead, she told herself she had to go to the pizza thing for her business, and it was only one time. She'd stay for an hour, tops.

Besides, homemade pizza sounded really good.

~

"I'M SO glad you decided to join us," Nadine said when she opened the door. Her eyes sparkled and she was holding a glass of wine in one hand. Instead of athletic clothes, she was wearing a long, dress-like sweatshirt in soft gray that looked both comfortable and cozy. Her feet were bare and her toenails were painted shocking blue. "Come on in!"

When Jacqueline stepped inside the yoga center, she smelled pizza and incense. An interesting combination.

"Oh, wow," she said, looking around. "This looks really nice. Very inviting."

The studio was a large room with tall windows on three sides, and the single interior wall was lined with mirrors. Although Jacqueline didn't think she'd want to watch herself while attempting any yoga positions, she thought the rest of the place was very inviting. Silks hung suspended by four corners from the ceiling like canopies, shimmering slightly with the movement of the air. Plants of all shapes and sizes sat where they could soak up the sun and provide fresh oxygen throughout the day. A Himalayan salt lamp glowed in one corner and was surrounded by candles in hurricanes or on stands. There was a second large cluster of candles and an incense burner, as well as an essential oil diffuser, in a different corner.

The candles were all lit, and one tall, upward-facing lamp was illuminated. A pile of large, colorful poufs and floor cushions made an inviting jumble against one wall. Next to them was a large basket holding rolled-up yoga mats.

"Thank you. I hope you'll join us for a class sometime," said Nadine.

"I'd love to," Jacqueline said, mostly honestly. The curvy, definitely not sleek and slender Nadine inspired her—if she could fold herself into a pretzel, Jacqueline could probably manage a Downward Dog. Eventually.

"Welcome," said Nadine, and before Jacqueline could resist, the yoga teacher folded her into a hug. She definitely had some tone and muscle beneath her softness, for the embrace was very solid. "We're really glad you're here. As a business owner, and as another female here on the court!"

"Thank you," Jacqueline said, carefully extricating herself. She wasn't a very huggy person—especially with people she didn't know very well. Or, in this case, hardly at all.

"Pizza's almost done," said Suzette gaily as she appeared from a back room—presumably a kitchen. Her silver-threaded curly hair was pulled up into a loose tail at the top of her head, and she was wearing an apron. Short t-shirt sleeves revealed defined bicep muscles below angular shoulders. "Oh, hey, Jacqueline! I'm so glad you decided to join us."

"I've brought wine," Jacqueline said, offering the bottle of Pinot Noir in an attempt to hold off another potential hug.

"Well, let's get her open so she can breathe," said Nadine. Her eyes sparkled with light and enthusiasm, and Jacqueline couldn't suppress a smile. It was difficult not to feel the vibrancy of the woman's energy, and to respond.

She followed Nadine down a hall, passing a powder room and into another section of the building. To her surprise, there was a full kitchen and living room tucked away on the other side of the mirrored wall in the yoga center. She wondered if Nadine lived here, and if so, where was the bedroom? Upstairs, maybe.

The kitchen and living room were another large,

open space, furnished with a well-used leather sofa set, a low coffee table, and colorful photographs of Northern Michigan flora and fauna on the walls.

"Can I do anything to help?" Jacqueline offered, feeling a little awkward.

"Yes," said Suzette. "You can help us finish this bottle of Cab so we can move onto the Pinot."

"I can definitely do that," Jacqueline replied. Both of the other women had wine glasses in their hands, and there was an empty third one on the counter.

For some reason, that little detail—that there was a glass ready and waiting for her—warmed Jacqueline, and suddenly she no longer felt awkward or like an intruder. She relaxed and slid onto a barstool.

"Mmm, I like this," she said after she tasted the Cabernet Sauvignon.

The three of them had gathered around a Formica kitchen counter, which opened into the living room beneath a row of short oak cabinets that had probably been installed in the eighties. Jacqueline and Nadine sat on barstools on the living room side, while Suzette —who seemed completely comfortable in Nadine's kitchen—checked on the pizza and pulled out cutlery, salad bowls, and regular plates.

"I love these Sunday nights," Nadine told Jacqueline with a grin. "Suzie just takes over my kitchen and I don't have to do anything but watch—and eat. And her *pizza*... Wait till you taste it. It's heaven."

"It smells incredible," said Jacqueline, whose mouth was definitely watering.

"That's why you always offer to host, Nadine," said Suzette, setting plates topped with salad in front of them.

"Damn straight," replied Nadine, pointing with her fork. "I provide the wine and salad, and someone else cooks... and I don't even have to *go* anywhere to have my meal served to me." She grinned, then took a healthy sip of wine. "I even bought a pizza stone to keep in the oven for when she comes over. I don't cook," she added with a shrug. "If it weren't for Suze, I'd live on hummus, mac and cheese, and tuna sandwiches. She's even ruined me for frozen pizza." She laughed.

"So, Jacqueline," said Suzette as she turned from checking the pizza—the open oven door had offered a tantalizing view of a cheesy pizza—"tell us how it's going over at Three Tomes." She leaned on the counter and began to work on her salad.

"Surprisingly well," Jacqueline replied, a little uncomfortable being the focus of attention. But the baker was only asking a simple, reasonable question. "We just opened on Friday, and we've had a steady stream of customers. And they're *buying* things." She still couldn't get over the amount of traffic and purchases. All her life, she'd heard about independent bookstores struggling to make ends meet. "I don't know whether it's because we just opened after being closed for so long and people are curious, or because the weather was so nice over the weekend and people were out, but I'll take it."

Jacqueline realized she'd used the pronoun "we," automatically including Mrs. Hudson and Mrs. Danvers in her thoughts, as if they were an instrumental part of the store. She sighed inwardly. It didn't seem that she had any choice.

"It's all of the above, but it's also the fact that this block of Camellia Avenue—the court in particular—is a little gem of a retail oasis," Nadine told her. "It's always busy, and people are always coming here, and most of the shops along here do really well." She gave

Suzette a glance, then went on, "That's why we wanted to get to know you, sort of."

"Right," replied the baker. "Just wanted to see what your vibe was. You know?" She grinned, and Jacqueline's initial pang of uncertainty vanished, for it seemed her "vibe"—such as it was—was okay with these two women, at least so far.

"You know how sometimes when you first meet someone, you really click?" Suzette went on. "That's how it was when Nadine moved in up here, right above my place. I'd only been in business for two months, and then this yoga place got put in right above me. I wasn't sure how that was going to go—after all, here I am making and selling all of these sugary, carb-heavy—"

"*Delicious* and very much *required*," Nadine interjected. "One *must* have baked goods in one's life. It's an unbreakable rule."

Suzette laughed. "Yes, well, *I* certainly think so, but I wasn't sure how a yoga teacher would react to it. You know the stereotype of yoga teachers, right? They're vegetarian—or even vegan—and they're fitness gurus—"

"She means they're usually skinny and toned," Nadine interjected.

"No, that's not what I meant—well, maybe—and anyway, they meditate and hug trees and yada yada. Not that there's anything *wrong* with that; hell, I'm as happy to hug a tree as anyone, and I do so regularly, and she's even got me to try meditating—"

"What Suze is trying to say," Nadine said, "is that she thought I was going to be all looking-down-my-nose at her and her baked goods because she had preconceived notions. But," she said, flipping her hands out and up by her shoulders in a "here I am" gesture,

"I don't fit the stereotype of a perky, *om*-intoning yogi."

"And you know what?" said Suzette earnestly. "That's part of why you're so successful. Most of her classes are full, and some even have wait lists," she said to Jacqueline. "I keep telling her she needs to start a YouTube channel."

"Right—the Chubby Yogi or something," Nadine said with a wine-infused giggle.

"You're not chubby, you're deliciously curvy," Suzette said, then looked at Jacqueline.

"I'm chubby and I'm fine with it."

Suzette shrugged. "She doesn't intimidate people who aren't fit because they know she won't judge them."

Jacqueline was smiling and nodding, because *boy*, could she relate to Suzette's preconceived notion about the yoga teacher. "And so you two clicked," she said, wondering for a moment if that meant they'd clicked romantically, or just as friends. She hadn't gotten a vibe that they were in a relationship, but she was open-minded enough to acknowledge it was possible.

"We definitely did click," said Nadine. "I'd just gotten out of a divorce and was putting my entire life savings—and my livelihood—at risk by opening this place. I used to teach middle school. That's how I came to yoga—I needed an outlet for my anxiety and stress," she said with a laugh. "And Suzette has not only been a huge support but a good friend. I've got two kids, upper teens, the youngest just about to grad-uate high school. Both girls, both really good kids, and my ex and I share custody—and things are really tight and hectic sometimes. Hence the need for medita-tion," she added, giving Suzette an arch look.

"I'm still working on that meditation part—and oh, I better get this bad boy out of the oven," said the baker, spinning around with a flutter of her apron.

Jacqueline didn't mind letting the two women do most of the talking. It was easier for her to get a handle on things that way, to settle in and figure out whether she liked these women—so far, yes, she did— and whether she could feel comfortable sharing her own history with them.

When Suzette put the pizza on the counter, Jacqueline goggled at it. She'd never seen a more delicious-looking pie, and that was saying something, since she was from Chicago. Cheese oozed everywhere, and the crust was crispy at the edges and not too puffy, like she'd be eating a pillow. It was topped with sliced tomatoes, something that was probably basil, red onions, and, on one half, slices of ham.

"I know, right?" said Nadine, obviously noting her reaction. "I love sex, but if I had to make a choice between getting laid and no more Suzette pizza, it'd be a tough one."

"That's what vibrators are for," Jacqueline said without thinking, then blushed. *Oh my God!* She couldn't believe she'd let that slip.

But instead of being horrified, the other two women burst into laughter. "I know! That's what I told her," Suzette said, using a pizza cutter to slice the pie into eight generous pieces. "Best of both worlds—take care of yourself and eat pizza. I don't need a man to be happy and fulfilled."

"Although they're nice to have around sometimes," Nadine said. She didn't wait, and instead reached over to slide a piece of steaming pizza onto her plate. The cheese hung in long, delectable strings, and Suzette severed them with a quick slice from the cutter.

"Hmmph," Suzette said. "Jury's still out on that. Ham or no?" she asked Jacqueline, hovering over the pizza with a server.

"Ham," Jacqueline replied.

"Suze's been divorced for eight years," Nadine said, already diving into her piece—which, Jacqueline noticed, did not have ham on it. "And had a not-so-good breakup, what, two years ago?"

Suzette nodded and served Jacqueline her piece. "I'm taking a break from men for a while. Could be forever. Maybe I'll become a lesbian."

Nadine snorted. "You don't *become* a lesbian. As my daughter—the lesbian—would tell you."

"I know, I know... but if it *were* a choice, I might consider it," Suzette replied, finally taking a piece for herself.

"But do tell, Jacqueline... looks like you've had a lot of action from that hottie Miles Massermey." Nadine waggled her eyebrows.

Jacqueline felt her cheeks heat up. "Um... he's been investigating a suspicious death," she said, trying to sound offhanded. "So, yes, he's been around a little. But there's been no *action*." Her cheeks got even hotter. Damned hot flash.

"Right," said Suzette. "But when he was in here last night—downstairs, I mean—getting a pie, he was looking over at your store the whole time, and he asked about you a few times. I had to ask him for payment twice."

"He's a hottie *and* a nice guy," Nadine said. "I get this whole Leif Erickson vibe from him, you know?"

"Definitely," Suzette replied, then moaned as she bit into her pizza. "OMG, I am a *brilliant* cook. Honestly, I should be cleaning up on *Chopped* or something like that."

"That you are," said Nadine, tucking a piece of dangling cheese into her mouth. "And this Pinot is perfect with it. Thanks, Jacqueline—or do you prefer Jackie?"

"Jacqueline's good," Jacqueline replied.

"So... what about you? Married? Divorced? Involved with anyone? Do you like to sleep with men, women, or both?" asked Nadine. "Have any kids?"

"I like men, and no, I'm not involved with anyone —unless you count a friends-with-benefits kind of guy I know back in Chicago. Les is my plus-one to things and stuff like that, and vice versa. But I wouldn't call us *involved* by any stretch." She made air quotes around the word. "And yes, I definitely get the Viking vibe from Detective Massermey," she added with a smile. "Definitely. Never married, but almost was about twenty years ago—then I caught him cheating and that was that. Never found anyone I wanted to trust again after that." She was only mildly surprised that such a personal statement had tumbled out so easily.

"Like I said... we don't need men to be happy and fulfilled," said Suzette.

"I know, and I fully embrace my feminist side, but I really did like being married," said Nadine. "I liked having a life partner and I liked having regular sex. It just didn't work out with Noah." She reached for the wine bottle and topped off her friend's glass, then said, "You driving, Jacqueline?"

"Nope," Jacqueline replied, and scooted her glass closer to the bottle. "I'm walking back to Chance's Inn."

"Oh, that's a really cozy place," said Suzette.

"It looks nice, but I've never stayed there," said Nadine. "But let's get back on topic."

"Which topic? We've run the gamut here: men, sex, food, lesbianism, and wine," said Suzette, grabbing her third piece of pizza.

"Miles Massermey," said Nadine. "Actually, much as I can enjoy looking at him, I don't think he's actually my type. He's just too... I don't know, imposing, I guess. A little intimidating and so very, very serious all the time. Maybe he reminds me too much of Noah, who commanded attention the minute he walked in the room. He's a neurosurgeon. Half the time he thinks he's God." She rolled her eyes a little. "The other half the time, he *knows* he's God. Anyway, what can you tell us about the suspicious death? Or should we talk about something else? That had to be a big shock to find a dead body at your place."

"I didn't actually find it," Jacqueline said before she realized where that comment might lead. Even though Nadine had interacted with Mrs. Hudson, Jacqueline wasn't certain she wanted to get too deep in conversation about her two helpers. She assumed Nadine and Suzette were under the same impression as her customers—that Hudson and Danvers were normal people playing roles. "But yeah, it was a shock. He was upstairs in the apartment—I hadn't gone up there the day before, so that was the first time I'd seen the place."

"Cuddy lived up there. It's a nice apartment," said Suzette. "So who died?"

Jacqueline was mildly surprised she didn't already know. "Apparently he was a distant cousin of Cuddy," she said, then went on to give the few details she had as they mowed through another few pieces of pizza. "And his sister showed up at the store yesterday evening too. She was not happy. Blamed me for her brother's death."

"Seriously? What a *witch*," Nadine said.

Jacqueline declined to comment on how accurate a description that might possibly be. Instead, she debated internally about bringing up the subject of the three crones down the street. She was just gathering her courage when Suzette stilled.

"Hey, Jacqueline... did you leave a light on at your place?" She was looking out the window.

"No, I don't think so." Jacqueline turned and looked out the window of Nadine's living room, which she now realized faced Camellia Court and was next to the yoga center on the second floor. "Where's the—Oh!"

She slid off the stool quickly, because the light wasn't on in the shop on the street level—it was on in the third-floor apartment, right where Henbert Stone had died.

13

"I just got new locks!" Jacqueline said, puffing a little as she and her two new friends jogged across the street. "Today!"

It was nearly nine o'clock, and since it was Sunday and the tourist season hadn't started, the block was deserted of cars as well as passersby. The streetlights were on, and the moon was half-full in a cloudy night sky.

Jacqueline couldn't help but glance suspiciously down the street at Camellia House. The old ladies' house was lit with a soft glow, but that didn't indicate whether they were actually in residence or not.

"Maybe Massermey's people accidentally left a light on, and you didn't notice it during the daytime," Suzette said as Jacqueline slid her new key into the front door's lock.

"Or maybe Mrs. Danvers did," Jacqueline said, forgetting about her desire to not talk about her "employees."

"Sorry to say so, but I doubt she'd do anything so careless," Nadine said as she followed Jacqueline through the doorway. "That woman looks like she spits nails. She's more judgmental than you are, isn't she, Max?" She paused to give the black cat a stroke over his long, sleek back. Max looked bored by the attention, but Jacqueline noticed that he didn't slink away, either.

Jacqueline hurried up the stairs to the tea room with the other women right on her heels. As they left Nadine's, they'd armed themselves with pepper spray and two of Nadine's daughter's golf clubs.

Before starting up the stairs from the pantry on the second floor, Jacqueline paused and held up a hand to shush her companions. She wanted to listen for sounds from above, but she also wanted to keep their presence a surprise for as long as possible. Nadine and Suzette nodded, and they waited for a moment. The only sound was that of their breathing, and Jacqueline was annoyed to realize hers was more than a little heavier than her friends'. She probably should start actually working out instead of just doing a few half-hearted stretches in the morning. Ugh.

There were no sounds from above, so the three moved quietly up the stairs that would open next to the pantry in the apartment kitchen. The light had been coming from the living room, right where Henbert's body was found—and where the three crones were burning "sage" earlier today.

Jacqueline led the way, brandishing the small pepper spray canister Nadine had given her. Right behind her, the other two each had their own golf club. Their plan was to spray first, then whale on the intruder with the drivers. Then they would ask questions.

Pushing open the door, Jacqueline let herself into the tiny back hall by the kitchen and pantry, noticing a stacked washer and dryer setup for the first time. She waited, but heard no sounds of life from the front of the apartment (she wasn't certain whether that was good or bad), so she gestured for Nadine and Suzette to follow her.

The three of them were in shadows as they eased toward the golden spill of light in the living room, creeping across the old linoleum kitchen floor. Between the kitchen and the living room there was a half wall against which a small dining table had been placed on the kitchen side, and the three of them kept in a low crouch as they made their way toward it.

The countertops smelled like lemon and vinegar, indicating that Mrs. Danvers had been hard at work, and there was no sign of fingerprint dust. All of the furnishings had been uncovered by now.

A thought struck Jacqueline, and she stilled. What if she found the *Rebecca* housekeeper on the floor, dead like Henbert Stone?

Was it even possible for Mrs. Danvers to die? She was corporeal, but she wasn't real... was she?

Wait. Hadn't Mrs. Danvers already died in *Rebecca*? Jacqueline actually couldn't remember if we knew for certain...

Pushing those strange thoughts away, Jacqueline braced herself, pepper spray at the level of her eyes (she checked to make sure the nozzle was facing in the opposite direction, and it was), and, heart pounding, rose to look over the half wall.

"Oh my God," she said and, dropping the pepper spray, dashed around the wall to the living room.

"What is it?" said Nadine, but she and Suzette were right on Jacqueline's heels, and they saw what she did: a still figure, collapsed on the floor.

Jacqueline had immediately recognized her by her spiky hair and slender figure.

"Andromeda!" she cried, kneeling next to her and

feeling for her wrist. A rush of relief blasted through her. "She's got a pulse," she told her companions as they crouched next to her. "And she's breathing—seems to be normal. Andromeda?" Jacqueline tried to be gentle as she shook Andromeda's shoulder in an effort to rouse her. She didn't react other than a very subtle change of breathing. "Her skin's clammy," Jacqueline said, feeling the dampness on Andromeda's arms and cheek.

"Andromeda, wake up," said Nadine, gently slapping her face. "You're right—she doesn't feel right."

"I'd better call 911," said Suzette, pulling out her phone.

"No," came a voice from the shadows. "I highly recommend you don't do that."

Jacqueline turned, her heart in her throat, as Egala Stone stepped into the small pool of light.

She looked the same as she had last night, except that her penciled-in brows were thicker and seemed more menacing. Her wash-and-set hair was neat as a pin, as if she'd just left the salon. She was dressed in black from head to toe, including gloves. A collection of long necklaces in silver and copper were strung around her neck, bumping her at belly height. They had many pendants and gemstones dangling from them.

"What is going on here?" Jacqueline demanded, rising. "What are you doing here? Suzette, call 911 and report a trespasser and tell them we need medical help. And call Detective Massermey." Her voice was calm, but inside, her heart was in her throat and her stomach twisted in knots. "Tell him I have another intruder."

"Do you want to end up like her? *Put down the phone*," Egala snapped. Her eyes gleamed with malevolence, and Jacqueline remembered the sparks of lightning that had emitted—or seemed to emit—from her fingers last night. And the way the books had tumbled to the floor when she gestured.

"Bite me," replied Suzette, already bringing the device to her ear.

Jacqueline heard the voice on the other end: "Nine-one-one, what's your emergency—"

Suddenly, the small electronic device was flying through the air. It made an ugly shattering sound when it hit the wall. Suzette gasped and stared at Egala, who'd removed her gloves and from whose fingers sparks had shot.

"What are you doing here?" Jacqueline asked, confused, angry, and more than a little frightened. "And what's wrong with Andromeda? What did you do to her?"

Egala calmly put her gloves back on. "It's of no concern of yours, since this is *rightfully* my place, but I must say, I *am* pleased that you're here, Miss Finch. This will make things much easier."

"What do you mean by that?" Nadine said, still crouched next to Andromeda. "And this woman needs help—unless you want to be considered accomplice to murder. We need to call for EMTs."

Jacqueline noticed that, despite her challenging words, Nadine didn't dig out her own phone. But she was positioned next to the still Andromeda, as if to protect her from Egala.

"Miss Finch is going to give me my rightful property," Egala said. "And once she does that, I'll tell you how to help *her*." She sneered at the crumpled body of Andromeda.

"Your rightful property?" Suzette replied as

Jacqueline struggled with how to respond. "You mean the store? I don't *think* so."

Jacqueline couldn't let anything happen to Andromeda; if the stupid witch wanted the bookstore, she could *have* it.

But even as she thought those words, Jacqueline felt a shimmer of uncertainty, followed by a very strong tug of possession. *No. This is your place. From your family. It was given to you.*

"All right," said Jacqueline, her mind darting between tunnels of fear, anger, and the craftiness she admired in TJ Mack's Sargent Blue. "So you want me to give the store to you? And if I do that, you'll help Andromeda?"

"I didn't say that I'd help her—I said I'd tell you what was wrong with her," replied Egala smugly. The malicious gleam in her eyes had grown stronger, and a little smile twitched at the corner of her mouth. "But you have to give me the property, free and clear."

"No. If you want it, you have to *fix* Andromeda," Jacqueline said. She was beginning to realize that her possession of the house must give her some sort of power or leverage. If Egala needed it "free and clear," that must mean Jacqueline had to do so willingly.

At least, she hoped that was the case.

"You have to wake her and make her healthy again," Jacqueline said. "Completely healthy. What did you do to her?"

Suzette and Nadine were watching with horrified expressions, and when Jacqueline indicated her willingness to give up the store, both of her new friends made strident sounds of negation. Jacqueline also noticed that Suzette seemed to be inching slowly back toward the kitchen—to run and get help? To pick up a golf club? Maybe the pepper spray.

Did pepper spray work on witches?

Good grief, I can't believe I'm actually thinking *this way...*

"The same thing happened to her that happened to my brother," said Egala. "Serves you right!"

Her words seized Jacqueline with horror. "Is she dead?"

"She will be if you don't cooperate," replied Egala. "And quickly."

For a moment, Jacqueline was ready to believe her... and then she stilled her freaking-out mind and looked coldly at Egala. "I didn't do anything to your brother. I think Cuddy Stone did something here, in this place, that protected it from unwanted intruders —like Henbert. But Andromeda has been here several times, and she's been unharmed. Until now. So whatever happened to her, *you* must have done. And maybe you did the same thing to your brother, too!"

Egala's eyebrows jumped a little. Clearly, she hadn't expected such pushback. Her reaction gave Jacqueline even more confidence. "How *dare* you—"

"If you want me to even consider surrendering this place to you, you're going to have to wake up Andromeda and prove to me that she's all right," Jacqueline went on. Despite her calm words, her heart was racing wildly. This moment reminded her of the time at the library when a small child began to choke on a piece of candy and Jacqueline had to do the Heimlich on him.

It was a wild, scary, horrifying episode, but she'd been calm and confident, and thanks to her training, knew what to do. While everyone stood around in silent horror, watching him turn blue, Jacqueline ordered someone to call 911. Then she took up the little boy and did what had to be done, fitting her arms around him in the proper position and thrusting up and in. The candy—which wasn't even allowed in the library!—flew from his mouth.

Afterward, in private, she seriously fell apart.

So she figured she might fall apart later, but for now, she wasn't letting Egala Stone lie to her or manipulate her.

And she didn't see Suzette any longer, either, which she thought was a good thing.

"You think you can order me around?" Egala said, her necklaces clashing wildly against her belly as her eyes darkened with fury. She ripped off her gloves. "You have no idea who I am or what I can do, do you?"

"I don't care what you can do—this is *my* place, and—"

All of a sudden, the room was filled with a blustery wind. Curtains, pillows, and even wisps of Jacqueline's hair began to fly about as if a tornado had taken up residence. A statuette from the fireplace mantel crashed to the floor, and a small metal bowl flew toward Jacqueline.

She ducked and heard it clang into the wall behind her. The roar of the wind filled her ears, buffeting her clothing and tugging her hair loose from its moorings.

"You think you can order me around here in *my family's home*?" Egala cried over the noise. She was whipping one raised hand in a sharp, fast circle, as if she was stirring the air. Her hair, which had been so perfectly coiffed only a moment before, now stood out like a writhing, dark halo. "This should be my place, and—"

"Well, it *isn't*," cried Jacqueline, incensed and out of patience. "Cuddy left it to *me*. I'm family *too*! And I want you to leave. It's time for you to *go*. Now, Egala.

Leave this place now, and take your damned tornado with you!"

She pointed to the hallway that led to the back entrance. Her hand was shaking and her mouth was dry, and the wind snapped and whipped at her, but she stood her ground.

The tornado faltered, and then suddenly it was gone. Egala's hair constricted back into neat Professor Umbrage curls, as if she'd just left the salon. Her hands dropped to her sides. She was still holding the gloves in one of them.

"You'll regret this," Egala said, hurrying toward the back hall far more quickly than Jacqueline expected. "You have no idea what you've just done. What hell you've unleashed."

"Yada, yada," Nadine said tartly, then ducked a little when Egala whipped back around toward them with a raised arm.

A little zip of lightning shot toward Nadine and Jacqueline, but for some reason, Jacqueline didn't even flinch. She felt the rush of heat and energy as the bolt blazed past her cheek, but she was too furious— and curious—to react.

"I told you to leave," she said, starting toward Egala.

The witch didn't slow down as she hurried out of sight down the hallway. Jacqueline followed and saw Egala open the door to the back stairs and hurry down. Satisfied that the crazy broad wasn't going to return, Jacqueline hurried back to the living room.

But if she'd hoped that Egala's exit would remove whatever curse she'd placed on Andromeda, Jacqueline was bound to be disappointed.

Andromeda remained still and unmoving on the

floor, which was now littered with pillows, knick-knacks, and even a small book.

"I'm calling 911," said Nadine, having fished the phone out of her pocket.

"Wait," said someone in a rushed voice from the kitchen. This time the speaker was welcome, for Jacqueline recognized her as Zwyla.

"Let us handle this," said Pietra as she and Zwyla, along with Suzette—who was panting slightly—swarmed into the room.

Jacqueline was surprised and relieved by their presence, but not so much that she didn't notice that neither of the older ladies seemed out of breath. Had they already been here, waiting for an opportunity to make an appearance? Or had they come from the front of the house instead of the back, where Egala had just been? Or had they just... apparated here?

Zwyla and Pietra knelt next to Andromeda, and Jacqueline could hear the murmur as they spoke to each other in low voices. Or maybe they were doing some sort of spell—who knew?

"Thanks for going to get them," Jacqueline told Suzette, gesturing to the two crones. "I wasn't sure what was going to happen."

"That bitch broke my phone," replied the baker as she crouched to pick up the pieces. "I was *pissed*. I *am* pissed." She held up the parts and said, "Since when does an iPhone break into pieces? Usually the screen just cracks. But it's completely ruined!" She was livid, and Jacqueline didn't blame her.

"Is she alright?" she asked, edging over to where Zwyla and Pietra still hovered over Andromeda.

When Zwyla looked up at her with worried, dark eyes, Jacqueline's heart sank. "Not yet," the older woman replied.

"Is she going to be?" Nadine asked, coming over to stand next to the group. Suzette crowded in behind her.

"I don't know," Zwyla said after a pause. Jacqueline's insides squeezed when she heard a noise that sounded like a soft sob from Pietra.

No. No. No!

"We should call 911," said Suzette.

"They won't be able to do anything," said Pietra in a wavery voice. She pulled heavily to her feet. "It's not that kind of... condition."

"But... she can't... It can't be like that man." Nadine voiced the same horror that was settling over Jacqueline. "Hedwin—whatever his name was. It *can't* be."

"We need to get her back home," said Zwyla.

"We'll help," said Suzette, but Zwyla waved her off.

"I've got her." The tall woman of eighty bent, and the next thing Jacqueline knew, Andromeda's slender, elfin body was draped gracefully over Zwyla's sturdy shoulder.

"What can we do?" said Jacqueline. Somehow she felt responsible, and even though she'd only known Andromeda for two days, she just couldn't imagine her being gone.

"I don't know," said Zwyla. Her voice was tight and her face set. She turned and began to walk slowly out of the apartment, Andromeda's arms dangling sadly, helplessly, down her rescuer's back.

"If it helps," Jacqueline said, and Zwyla paused, turning carefully with her burden to listen, "Egala Stone claimed whatever is wrong with Andromeda was what happened to her brother. I didn't think that was true, because Andromeda has been here before, and if there was a—a—curse—I mean, some sort of danger," she said with a glance at Nadine and Suzette, "surely it would have bothered her before... but maybe Egala wasn't lying."

Zwyla nodded. "All right. Thank you for that information." Then, sober and staid, she continued her way down the hall.

"Usually it's Andi who does all the healing stuff," Pietra said. Her eyes were wide in her moonlike face, and Jacqueline saw that they were bloodshot with tears. "We'll figure it out," Pietra said, staring after her friends. "We *will*. We have to."

14

Jacqueline wanted to follow the older women back to their house, but she knew there was no reason to do so. There was nothing she could do to help Andromeda.

And maybe they wanted to be alone to do whatever they needed to do for their friend, she thought. An image of them huddled around the cauldron in the herbary popped into her mind... but the image included Andromeda, which made Jacqueline terrified and sad and even more worried. *Please let her be okay.*

She decided to put the thought out of her mind for now—she'd definitely go down to their house tomorrow and see if there was any news—but for tonight, she decided to spend a little more time in the apartment.

Was there something about this place that was drawing people here? First Henbert, then the three ladies with their sage, now Andromeda and Egala.

"What happened here?" Suzette said, looking around the messy living room with wide eyes. "Did you have a fight?"

"That woman—what was her name, anyway?— threw a hissy fit," replied Nadine. She'd already begun to straighten things up, putting pillows back on the sofa. "Is there a broom somewhere?"

"I don't know," Jacqueline admitted. She suddenly felt shaky and lightheaded as it all sank in, everything that had just happened. She'd actually stared down and stood up to that violent, angry woman who had some sort of witchy powers.

If Jacqueline hadn't been here in the thick of it all, she would never have believed what had happened.

"By the way," said Nadine, looking at Jacqueline, "you were effing *amazing*. Brave as shit all the way through. I was just standing there trying not to pee my pants—which is damned near impossible when you've had two kids and everything down there's not quite as tight as it used to be."

"Oh, well, I guess I just got mad," Jacqueline said, feeling very awkward as the two women looked at her in admiration.

"You should have seen her, Suze—she was standing there in the middle of the freaking tornado and it didn't even faze her a bit," Nadine said.

"Tornado?" Suzette asked.

"Yeah—that crazy woman unleashed a tornado sort of thing in here," Nadine told her.

Suzette frowned. "Like, she just started throwing things around? She must have been pretty pissed."

"No, no... I mean a real, actual, room-sized tornado. She was kind of stirring the air with her hand, wasn't she?" Nadine looked at Jacqueline.

"It seemed like it," Jacqueline replied.

"Um... whatever you say," Suzette replied, looking around with skepticism.

"Don't look like that," Nadine admonished her. "You're the one whose phone went flying through the air—and she didn't even touch it."

Suzette pursed her lips, then nodded. "Yeah, I guess so. But an indoor tornado? For real?"

"Does this look like someone just started throwing things around?" Nadine said. Her arms were filled with curtains and curtain rods. "She literally made the air spin. And you should have seen Jacqueline here— she just stood right up to her! Told her to leave, right in the middle of everything. She had her hands on her hips, her hair was all flying around—Hey, what's that?"

"What?" Jacqueline said.

Nadine came closer, and Jacqueline managed not to flinch as the huggy yoga teacher moved into her personal space. And before Jacqueline could back away, Nadine touched her on the cheek. "Right here, there's a mark or dirt or something."

Jacqueline reached up to feel her face and remembered the searing blaze from Egala's lightning bolt. "She *burned* me," she said, but her skin felt smooth and unmarked. "Is there a mark?"

"There's something," said Nadine, looking at her with a tilted head. "And your hair..."

"What about my ha—" Jacqueline caught a glimpse of herself in the round mirror that hung over the fireplace. "Holy crap!"

Her hair—which had been up in its normal, neat, professional French twist—was now a wild, tangled mass of curls. That was freaky, because her hair had always been stick-straight. She looked like the model on a historical romance novel—or, more accurately, like she'd looked when she got a perm back in the late eighties to combat said stick-straightness.

Now not only had she turned into Annie (thank goodness her hair wasn't as copper-penny bright), but there was also a two-inch-wide streak right in the front, like she'd gone to a salon for a highlight that went wrong.

Not a white streak, but a jet-black one, in the middle of her red hair.

"You didn't have that dark highlight in there before, did you?" Nadine said.

"She burned my hair!" Still looking in the mirror with something between fascination and horror, Jacqueline touched the swatch of black. It didn't feel any different from the rest of her hair, thank goodness. The last thing she needed was a huge clump of hair to fall out right in the front of her scalp. "And... my freckles! They're... darker."

Jacqueline had always had freckles as a child—the bane of being a redhead with fair skin. They'd faded over the years—but, unfortunately, not because of the lemon juice she'd tried to bleach them with during her middle school days. Just the other day she'd noticed that a little cluster of them seemed more noticeable all of a sudden—and now, those same six little freckles stood out like dark caramel spots on her left cheekbone.

Had Egala's zip of lightning somehow caused that darkening?

"I think it looks cool," said Nadine, peering a little too closely at Jacqueline's skin. Surely she could see the moonscape size of her pores, and the wrinkles, and the rest of her freckles that had never completely faded. Not to mention the age spots and the subcutaneous zit lurking next to her nose. "Six little dots— they make like a subtle star shape on your face. Marilyn Monroe would have killed for those beauty marks."

"I'd hardly call them beauty marks," Jacqueline said. "They were left by a damned witch!"

The minute she said those words, she regretted them. Now her new friends—yes, she'd already come to think of them as friends—would think she was totally nuts.

"You could look at it that way," Suzette said, reappearing from the kitchen with a broom and dustpan, "or you could look at it as a badge of honor that you faced one down and won. She did leave when you told her to, didn't she?"

Jacqueline's shaky knees finally gave out. Fortunately, the sofa was right behind her. "Am I going crazy?"

"Nope," both of her friends said in unison.

"Not unless we're going with you," Nadine added.

Neither of them seemed to be put off by the term "witch," although in fairness, they might have thought she used the term figuratively.

"She did leave," Nadine said. "Like—right away. I got the impression she didn't have a choice."

Jacqueline nodded. "I did too."

"What exactly happened?" Suzette asked. She'd been sweeping up broken porcelain and glass on the hardwood floor and tile in front of the fireplace.

"Jacqueline got pissed and told her to go, and she actually did. And she turned off the tornado, too," said Nadine.

"It really seemed like Egala had no choice but to leave," Jacqueline added. "It was kind of strange."

"It's your place," said Suzette, looking around for a place to dump the pieces of figurine. "You own it, and you told her to leave, and she had no choice but to do so. You know, legally."

Nadine shook her head. "I think it was more than that. She didn't even hesitate. It was like some sort of force made her walk out of the room—or maybe she was afraid of what would happen if she didn't leave. Which implies something else."

"Like what?" Jacqueline asked.

"Like... maybe you have some sort of power over her?" Nadine said. "Because you own the place?"

"Hmm. Maybe." Jacqueline was unconvinced. "All I know is that she left when I told her to. And, honestly, I couldn't believe it actually worked." She gave a nervous laugh.

"You should have told her never to come back," Nadine said. She'd moved to the window and was standing on tiptoes trying to put the curtain rod back up. "*Ow!*" she cried when one end of the rod fell and bopped her on the head.

"You can leave that, Nadine," Jacqueline said. "I'll take care of it tomorrow. Right now, I think I need a big—*very* big—glass of wine."

"Wine? I think this episode calls for something heftier than a Pinot—no offense to any Pinot whatsoever. I've got some bourbon stashed away for just such an occasion," said Nadine, rubbing her head where the curtain rod hit. "I usually break into it after I see Renee. The ex's new wife," she added for Jacqueline's benefit. "*She* thinks he's God *all* the time."

"And there's pizza left," Suzette reminded them. "We were interrupted mid-pie."

Jacqueline hesitated. Something told her she needed to stay in the apartment... at least for a while. She hadn't spent any time here, and it seemed to be the center of *something*.

And whatever that something was had killed Henbert Stone and seriously impaired Andromeda. Jacqueline shivered. Would she be in danger as well? Did it only happen when someone was here alone?

"What's wrong?" asked Suzette.

Jacqueline told them, and to her relief, both women nodded in understanding.

"Let's go get the pizza and bourbon and bring them back here," suggested Nadine. "If you don't mind the company, Jacqueline."

"I'd be grateful for the company," Jacqueline replied, "but I really hate to impose—"

"Don't be silly!" Suzette exclaimed. "It's not an imposition. Something is obviously going on here, and three heads are better than one. Besides, I have some of my famous butterscotch brownies that need to be eaten, since the bakery is closed tomorrow."

"Yes!" Nadine did a fist pump. "Jacqueline, you haven't lived until you've had Suzie's blondies. She puts toffee chips in them—and no nuts!"

How could Jacqueline say no to pizza, bourbon, and brownies?

She didn't even try.

~

"So let's talk about this," said Suzette.

It was nearly eleven o'clock, and they'd finished eating pizza and brownies, and had made significant inroads into the bottle of bourbon—all in between cleaning up the cyclonic disaster.

"Talk about what?" Nadine was sitting on a large blue pillow on the floor, leaning against the wall by the fireplace. She was sitting with her legs bent pretzel-style, her glass balanced on the side of one chubby ankle. Jacqueline noticed she had a small symbol tattooed on the same ankle, but she was too far away to make out exactly what it was.

"About the fact that someone died here and that someone else got very hurt or sick—or whatever is wrong with Andromeda." Suzette was curled up on one end of the sofa, which was positioned in front of the fireplace. Jacqueline sat at the other end with her feet on the small table between the fireplace and sofa, ankles crossed, a pillow beneath them. "It can't be a coincidence."

Jacqueline shook her head and realized the room was a little slow and murky. The bourbon had had a calming effect... something she definitely appreciated after the last few days. "I don't think it's a coincidence, but I don't know why. Detective Massermey said the cause of death was indeterminate, and..." Her voice trailed off before she could go on to tell them what the three crones had basically confirmed—that there was some sort of curse that had killed him.

"And...?" Nadine prompted her.

Jacqueline shrugged. "I don't know."

"What, do you think the place is cursed or something?" said Nadine. "First Henberg, then Andromeda? That crazy lightning-finger lady—what was her name again? Equala? Dang, they have weird names in the Stone family—except for you. I love Jacqueline, and I love that you don't shorten it. Anyway, the crazy lady made it sound like whatever happened to her brother also happened to Andi."

"But Andromeda has been here at least two other times since Henbert was found, and she was fine both times. I think Egala was lying when she said the same thing happened to Andromeda and Henbert. I think *she* did something to Egala. And maybe she even killed her own brother."

"Unless..." Suzette made fish lips as she mused. "Unless Henbert and Andromeda did something that *caused* whatever happened to them to happen. Like, tripped a switch, so to speak, or set off a booby trap.

And they were both, presumably, alone when whatever happened happened."

Jacqueline nodded. "Yes, that's all true. But then Egala showed up right after Andromeda got—whatever? I'm not sure. It seems more than coincidental that she was here when it happened."

They sat in silence for a long moment, then Nadine spoke. "Well, I don't get any sort of really strong vibe here—negative energy, I mean."

"That could be because those three crones from across the stree—Oh, crap, did I say that out loud?" Horrified, Jacqueline clapped a hand over her mouth as the other two women burst out laughing.

"The three crones! That's simply perfect!" said Suzette, her eyes bright as she lifted her glass to toast. "Not that there's anything wrong with being a crone."

"I guess. We're all going to be there at some point. My friend Stacey used to say that women are pretty much written off once we hit forty-five. No one wants to hire us, we're done having and raising children—if we had any, which I didn't—and sex isn't really on the table anymore," Jacqueline said.

"That's nuts," said Suzette, her eyes wide. "All due respect to your friend, but I totally disagree."

"So do I," said Nadine. "First of all, sex is always on the table for me, vibrator or not. And there's no way I feel written off. I've got a new business going quite well—that I started when I turned forty-five, by the way. I'm ready to embrace my croneness whenever I get there—hell, sometimes I already act like one, all cranky and badass and not giving a flip! We need to *own* our womanhood—all parts of it—and crone is just as important a stage as maiden and mother."

"Personally, I think it's the *most* powerful," said Suzette. "By the time you get to be a crone—or wise woman, which is the other name for it, but I really feel like we should own the word crone, too, you know? We'll *own* 'crone'! Take away any negative connotations and make it a powerful word—you know, like how the Millennial LGBTQers have embraced the word 'queer' and made it their own again.

"Anyway, by the time you get to this phase, you know who you are and you realize you don't give a crap about what anyone thinks of you. We're not washed up *at all*. I mean, look at Helen freaking Mirren!"

"Right?" agreed Nadine enthusiastically. "She's more badass now than she was twenty years ago. And Sharon Stone and Robin Wright—"

"Not that any of us look as good as they do, but *still*," Suzette said.

"Girl, your arms are way more cut than Sharon Stone's," Nadine admonished her. "And it's not about the looks anyway. It's about the *attitude*."

"True," Suzette said. "Anyway, when we women get to the crone phase, we really come into our *power*: knowing who we are, being comfortable with that—and with having many years of experience behind us. Wise women."

Jacqueline had been listening to Stacey's opinions for so long that she wasn't certain she agreed with her new friends, but their opinions and expressions thereof were certainly entertaining. "That not-giving-a-crap part might have something to do with a lack of estrogen," she said with a grin, "but ask me if I care."

"Do you care?" Nadine giggled, making Jacqueline wonder if her new friend had an early yoga class tomorrow and whether she'd be hurting from bourbon, wine, and too much brownie.

"Nope," Jacqueline replied. "Besides, look at my

hair!" She fluffed the curls, catching sight of herself in the mirror that hung over the fireplace.

It was strange, seeing herself with a cloud of hair around her face instead of it being pulled back into a smooth, professional twist. It wasn't a bad look, she decided. And with all the curls, her hair didn't even reach her shoulders, as it did when it was straight. She wondered if the curls were a permanent (ha!) change or if they'd wash out.

Then she gasped and bolted to her feet, turning around.

"What is it?" Suzette and Nadine chorused, standing as well.

Jacqueline looked around the living room. No, there was no one else there.

"What's wrong?" Suzette said as Nadine walked over to where Jacqueline was looking.

"I... thought I saw something," Jacqueline replied. "Reflected in the mirror—someone behind me."

"No one is here but us," Suzette said.

Jacqueline turned back to the mirror over the fireplace. The whole thing was a circle, measuring, she guessed, four feet across. The mirror itself was small —maybe only two feet in diameter—but it was encircled by a wide, ornate frame made from silver. It would be very heavy, and Jacqueline hoped it was mounted sturdily enough. The design of the frame was beautiful—it looked as if leaves and vines had been wrought in the silver, and as Jacqueline looked at it, they seemed so realistic as to actually be fluttering gently, as if a tender breeze was moving through the room.

But that was silly.

Or... maybe it wasn't.

She shook her head, still caught by the reflection

in the mirror. Her face, with its strange new nimbus of hair and the small, starlike mark on her cheek, was centered in the mirror. She felt as if she were being drawn toward the reflection, to the mirror.

"Jacqueline, are you alright?"

"I... Yes," she replied. It wasn't a malevolent feeling or an unpleasant experience, this compulsion to look in the mirror. "It's the mirror," she said, speaking slowly yet not really thinking about the words. They just spilled free, as if her brain was working things out as she spoke.

"What about it?" Suzette said. She came to stand next to Jacqueline, and although her reflection was visible, it was Jacqueline's face that seemed to dominate the reflection.

"It's a beautiful piece," Nadine said, joining them as well. She stood on the opposite side of Jacqueline, and their three faces—with Jacqueline's in the center, larger and more prominent—stared back at them. "And now I'm getting some serious vibes in the room." She gave a little shiver and rubbed her arms.

"Maybe it's the bourbon," said Suzette.

"I don't think so," replied Jacqueline. "Did you see that?" Her voice pitched higher as the other two gasped.

"Yes!" Nadine replied.

"It was like a flutter... at the edge of the image," said Suzette. "Like someone's hair?"

"*Is someone in the mirror?*"

15

As soon as she spoke, Jacqueline saw a flash of light or some brightness coming from inside the mirrored image. Like, from *inside* the glass.

Nadine and Suzette whirled to look behind them, but Jacqueline didn't. She kept watching the mirror.

And then, to her shock and fascination, a new face became visible in the reflection. Jacqueline could still see her own visage, and those of her friends—who'd turned back to look at the glass again—but the new face superseded theirs, turning the three originals into murky images.

"What the..." Suzette breathed.

Apparently, she and Nadine could see it too.

"I'm not freaking out," said Nadine. "Nope. Not at all..." But she reached over, grabbed Jacqueline's wrist, and squeezed. For once, Jacqueline didn't mind the touchy-feely stuff, for that meant that one, she was awake, and two, someone was there with her.

The face was that of an old woman: very pale—almost ghostly—wrinkled, with eyelids that sagged so much that the folds probably obstructed her vision. Her lips were thin, with countless lines radiating from them. She had gray and white hair that straggled around her face in wisps, and the detail in the mirror was so clear that Jacqueline could see the fine covering of hair over the woman's cheeks. There was a very large mole on the side of her chin that looked like a tiny, bun-less hamburger.

"Who are you?" Jacqueline asked.

"Nema," replied the woman. Her voice was clear and strong, as if she were standing right next to them.

Somehow, Jacqueline had expected the woman's response to be "Cuddy Stone," so she was thrown for a loop. "Are you... What are you doing here? In there?"

Nema smiled, and Jacqueline fancied she shrugged, but her shoulders weren't visible. "Whatever I need to do," she replied.

"Oh great, just what we need," said Suzette into Jacqueline's ear, "a bunch of non-answers from a ghost in a mirror."

"Are you a ghost?" Jacqueline asked, hoping Nema hadn't heard her friend's comment.

"I'm whatever I need to be," replied the old woman, prompting a stifled sigh from Suzette.

"Do you know what happened to Andromeda?" Jacqueline asked. "Can you see into the room? Did you see what happened to her?"

Now the old woman smiled and gave an abbreviated nod, then her expression turned sober. "I can see, when I choose to and when I'm allowed to do so. Andromeda will die—"

"*No!*" all three of them cried.

"No, no," Jacqueline said, stepping closer to the mirror. "There has to be a way to save her... isn't there? Please tell me there is..."

"I was about to say *unless*," replied Nema in a crisp tone. Her wrinkled lips pursed with irritation, and

Jacqueline could see the hairs bristling from around her mouth like a Venus flytrap.

"Unless what?" Nadine demanded. She was still squeezing Jacqueline's hand.

"Unless you rid yourself of Egala Stone. Permanently."

"Um..." Jacqueline said. Shock and horror flitted through her. What the hell did that mean? Permanently, like... death? She shivered and, for the first time, felt very uneasy about the woman in the mirror.

"What happened to Henberg or Henwig or whatever his name is?" said Nadine. "Did you see that too?"

Nema gave Nadine a look that clearly asked why she was even speaking. Instead of responding to Nadine's question, she said, "You haven't much time. Andromeda's life is flitting away as we speak. And she'll take her friends' lives with her."

"*What?*" Jacqueline cried. Somewhere in the back of her mind, she realized how crazy it was that she was having a conversation with a woman in a mirror, à la Snow White, but for the moment it didn't matter. "You're saying all three of the—the crones are going to die?"

"You catch on fast," replied Nema, rolling her eyes. "I can see why Cuddy left the place to you." Even more sarcasm.

"What happened to Henmeg?" asked Nadine. "There's a whole police investigation, and Jacqueline's in the hot seat over it, and—"

"Who is that person speaking?" Nema said, looking around Nadine as if talking into the ether. "Why does she keep interrupting?"

"*I* would like to know what happened to Henbert Stone," said Jacqueline.

The old woman heaved a sigh. "All right, if you must know, I cursed him."

"You did *what*?" Jacqueline said as her two friends took very large steps away from her, as if to remove themselves from the scope of the mirror's reflection. Nadine dropped her grip on Jacqueline's wrist and scooted even further away.

"I was protecting the house for you," Nema replied.

"Oh...kay," Jacqueline said, giving her head a little shake. "Why?"

"Because Egala and Henbert wanted the place, of course. Haven't you been paying attention to anything they've been telling you?"

"Yes," Jacqueline responded. Always the teacher's pet and rule follower, she was unable to ignore a direct question. "Who do you mean by they?" she added.

Nema gave a gusty sigh, and Jacqueline swore she felt the air move. *That* was creepy. "Everyone—Zwyla, Andromeda, Pietra, Egala—all of them. Haven't all of them told you about the family feud, and that Egala and Henbert—by the way, it's Hen*bert*, all right?" Clearly, that was directed at Nadine, who'd edged even further away from the reflection of the mirror. "That they wanted the property?"

"Right, right," Jacqueline said. "It's kind of a lot to take in, you know. And I don't even know how I'm related to the Stones."

The old woman's brows rose into inverted vees. "Like I said, I can definitely see why Cuddy left her the place," she said, again speaking as if into the ether.

"So let me get this straight," said Suzette, bravely stepping back into the circle of the reflection. "Jacqueline has to permanently get rid of Egala Stone in order to save Andromeda—and Zwyla and Petey? What exactly does that mean—permanently get rid of?"

"Broken, moldering, *witching* bones, who *are* these people?" Nema muttered. Then she fixed her eyes steadily on Jacqueline, capturing her with a cold blue gaze. "If you want to save your friend and keep the house, you have to destroy Egala. That's it."

"But I can't just—" Jacqueline sputtered.

"Destroy her. To use your favorite word: *literally.* Do it or not, that's your problem. Not mine."

And then, all at once, the face was gone.

16

Needless to say, Jacqueline did not sleep well that night. She couldn't blame it on too much bourbon or brownies—or even night sweats. No, she couldn't sleep because apparently she was required to rid herself of someone in order to keep a house she'd legally inherited—as well as save the lives of three old women.

It not only didn't make sense, it was simply an impossible prospect. As if meek and mild librarian Jacqueline Finch had the faintest idea how to destroy someone—even if she had the intention of doing so. Which, of course, she did not.

But... what about Andromeda?

She closed her eyes tightly. Something had to be done to save Andromeda, but by her? If so, how? *Why?*

The whole situation was impossible—not to mention ridiculous.

There had to be another way.

There *had* to be another way.

There must be. And she was going to figure it out. She might not be Lara Croft or Ellen Ripley, but she was a freaking librarian. She knew about a *lot* of things—some more relevant than others—and what she didn't know, she knew how to find.

So when she finally dragged herself out of bed in her cozy room at the bed-and-breakfast, Jacqueline gave herself a good talking-to in the mirror between brushing her teeth, doing her stretches, and getting into the shower.

First, she was going to go back to the apartment and look around in the daylight. Alone. She felt as if she was missing something.

Then she was going to march herself straight over to Camellia House and talk to Zwyla and Pietra and, hopefully, get some good news about Andromeda. At the very least, she was going to insist they tell her who this Nema person was and why she was in the mirror. Jacqueline was certain Zwyla and Pietra would know.

Maybe, Jacqueline told herself as she stepped out of the shower and wrapped her hair in a towel, Andromeda would be awake and chipper and cheerful—and maybe even with a different color to the tips of her hair. Maybe everything that went on last night had just been... well, some sort of weird event that had resolved itself overnight. Maybe Zwyla and Petey would laugh at Nema's dire prediction and tell Jacqueline it was as absurd as it sounded.

And it wasn't as if Jacqueline had any idea where or how to find Egala Stone, even if she *wanted* to try to remove her permanently.

Not to mention, she had a freaking bookstore to run.

But when she took off the towel she'd wrapped around her shampooed hair and saw that her Annie curls had not, in fact, washed out, Jacqueline's heart sank. Not only that, but the little six-freckle cluster was still visible on her left cheekbone, darker than even when she was eight. Under other circumstances, she might actually find it intriguing or attractive, but not now. Not in this situation.

She sighed.

I should never have left Chicago. I could have found another job and another house and other people to hang with.

It would have been a lot easier than coming to Button Cove.

STRANGELY ENOUGH, being in the apartment above the bookstore after last night didn't bother Jacqueline at all.

She didn't feel creeped out about the space. In fact, shockingly, she felt more possessive of the high-ceilinged living room and the neat, compact kitchen than she had previously. She even poked into the larger of the two bedrooms and had the vision of a comfy queen-sized bed tucked on the inside wall, across from a pair of tall windows that let the sun shine in. With a bright blue and yellow quilt and a pile of throw pillows—

She stopped herself mid-thought.

Am I really thinking about living here?

Maybe.

Even with weird entities living in a mirror?

Maybe... not.

It would *be very convenient...*

Jacqueline shook off the thought for now. She would have to find somewhere to live very soon, for she couldn't keep paying to stay at the inn even though they'd given her a reasonable weekly rate because it wasn't tourist season—but right now she had other things on her mind.

Like whether the mirror over the fireplace would look any different to her in the starkness of daylight.

The living room was also bright and sunny today; if Jacqueline didn't know any better, she might think the apartment was showing off its best, coziest, most attractive and inviting self in order to entice her to move in here. The sofas would have to be replaced—they were a little ragged, and paisley was not her style —but the long wooden table in front of the fireplace could stay.

And the mirror.

She looked up and found herself reflected back: unfamiliar curls of auburn, slight frown lines between her brows (she automatically smoothed them out), and the large hazel eyes she'd always thought of as her best feature. Not bad for forty-eight, she thought, even as she acknowledged the sagging at her jowls and the beginnings of horizontal wrinkles across her throat. Though where the hell were her eyebrows disappearing to?

She could stand to lose ten, maybe fifteen pounds —who couldn't?—but all in all, she decided forty-eight didn't look that terribly scary. Even the new look of her hair didn't bother her, though normally, tousled curls made her think *messy*.

Turning away from the mirror, Jacqueline decided it was time to give the living room a close examination. This was where both Andromeda and Henbert Stone had been found, so whatever happened must have happened here, right in this room.

She knelt on the floor and looked up and around from that vantage point, searching for she had no idea what, but Suzette's words stuck in her mind. Some sort of trigger or booby trap that caused a curse... What on earth would that look like, anyway?

It occurred to her after several minutes of crawling around on the rug, pushing on the bricks of the fireplace and the tiles of its hearth, examining the mantel and the bookshelves, and looking behind the pictures on the wall that maybe she shouldn't be doing this alone. After all, if a curse or something was triggered and she got caught in its crossfire, she was cooked.

But she didn't feel anything strange or malevolent or *off*, or threatened in any way. The place felt like *hers*.

She belonged here. Somehow, she knew whatever had hurt Andromeda and Henbert wasn't a danger to her.

"Nema," she called, standing in front of the mirror. "Are you there?"

Nothing happened. Jacqueline waited, then called again. "Nema! Are you in there? Helloooo!" She rapped on the mirror with her knuckles.

She waited again and was just about to give up when something flickered in the reflection. "Nema?"

"What?" The old woman looked as annoyed as she sounded. Her straggling gray hair looked like a wild spiderweb around her head. The unfortunate hamburger mole on her chin seemed even more prominent in the daylight.

"Did I wake you up?" Jacqueline asked, surprised and confused. Who'd have thought a mirror entity had to sleep?

"Oh, it's you." Nema blinked groggily, and then her eyes brightened. "Did you do it?"

"Do what?" Jacqueline replied, even though she knew what the woman was talking about.

"*Egala Stone*," Nema replied in a decidedly grouchy voice. "Did you get rid of her? Destroy her?"

"No, I did not," Jacqueline replied in her firmest librarian voice. "And I have no intention of 'getting rid' of anyone—literally, anyway. I have no problem telling her to leave my house, but I'm not going to, well, hurt her or anything."

Nema's eyes sparked—literally—and Jacqueline stepped a little to the side. She didn't know whether lightning bolts or flames could come through the mirror, but she wasn't going to chance it. When she smelled a faint sizzle, she knew she'd made the right decision.

"What do you mean you have no intention of getting rid of her? Do you understand what that means?" The old woman's gaze was furious, and her eyes blazed. Apparently, she was wide awake now.

"Well, you told m—"

"If you don't do as I say, you're going to have a lot more problems than a sick witch," Nema went on. "And her friends, Zwyla and Petey! Don't forget her friends! Do you understand?"

"But I—"

"I told you what you have to do! Now do it... or you'll be very sorry." And with those irritable words, she faded away.

Well, that was rude. And unsettling. Hadn't Nema said "do it or not, it's your problem, not mine" last night? And now she was upset that Jacqueline hadn't done anything about Egala.

Jacqueline stared at the mirror for a few minutes, then when she noticed her reflection and the frown lines between her brows and around her mouth, she forced herself to relax.

If Nema was so determined that Jacqueline should destroy Egala—not that she was going to—you'd think she'd stick around and give her more details.

Sighing, Jacqueline passed a hand over her face. When she looked up, her attention fell on the happy-looking Victorian house at the end of Camellia Court.

Time to visit the witchy trio.

She sure hoped they'd have answers.

THEY MIGHT HAVE ANSWERS, Jacqueline thought when Pietra opened the door to her knock, but they didn't have good news.

The expression on Pietra's face told Jacqueline everything she needed to know. "Come in," Pietra said in a far more subdued tone than Jacqueline had ever heard her use.

Jacqueline didn't ask the obvious. She merely followed the older woman into the house and through the door hidden behind the tapestry.

The herbary smelled of many things, most of which Jacqueline couldn't identify. Definitely lavender and maybe some rose, but whatever else the crones were using for Andromeda was unrecognizable to Jacqueline.

Zwyla turned from where she was grinding something in a mortar and pestle, and Jacqueline nearly gasped. The regal woman's face appeared exhausted. It was damp with perspiration and had an unhealthy cast to it, and her eyes were puffy. Her lips were pale and looked dry, and the whites of her eyes were cloudy. She wasn't wearing a head wrap today, and her smooth head showed a hint of fuzz in the back, as if she hadn't taken the time (or the energy) to shave it.

"It's nice of you to come," Zwyla said, and Jacqueline realized she was sitting instead of standing.

"Let me do that, Z," said Pietra, pushing over to Zwyla at the counter. "You need to lie down."

"I can't," replied Zwyla. "We have to try this..." But her voice trailed off and Jacqueline could see the way her hand trembled.

"We were in a rush and used the coffee grinder first," Pietra explained, glancing at Jacqueline, "but Z thinks we should have ground this butcher's-broom by hand because it's so important to the recipe, and because of the intentions that we can instill in it as we do the motions."

"That's right. Putting an electronic or piece of machinery between the hands doing the work just adds another layer of separation," said Zwyla. She sounded as if it was great effort to push out the words. "Andi wouldn't have made such a stupid mistake. Do you have the valerian?"

"Go lie down," Pietra said, her voice tight and high. "I won't be able to pick you up if you collapse here, and you know it."

"Can I help?" Jacqueline asked, stunned and suddenly terrified. Without being told, she knew that whatever was taking the life from Andromeda had also moved on to Zwyla—just as Nema had warned. "I want to help."

"Make her lie down," Pietra said grimly as she ground fragrant spices and herbs and who knew what else in the large stone mortar. Jacqueline definitely smelled black pepper.

"I'll check on Andi," Zwyla said, her voice gritty but stubborn.

"Go with her and make sure she lies down too," Pietra said, focused on measuring out something purple and crumbly from a small jar. "I don't need to be distracted from this."

"Don't forget the valerian—seventeen snips with intention," Zwyla said as Jacqueline followed her from the room. Behind them, she heard Pietra murmuring something that sounded like an incantation.

For some reason, it no longer felt weird to her.

Andromeda looked even worse than she had last night, but Jacqueline was relieved to see her chest rise and fall with even breathing. That was something, at least.

The patient was lying on a narrow bed in a welcoming, sunshine-lit room that looked more like an infirmary than a bedroom. Pretty yellow curtains fluttered at the windows, which were open to allow in the fresh spring air. There was a second small bed and a trunk that Jacqueline guessed held clean linens, along with a small prep table. Many candles of different sizes and shapes were stationed about, and there was an agate bowl holding a variety of healing crystals. What appeared to be an eagle feather sat in a vase next to the bed, and Jacqueline wondered if it had come from the bald eagle that she'd seen perched on the top of Camellia House.

A large sage bundle wrapped with string—a smudge, Jacqueline knew it was called—rested on a small clay tray in the corner, its pungent smoke wafting gently over the room. It smelled like marijuana.

"I've brought you more poultices," Zwyla said to Andromeda, and as Jacqueline watched, she began to lay pieces of warm, damp cloth over the patient's forehead, chest, and belly. She wrapped strips of the fragrant cloth around the patient's wrists, ankles, and feet, all the while murmuring softly. This new floral scent filled the room, and again, Jacqueline couldn't identify it. She would ask later; now didn't seem to be the right time. Whatever it was, it felt powerful.

"Honeysuckle and the spadices from peace lily, along with a juice made from Venus flytrap. They're helping to hold the curse at bay," Zwyla told Jacqueline when she was finished, saving her from asking. "They're keeping it from completely taking over her energy, helping her to fight it off. That's all we can do until we find a fix. We've been trying every banishing and protection spell we can think of." Zwyla drew the back of her hand across her face and sighed. "Thank the stars you found her last night. This morning would have been too late."

"Maybe you should have some of those poultices too," Jacqueline said. "It's happening to you, too, isn't it? Whatever has Andromeda."

Zwyla nodded reluctantly. "I don't know how—it must be a very powerful curse in order to jump from her to me."

"It'll go to Pietra next," Jacqueline told her. "Nema told me."

"Nema?" Zwyla collapsed into a chair as if she could no longer fight to stay upright.

"The woman in the mirror," Jacqueline said.

Zwyla shook her head wearily. Her eyes looked even glassier than before, and a trickle of perspiration ran over her elegant cheekbone. "I don't know who that is."

Jacqueline felt a stab of uncertainty. She'd been sure the three women would know about Nema, and would be able to advise her on how to proceed. "She seems to inhabit the mirror above the fireplace in Cuddy's apartment," she explained. "She appeared to me and Nadine and Suzette last night and told me... she told me that Andromeda wasn't going to make it—

and neither would you and Pietra—if I didn't get rid of Egala Stone. Destroy her."

Zwyla blinked, and Jacqueline could see her processing—or trying to—what she'd just said.

"In Cuddy's mirror," Zwyla repeated. "The big silver one over the fireplace." Then she muttered the very versatile, old-fashioned, earthy English word whose use is bleeped out from film and television. When she looked up at Jacqueline, her eyes blazed with comprehension from an otherwise drawn expression. "Petey. Get Pietra."

Jacqueline hastened to comply. Although Pietra didn't want to be taken from her work, she followed Jacqueline back to the infirmary, carrying the shallow elliptical wooden bowl that held whatever concoction she was making. She held sharp little copper scissors and was cutting up tiny white blossoms that looked like lilacs, but didn't smell like them.

"I have to keep count," she said, then continued to snip at what Jacqueline concluded was probably valerian. She knew that the herb was good for sleeping, but apparently it had other uses as well, because she didn't think Andromeda needed to sleep any more deeply.

"Tell her," Zwyla said when Jacqueline and Pietra returned to the bedroom.

"Shh, let me finish this," Pietra said. She stood there, snip-snip-snipping at the tiny, fragrant blossoms. Jacqueline heard her counting and muttering, and a murmur from Zwyla as if she too was joining her intention or strength to the incantation.

"*Seventeen*." Pietra closed her eyes for moment, her lips moving silently as she pressed her hands into the bowl, gently sifting through its contents. Then she opened her eyes. "All right. What is it?"

"Tell her what you told me, and everything—exactly everything—that Nema said to you. Andi, are you listening?" Zwyla reached over to place her hand on Andromeda's bare arm. She waited, then nodded. "Good. All right, go ahead."

Jacqueline told them everything that had happened, interrupted only by Pietra saying, "I thought your hair looked different!" When she finished telling them about the conversation with Nema both last night and this morning, the two crones exchanged looks, and then Zwyla glanced at Andromeda. She closed her eyes as if listening, all the while keeping a hand gently on her friend's arm. She nodded and listened more and then opened her eyes.

"We're right, aren't we?" Pietra said. Zwyla nodded, and her friend snapped, "All right, then, that's enough of that. Lie down *now*. I can finish this." She pointed to the other infirmary bed, and to Jacqueline's surprise, Zwyla pulled heavily to her feet and made her way slowly to the bed.

Her difficult movements belied the spark of comprehension in her eyes, but Jacqueline was horrified at how quickly Zwyla had deteriorated in only a few minutes. Her own hands were clammy and her insides churned.

I've got to help them. I've got to do something.

"Thank you for telling us all of this," Pietra said, and with a flicker of terror, Jacqueline noticed the dampness beginning to collect on the third crone's forehead. "The woman in the mirror is really Crusilla Stone, not their ancestor Nema," she said. "Z, you stay here. I'll be back with some of the poultices for you. *Don't you dare get up.*"

Pietra hurried back to the kitchen with a grace and

speed that left Jacqueline behind in the confusing warren of hallways in the house.

Crusilla? Wasn't that Egala and Henbert Stone's relative—from the anti-Cuddy wing of the family?

By the time Jacqueline found her way back to the kitchen (like her own building, the house seemed far bigger on the inside than it did from the outside, and definitely more confusing), Pietra was already busy using tongs to soak strips of cloth in whatever was simmering in the cauldron over a low flame. The scent of honeysuckle was strong, and Jacqueline saw the pile of elegant white spathes of peace lilies, each denuded of its spiky yellow spadix. Pietra murmured to herself, and Jacqueline waited patiently, looking around the herbary.

She was surprised to see coffee beans—both green and brown—in open jars on one of the counters. And a bowl of black peppercorns, as well as several bowls of salt in colors ranging from white to gray to pink... and even a greenish blue! The largest Venus flytrap plant she'd ever seen sat in a pot, reminding her of *Little Shop of Horrors*, and she could see where the little, trap-like flowers had been cut off. Next to the plant was a small bowl where the pods had been muddled into the juice used in the tea for the poultices.

When Pietra finished at the cauldron, she began to add the dripping strips of cloth to a small bowl. "I need to put these on Z now. Let's talk while I do that—soon I won't be able to." Her words were so matter-of-fact that Jacqueline felt terrified.

Her heart in her throat, she once more made her way to the infirmary, this time in Pietra's wake. The sweet, calming scent of honeysuckle accompanied them.

"All right, so the woman in the mirror calling herself Nema is really Crusilla Stone... how do you know that?" Jacqueline asked, pulling her thoughts together. Apparently, it *was* going to be up to her to help the three older women. "Why would she be telling me to destroy Egala if they're on the same side of the family feud? And most importantly, *how did she get in my mirror?*"

"Zwyla suspected it, just based on what she said to you—Nema was the name of one of the Stone family members from centuries ago. I agreed, and Andi confirmed it," Pietra told her. "Andi saw her in the mirror before. Besides, that mole is unmistakable."

Jacqueline glanced at the still, reposed Andromeda and decided not to ask how on earth that information had been communicated. "But why would she want me to get rid of Egala if they're on the same side of the family feud?"

"Maybe they aren't," murmured Zwyla weakly.

"So something changed among the family alliances, and now Crusilla wants the house?" Jacqueline said. "So she wants me to get rid of her competition for her?"

"Makes sense to me," said Pietra, placing the last of the fragrant cloth strips on Zwyla's forehead. "She's allying with you now, since you inherited the place?"

"If that's the case, then maybe that's what happened to Henbert. She—Crusilla—cursed him. And then she cursed Andromeda," Jacqueline said slowly. "But why Andromeda?"

"Because Andi recognized her, probably, and because Crusilla knows we can help you. Which is why she's trying to get rid of us," Pietra said. "Did she tell you how she wanted you to get rid of Egala?"

"No." Frustrated, Jacqueline scrubbed her face with her hands. "And there's no way I'm going to, you know, kill someone or destroy them or whatever. What I really want to know is how I can get that nasty witch out of my mirror and out of my apartment. As far as I'm concerned, those two crazy women can battle out their own family issues without me. I'm representing the *sane* branch of the family."

Zwyla's lips moved in what Jacqueline interpreted as an effort to smile, and Pietra nodded eagerly. "That's the spirit—no pun intended." But her smile faded.

"And what's so damned special about the house?" Jacqueline asked. "I mean, it's wonderful and everything, and the store is just perfect, but it seems like there's a *lot* of activity around it, and, well, it just doesn't seem so valuable that the entire Stone family is in on a big fight for it. What am I missing?"

Pietra tsked, shaking her head. "Apparently, a lot."

"Well, then *maybe* you ought to fill me in like I asked you all to do yesterday," Jacqueline said from between gritted teeth. "Honestly, I feel like Harry Potter talking to Dumbledore! Everyone knew everything about what was going on around him—especially in the fifth book—and no one felt the need to tell him, even though he was in the thick of it and he was the one who had to save everyone's bloody lives. It happens in books all the time, and sometimes I have the patience for it and *sometimes I don't*. This is one of the times I don't have the patience for it." She felt the blaze of fury coming from her eyes and the surge of determination rush through her.

"Right," Pietra said, looking at her with wide, admiring eyes. Then she glanced at Zwyla. "I *told* you she had it in her, Z. I *knew* it. Look at her face!"

Jacqueline merely glared at her silently, and Pietra got the message. "Right," she said again. "Well, first of all, *obviously* the house is special—you had to have figured that out at least, with Mrs. Danvers and Mrs. Hudson—"

"And now Miss Gulch," Jacqueline added gloomily.

"Oh, dear... really? From the movie or the book?" Pietra asked.

"She wasn't in the book," Jacqueline replied tightly, deeply regretting her interruption. If there was one thing she'd learned about Pietra, it was that she loved tangents. "Go on about the house being special."

"Well, as I said, you already know that it's different and has unique properties—and the reason is that it sits in a high-energy location on the earth. Like a focal point, where several ley lines come together. The Native Americans who lived here—specifically Mystera's mother's Anishinaabek tribe—recognized the power and energy of this location, and so they've been honoring and protecting it for centuries.

"Incidentally, our house is also in part of that same energy system," Pietra went on. "In fact, Camellia Court itself is filled with great and divine female energy and broad potential. That's why it's named *Camellia* Court, you know."

Jacqueline nodded as something stirred in the back of her librarian's mind. "Right... there's a lot of mysticism surrounding flowers, isn't there? And camellias are believed to represent and enhance prosperity and confidence, if I remember correctly."

"Oh yes, but more importantly for our purposes, camellias help one align with the divine feminine. They also help open oneself to the receptivity of everything the Earth and the Universe have to offer. Including and especially," Pietra added with a wistful smile, looking at the two other women in their sickbeds, "friendship."

"It's too bad camellias don't grow here in Michigan," Jacqueline said.

Pietra gave her an indulgent smile. "They do in our yard."

"Of course they do," Jacqueline replied, smiling back.

But their respective grins faded. There was little to feel optimistic about right now, for Pietra's face was turning wanner and wearier by the moment.

"Suffice to say," Pietra said, sinking into the chair Zwyla had previously sat in, "the property at Three Camellia Court is worth a lot to those who understand its power. And the Stone family—the rest of them, anyway—know that."

"So why did Cuddy Stone leave it to *me*?" Jacqueline asked. "I called my parents to ask how I'm related to her, and neither of them really know. Something about a great-great-great—I have no idea how many greats—grandparent being the illegitimate daughter of a Stone, and she was raised by my mother's side of the family." She shook her head. Knowing all of this other information—information she'd sensed, she supposed, at an intuitive level—just made her more desperate to understand: *Why me?*

"You'd have to ask her," Pietra replied.

Jacqueline opened her mouth to respond, then decided against it. Instead, she said, "All right, but what can I do to help you three? I want to, but I can't—I can't *kill* or get rid of someone else, even for you three."

Pietra nodded. "That's how we knew—or suspected—that Nema was Crusilla. Ones like us—witches, crones, wise women—whatever you want to call us, but I prefer the last, obviously—don't cause harm to others and don't try to control the actions of others. And anyone who wishes you well isn't going to insist or even ask you to do something to harm another."

"What if..." An idea was blossoming in Jacqueline's mind. It was a crazy idea, but then, she was living in craziness right now. "What if I told Egala that Crusilla asked me to get rid of her? That might make her mad enough to leave me alone, and those two can fight with each other."

"You could try it. I don't really know," Pietra said, and Jacqueline heard the increasing strain in her voice.

Her chest tightened. "Is there anything I can do for you? I don't want to leave you here..."

"The only thing you can do is to break the curse," Zwyla said, and it sounded more like a breath than actual words. But Jacqueline discerned them, and the starkness of the situation settled over her like a heavy black cloud.

She wanted nothing more than to break the curse... but she had no idea how.

17

Jacqueline reluctantly left the three older women. The only thing that made her feel slightly relieved was that Zwyla and Pietra were still awake and conscious, and the strips of poultice seemed to be keeping the curse at bay. The two women were weak but able to get up and carefully make their way to the herbary, where, Zwyla assured her, they would continue to try new remedies—the first of which would be the tea with valerian, butcher's-broom, and coffee beans, which was nearly ready.

As Jacqueline left, she heard Zwyla send Pietra out into the backyard to gather some rue for yet a different infusion.

Heart in her throat, worry coursing through her, Jacqueline walked quickly toward Three Tomes. The temperature had dropped a little, and she shivered. A glance to the west showed rain clouds gathering, and she felt the wind picking up a little.

A shadow flitted across the street in front of her, and she looked up. The eagle was back, and for a moment, Jacqueline stood there, feeling the wind toss her curls and the cool breeze lift small prickles over her skin. She couldn't seem to look away and watched the aviator's majesty as he circled, dipped, swooped up, and then flew off toward the puffy gray clouds.

When he was nothing more than a small, dark speck against the threatening storm clouds, she finished the few more steps to Three Tomes.

The store was closed on Mondays, fortunately, so she would have the place to herself... for when Jacqueline needed an answer, she always knew where to turn: books. She could look up anything to help anyone, and now she'd be doing it for the three wise women.

It stood to reason that if the bookshop had been owned by Cuddy Stone, who seemed to have her own metaphysical abilities that included protecting books from spills and crumbs—and presumably, bringing book characters to life—that there would be resources within that might help Jacqueline find the answer.

As she approached the front door of Three Tomes, she heard her name and turned. Suzette had come out of the bakery and was hurrying across the street.

"How are you?" Suzette said, then glanced down the street at the blue Victorian with its colorful, tangled garden. "How's Andromeda? You just came from there, right?"

Jacqueline shook her head, shocked when her voice failed and the back of her throat burned. She'd only known the three old ladies for a few days, and already she'd become far too attached to them.

"Oh no," Suzette said, squeezing Jacqueline's arm. "Is she...?"

"She's fighting it," Jacqueline managed to say. "But now the other two are starting to—to get sick. I've got to find a way to break this curse," she said, uncaring that Suzette might not know, understand, or believe what was going on.

"I'll help you," said Suzette immediately. "And I know Nadine will too. We have to figure it out. We'll do it together."

Jacqueline's eyes stung. She nodded and was mortified when a tear popped from her eye and plopped onto her cheek. Damned hormones. "Thank you."

"I'll text Nadine," Suzette said, pulling a shiny new smartphone out of her pocket. "I went to the store and got a new phone first thing this morning. Cost me way too much, but I needed an upgrade anyway, so here I am. Thanks to that Nema bitch. *Not.*"

Jacqueline unlocked the door of the bookstore and let them both in. The place was quiet and empty, and she was grateful for that. She needed a tissue and a good, strong cup of coffee—no tea—this morning.

"I just love the smell of books," Suzette said, inhaling audibly. "Especially old ones."

"So do I," Jacqueline replied, and made a beeline for the cabinet holding some of the oldest of the vintage books. Maybe there was something in there to help her with breaking the curse.

First editions of *The Mysterious Affair at Styles,* Phyllis A. Whitney's *Step to the Music,* and *The Bungalow Mystery* distracted her, however. Jacqueline was compelled to pause for a moment, sighing over them and stroking their spines.

The Nancy Drew was one of the actual first printings of the first edition, with blank endpapers and orange printing on the front and spine of a smooth cobalt-blue hardcover. Later printings of the first edition had orange silhouettes printed on the endpapers and spines, so they weren't as rare or valuable. *Bungalow*'s dust jacket wasn't in perfect shape by any stretch, for it had some spotting and the edges were ragged in areas, but it was the original—which was nearly impossible to come by for a book that was nearly a century old. In an effort to make the books look more authentic, some sellers and collectors of first printings of first editions had facsimile dust jackets made—obviously disclosing that they weren't the originals.

Jacqueline saw Suzette looking at her with an amused expression. "Sorry," Jacqueline said with an embarrassed smile as she clutched the Nancy to her chest. "This is a very rare book, and I just had to pet it for a minute."

"No judgment here," said Suzette. "That's how I feel when I walk by a confectioner's shop and see the flowers made from fondant or royal icing. I just don't have the patience for that sort of work, but boy do I admire those who do."

"I just thought I'd look through the cabinet here to see if there was anything—Oh!" Jacqueline stifled a gasp when she saw the shadow move from out of the corner of her eye. "Oh, hello, Miss Gulch," she said, trying not to sound as unenthusiastic as she felt. *Great.*

When she saw the skinny woman dressed in a buttoned-up Victorian-style dress and black hat, Suzette made a quiet noise of her own that Jacqueline interpreted as one of startled recognition. Jacqueline suspected it was the Miss Gulch's blade-like nose and pointed chin that really gave the clue. Not to mention the glower she wore.

"Good morning," said the spinsterish woman in a crabby voice. "Where have *you* been? Sun's been up for hours now—what you can see of it, anyway—and the day's half gone!"

Since it wasn't even ten o'clock, Jacqueline rolled her eyes. Then she drew in a deep breath. "What can I do for you, Miss Gulch?" she said in a calm voice she hardly recognized as her own, considering the state she was in.

"Well, you ought to be taking better care of things here," said Miss Gulch. Her lips were pinched into a tight circle and her chin jutted out. "Floor needs to be swept, shelves need to be dusted—"

"Thank you very much," Jacqueline said. "I'll pass on your suggestions to Mrs. Danvers, as she's the housekeeper. But now, I'm busy with another problem, and since the store isn't open today, I don't think—"

"And that's another concern," Miss Gulch went on, lifting her large, beaky nose as if she smelled something rank. "Having the store open on the Sabbath, but not on a Monday? What on earth are you thinking? The Sabbath is the Lord's day of rest, and therefore we should rest too. It's not a day to be making money. It's a day of quiet reflection."

"Tell that to the churches who send around their offering baskets every Sunday," muttered Suzette, causing Jacqueline to choke back a giggle. They exchanged looks, and she saw the unholy (ha!) humor in her friend's eyes.

"Oh, is that Sebastian?" Jacqueline made a show of looking behind Miss Gulch.

Her diversionary tactic worked, and the spindly spinster whirled around with a low cry. "Now, where did that sweet little devil get off to?" she said in the sugary voice she reserved for the cat. "Come here, kitty!" She went into the mystery room, still crooning hopefully—and still seeming to favor her left leg. Had she been injured?

Nonetheless, Jacqueline wasn't willing to spend time on the Miss Gulch problem at the moment, so she jerked her head toward the stairs to the café.

Suzette got her message to follow her up. Once at the top of the stairs, they hurried to the back of the tea room and sat on a large sofa.

"I don't think this was here yesterday," Jacqueline said as she sank onto the green tweed furnishing. She couldn't imagine finding a green tweed sofa to be attractive in any other environment, but for some reason, it worked here at Three Tomes. It was a bright spring-green color threaded with light blue and yellow. There were comfortable pillows of those same colors arranged on the cushions, and a long, low black table in front of it. Maybe Mrs. Danvers had dragged it out from somewhere, or maybe Jacqueline had just been too distracted to notice it.

The tea room wasn't as sunny and inviting today due to the clouds quickly gathering outside and the cooling temperature. A fire in the fireplace on the near wall would be just perfect, but Jacqueline didn't have the energy to figure out how to make one. She didn't even know if the fireplace was usable. If it wasn't, she'd fix that as soon as possible. There was nothing better than curling up with a good book near a crackling fire. On a day like today, when the store was open, she'd have fires going in all five of the fireplaces and people could drink tea and eat cupcakes with abandon!

"So when did *she* show up?" asked Suzette, gesturing downstairs with a horrified look.

Jacqueline grimaced. "Yesterday. I have no idea what she's doing here." She wondered whether Suzette thought, as the obviously customers did, that the literary characters were simply employees playing a role. Based on Suzette's question, Jacqueline suspected that wasn't the case. But before she could broach the subject, they heard a knock on the front door of the shop.

"It's Nadine. I'll let her in." Suzette popped up and loped off and down the stairs. Moments later, she and the yoga instructor appeared, the latter carrying a closed umbrella.

"I thought you weren't open on Mondays," Nadine said as she dragged a chair over to the couch. "That customer down there looking for Sebastian—she really reminds me of the mean bicycle lady in *The Wizard of Oz*. The one who tried to steal Toto."

"That would be Miss Gulch," said Jacqueline. "And that's exactly who it is. She's not a customer, because you're right—I'm not open on Mondays. But I *am* open on Sundays, and Miss Gulch doesn't think that's appropriate." She looked at her friends as Suzette plopped down on the couch next to her. "I know you hardly know me, and you probably think I'm stark raving mad, but I swear that until I arrived here in Button Cove, I never had anything like this kind of stuff happen." She closed her eyes tightly for a moment, then opened them again.

"It's all right, Jacqueline. The first time I met Mrs. Hudson and got into a conversation with her, I realized things were a little different in this place," Nadine said. She reached over and squeezed Jacqueline's hand. "At first I thought she was just playing a role, you know? But then it became obvious she wasn't." Nadine shrugged. "I gave up trying to explain it and just went along with it. But, not gonna lie, I've been wondering why someone hasn't figured out how to send that Mrs. Danvers person back to wherever she came from."

"She's a real piece of work," Jacqueline agreed on a gust of laughter. "The thing is, it seems that Danvers and Hudson are regular fixtures around here, and have been for a long time—and, crazy as it might sound, I've already gotten used to having them around doing all the work I can't get to. They know more about running this shop than I do.

"But with Miss Gulch arriving on the scene, I get the impression it's not the same thing. She told me yesterday she didn't know what she was doing here or why—that she was looking for Toto and suddenly showed up here. It's obvious Hudson and Danvers know why they're here, and even *choose* to be here. So what's different about Miss Gulch?"

"I don't know," Nadine started, but Jacqueline couldn't seem to stop talking.

"Are there going to be others? I don't think I could *handle* it if there were others." Jacqueline buried her hands in her hair and was mildly surprised to find it curly and not sleekly pulled back. "And how many more are there going to be?"

"If it's any consolation," Suzette said, "one, I don't think you're crazy—in fact, I think you're holding your own pretty damned well considering what's been going on—and two, I've never noticed any other... well... *unusual* people here other than Danvers and Hudson before."

"So you're saying it's *me*?" Jacqueline said with a pained laugh. "Oh my God, I *knew* it! I had this thought the other day after Egala Stone showed up here and accused me of killing her brother and of stealing something from her—the store—and immediately I thought of *The Wizard of Oz* and the Wicked Witch of the West accusing Dorothy of killing her sister and stealing her ruby slippers. But then I consoled myself by remembering that never happened in the book, so even if book characters actually manifested themselves here in the shop—I cannot believe I just said that out loud!—even if characters came to life from books, that wasn't going to happen because it didn't occur in the original book. And yet here I am."

"Here *we* are," said Nadine. "We're in this with you, Jacqueline—we've seen almost everything you've seen and experienced, so it's not just you."

"That reminds me," Jacqueline said. "I went upstairs again this morning, and I called Nema back into the mirror to talk to her." She went on to explain what happened in the flat, and then what was happening with the three crones.

By the time she was finished, both of her new friends' expressions were grave.

"How much time do you think we have?" asked Suzette.

Jacqueline's eyes misted again at her use of "we," and she shrugged. "I don't know. They're trying to stave off the curse, but both Zwyla and Pietra are getting weak. I came over here because I thought maybe there's some sort of resource I could use to help." She stopped short of saying "spell book," even though she was certain Nadine and Suzette knew what she meant.

"That's a good idea," said Nadine. "We can help you look. Some sort of spell book or something?"

"Thank you," Jacqueline said, suddenly overwhelmed by emotion. Her eyes burned, her nose was beginning to drip, and the back of her throat was scratchy.

She'd never made friends easily. Stacey had been her closest, her soul-mate girlfriend for decades, and no one had ever taken her place—or could. Between the loss of Stacey and Josh's cheating, Jacqueline had learned it wasn't safe to open herself up to other people.

But now, she felt as if she not only didn't have the

choice but to accept the friendship from Nadine and Suzette... but also that she *wanted* to do so.

And that was just as strange and scary as the thought that she might have to save the lives of three wise women, by using, well... actual metaphysical skills and supernatural information and herbal remedies instead of just looking things up.

Jacqueline simply wasn't ready to use the word *magic* to describe what she was expected to do.

18

Jacqueline left Nadine and Suzette to rifle through the books in the store while she went up to Cuddy's apartment in case there was something there on one of the bookshelves.

And besides... she had a few things to say to Nema, a.k.a. Crusilla.

A little shocked by her emboldened self—maybe her new curly hair and star-shaped beauty-mark were indications that she had changed and decided to take charge of things instead of just looking stuff up—Jacqueline marched upstairs from the tea room's stairway.

"Nema!" she called as soon as she came into the living room. She rapped on the mirror impatiently. "Nema! I need to talk to you."

This time when she appeared, the old woman didn't look as groggy—but she was still disgruntled. "Well, did you do it?" The hamburger mole jumped impatiently on her chin as she spoke.

"No, I didn't." Jacqueline stood with her hands on her hips, positioned slightly to the side in case of stray lightning bolts. "*Crusilla.*"

The old woman's expression changed to one of surprise, then, to Jacqueline's astonishment, her actual *face* changed into something completely different. After the metamorphosis, a pale-skinned woman of indeterminate age with yellow-blond hair and dark eyes stared back at her. She had a sharp widow's peak that accentuated winged brown eyebrows and a narrow chin. Everything about her had changed except for the mole on the corner of her triangular chin.

Yikes. Forget the blond hair and widow's peak; if she were in charge, Jacqueline would've put all her metamorphosing efforts into getting rid of that mole.

"So you've talked to them, have you?" Crusilla said, pursing her lips. "Those batty old hags."

Jacqueline had no patience for beating around the bush. Not when three wise women were growing weaker every moment. "If you want my help, I need answers. What is it you want me to do to Egala—specifically? How can I get rid of her? How can I find her? I don't even know where she is. *And* if you wanted her gone so badly, why didn't *you* do something about her last night when she was here?"

Crusilla's eyes widened at this verbal attack, and Jacqueline automatically braced herself for zipping sparks and flying hexes. But nothing shot through the mirror. Instead, Crusilla looked thoughtful. "You ask excellent questions."

"I'm a librarian," Jacqueline said coolly. "I'm used to finding answers for people, but one has to have the questions first. And those are mine."

"Very well. To answer one of your questions—I didn't want Egala to know I was here. She would have recognized me right away."

"Yes, I can see that," Jacqueline said, resisting the

urge to touch her own chin in the place Crusilla's mole was. She realized with a start that the star-shaped beauty mark Egala had left on her could just as easily be a hamburger mole, and she shuddered. "But why," said Jacqueline, "do you want to get rid of her anyway? Aren't you on the same side of the Stone family feud?"

"There's only one side of the family feud," Crusilla replied, "and it's *my* side. Only one person understands the power of this place, and that's *me*."

Jacqueline's eyes narrowed. "So that's it. If I do whatever it is you want me to do to get rid of Egala, somehow the place will come to you instead of remaining mine? So why would I do that?"

Crusilla seemed to realize her mistake, for she backtracked quickly. "Not at all; it'll still belong to you, since Cuddy willed it to you and you *are* blood-related, but I'll be here too—you and I, members of the Stone family, will continue our legacy. I'll be here too, to help you. Right here." Even though Jacqueline couldn't see her hands, she could tell by her shoulder movements that the old woman was indicating her presence in the mirror. "I guide you and teach you," she went on, smiling beneficently. "You have no idea what abilities and powers I can give you."

"I see." Jacqueline pretended to consider the situation, although inside she was shouting: *Oh hell no!* "That sounds very intriguing. The only problem is, I really can't have the deaths of Andromeda and her friends on my conscience. Isn't there a way we could work together on getting rid of Egala but saving them?"

Crusilla pursed her lips again, revealing that not all of the spiky hairs that grew there had disappeared during her metamorphosis. "Perhaps... but why should I trust you? I could help you save the others, and then you might decide not to banish Egala."

"You think I want *her* hanging around here?" Jacqueline asked. "If you could have seen what she did to the books downstairs—and look at *this*." She flicked a hand against her wild curls. "I look like Little Orphan Annie... do you even know who that is?"

She paused to give that some thought. Who *was* Crusilla, anyway? Was she some sort of spirit or phantom, or was she a real person who'd inserted herself into the mirror? Even if Jacqueline didn't want her around, she wondered if the mirror was the only place Crusilla could live... like a djinni in a bottle?

Destroy the mirror, banish the woman...?

"Hmm." The woman in the mirror was considering.

But before she could say anything further, Jacqueline heard the sounds of footsteps coming from the back of the apartment. A deep voice called, "Ms. Finch?"

To her mortification, Jacqueline felt her stomach do a pleasant little flip when she recognized Detective Massermey's voice. And then she realized what was about to happen, so she turned and fairly bolted from the living room to meet—and forestall—him in the back hallway. The last thing she needed was for Crusilla to appear to Massermey.

"Good morning, Detective Massermey," she said, trying not to sound out of breath, as if she'd rushed to greet him. (Oh great—what if he thought she'd rushed to greet him?)

"Ms. Finch," he said, looking at her curiously.

Damn. He *did* think she'd rushed to see him!

"You did something different—to your hair, I mean," he said, and Jacqueline blushed and relaxed a little—that was why he was looking at her like that. His voice had gone a little deeper. Kind of sexy. "It looks nice."

"Thank you," she said, angling to keep him from looking past her toward the living room. She didn't know whether Crusilla would remain visible (and vocal) while he was there, but she didn't want to take the chance. No one had mentioned any sort of phantom disturbance or mirror-ish appearance when the crime scene people were there, but she didn't want to take any chances. "Um... I was just heading down to the tea room for a cup of coffee. Why don't you join me?"

"Sure," he said, standing aside so she could pass by him to the stairs. "I know you aren't open today, but Suzette was here and said I should come on up. I hope it's no trouble, but I could really go for a cup of coffee. Usually Mrs. Hudson insists that I have tea when I'm here," he added grimly. "I'm not really a tea sort of guy."

"Mrs. Hudson isn't here," Jacqueline told him as they started down the stairs. At least, she didn't think the Holmes landlady was there. She wondered if Massermey realized who Mrs. Hudson was. "So I think we can sneak a cup of coffee without her knowing."

Massermey rumbled a pleasant laugh. "That would be nice."

Jacqueline was surprised to discover that neither Suzette nor Nadine was on the main floor of the shop, through which she had to pass to get to the front steps to the tea room. Nor, thankfully, was Miss Gulch anywhere to be found.

"All right, let me see about some coffee," Jacqueline said. She was feeling a little flustered for some reason, and when she got behind the counter to look around for coffee (surely there was some *somewhere*), she fumbled a cup, and it bounced, miraculously didn't break, then slid across the counter.

Massermey caught it just before it rolled onto the floor. He replaced it on the counter with a flourish.

Jacqueline, whose face was hot after the near disaster, busied herself looking for coffee and trying not to notice the detective's hands. They *were* big—and strong-looking, and freckled, and sprinkled with light blond hair.

"Ah! Found some," she said, extracting a box of instant coffee that had been shoved behind at least twenty boxes and canisters of tea.

"Thank God," he breathed, and gave her such a relieved smile that she couldn't help but laugh.

"I feel the same way," Jacqueline said. "It's instant, but beggars can't be choosers."

"It's got to be better than the sludge at the office—I know that's clichéd, but it's clichéd for a reason. Cop coffee is the worst because most of us disdain the Keurigs of the world. We want our fuel strong and bitter—just like we are." He gave a little chuckle. "Or at least, how we want perps to think we are."

"Right," she replied with a smile. "So... how was the pie? With your daughter?"

His grin was sudden and broad. "Great. I just love having her home. She's so busy that when we get the chance to spend time together, it's special. She's working at the zoo this summer, which is why she's here in town. She gets up really early to go help feed the animals and is usually gone by five thirty. Which is bonkers, considering that she used to sleep till noon every day when she was a teen. And obviously my hours are crazy, so we have a hard time crisscrossing."

Jacqueline smiled again. "I can imagine. So, uh, what can I do for you, Detective?"

She said—and meant—the words very innocently, but there was a flash of something in his eyes—heat? humor?—before he masked it as something more professional. "I wanted to give you an update on the post-mortem," he said. Now his expression was serious, even concerned.

Jacqueline frowned as she dumped packets of instant coffee into their respective cups. "Is that... normal? In a criminal investigation? I didn't even know Henbert Stone, so why would I need to know? I mean, that happens all the time in books—the non-detective character gets to find out confidential information he or she has no business knowing because that's how fiction works... but in real life it seems strange."

Then a thought struck her—a horrible thought that she mentally shoved away as hard as she could. But it sort of stuck there anyway, in the back of her mind. What if *she* was becoming a character in her own book?

No, no, no... that was silly. Just because fictional characters came to life and walked onto the scene at Three Tomes didn't mean *she*, a real person, was going to end up as a character herself. Absurd.

And if she did... who the hell was writing it?

No. She wasn't going to entertain that possibility for one instant.

"Right," Massermey replied. He looked a little surprised. "That's actually a pet peeve of mine when I read certain novels or watch TV." He grinned, and Jacqueline felt her whole body flush with heat. Damned hormones. "And normally, you're correct—there'd be no reason for me to tell you the details of the postmortem... but in this case, I feel like you should know. Since it happened in your house. And you are related to him—however distantly." He looked at her closely, and the little bit of heat she'd been feeling ebbed. "You didn't mention that the other day when I asked whether you knew him."

"Right," Jacqueline replied, her cheeks warming. "I honestly didn't think about it, Detective. We're so distantly related that even my mother doesn't really know how, and I had never even heard of him—or Cuddy Stone, for that matter—until I came here to Button Cove."

He nodded, his lips pursed a little, his eyes still fixed on her. "I see. I guess family trees can be pretty complicated, can't they?"

"Mine is clearly no exception," she replied, thinking of all the different factions of the Stone feud. She poured hot water, which was conveniently on demand here in the café, into the mugs. "How do you like it?" she asked, then felt the heat rush over her face. Enough with the double entendres! What was *wrong* with her?

To her relief, Massermey didn't seem to pick up on it (maybe she was being a little too sensitive), for he just shook his head. "Black is fine. I only allow myself one sweetened coffee a day, and that was first thing this morning." He sniffed the brew, sighed with pleasure, then sipped before speaking again. His expression was serious when he did. "Anyway, I wanted you to know because the results of the postmortem are... frankly... inexplicable."

Jacqueline's insides turned to ice despite the trickle of hormone-induced perspiration running down her spine. She supposed if a regular doctor did a postmortem on someone who'd been cursed dead, they wouldn't have an explanation either. "Go on."

She wrapped her hands around the mug as if to anchor herself for whatever he was about to say.

Massermey pursed his lips, causing his mustache and beard to bristle. "The pathologist says Henbert Stone died because his heart was frozen."

Jacqueline blinked. "You mean... like ice."

"Yep."

"And the rest of him... wasn't."

"Nope."

They looked at each other for a minute, then he shrugged, breaking what had been a comfortable connection of shared astonishment. "Like I said," Massermey continued, "inexplicable. The heart was still frozen two days later. It's only now beginning to... uh... defrost. Or so they tell me."

"Wow." Jacqueline didn't know what else to say, so she took a sip of coffee. That must have been one hell of a curse.

"They can find no cause for something like that," Massermey went on, his big, freckled, blond-haired hands gesturing over the counter.

"No marks on his body where he might have been injected with something that caused it?"

He shook his head. "No cause. His body was otherwise completely unmarked. I thought you should know in case... well, if it happened in your apartment, something had to cause it. And I would hope it doesn't happen again." He began to turn the mug in slow circles on the counter. "Are you going to be living up there?"

"I'm thinking about it," she replied. "I wasn't going to—I didn't want to live that close to the shop so I could have some work-life balance, and I wanted a small garden. I figured I could rent it out... but it's a really nice place."

"Except for the dead guy," Massermey said, his eyes crinkling slightly at the corners.

"Yeah," Jacqueline replied, smiling back.

He sobered. "The thing is... whatever caused that could still be in there. Although no one else seems to have succumbed to any sort of injury other than Henbert Stone—and there were a lot of people in and out of there over the last few days. Right? No one else has had any issues?"

The way his blue eyes connected with hers made Jacqueline feel like a butterfly pinned to its mounting block.

Could he know about Andromeda? Her mind raced through many different thoughts and scenarios as she tried to figure out what to say... because if Andromeda died, and the other old ladies did too, Massermey would surely hear about it. And he wouldn't necessarily connect their demises to the apartment, but he might. He knew they'd been up there.

And he seemed pretty sharp.

And gossip did tend to spread.

And if they died from the same thing as Henbert... it would be an obvious connection.

Besides, cursing someone to death *had* to be a crime. It was murder. Egala or Crusilla Stone were still subject to the legal system... weren't they?

This was all so confusing and strange, and suddenly, Jacqueline really just wanted to go back to Chicago. *Really* wanted to throw up her hands and just go back to the city and figure out a new life there.

"Ms. Finch?"

"Andromeda isn't feeling well. She was up there last night," she said in a rush. "We found her lying on the floor."

Massermey's eyes widened a little, then his mouth tightened grimly. "Is she in the hospital?"

"N...no," Jacqueline replied, feeling like she was beginning to sink into quicksand. How was she going to explain *that*? She should have just kept her mouth shut!

Massermey started to speak, then he snapped his mouth closed and shook his head. He muttered something that sounded like *crazy* and could have been *witches*, but surely she hadn't heard him correctly.

His questions and her answers had brought back to mind how urgent it was for Jacqueline to figure out a way to help the three crones, and so she gave the detective a professional smile and said, "I appreciate you giving me this information, Detective. Thank you for stopping by, but I should let you get back to work."

He gave her a look, then slid off the stool he'd been using. "I thought you should know. And thank you for the coffee. It really hit the spot."

"Just don't tell Mrs. Hudson," Jacqueline said with a smile.

He smiled back. "It'll be our secret. Make sure you hide the rest of that instant coffee somewhere so we have it for next time." He winked, then sobered. "I guess I'd better stop by Camellia House," he said. "See how Andromeda is doing."

"Oh, I'm sure that's not necessary," Jacqueline replied, imagining his reaction when he found all three of the women in dire straits—or in their herbary in mid-concoction.

"Oh, it is," he replied. His eyes were all cop. "It is. Have a good rest of your day, Ms. Finch."

And before she could say anything else, he gave her a brief wave and hurried down the stairs. Moments later, she saw him striding along the street to the crones' house.

Damn.

Jacqueline dithered. Should she follow him? Try to run interference?

Before she could make a decision, she heard footsteps bounding up the stairs.

"Well? What did he want?" Suzette asked. Nadine was right behind her, and they were both looking at Jacqueline with gleeful expressions. "We made ourselves scarce, for obvious reasons."

"What obvious reasons?" Jacqueline retorted, but she couldn't hold back a grin. Then it faded. "He's going over to Camellia House right now. I'm trying to decide if I should go there too and do—I don't know what. Something."

"I'm pretty sure those three women are more than capable of handling him," Nadine said. As if in agreement, low, long thunder rumbled in the distance.

Jacqueline grinned, then her smile faded. "Under normal circumstances, I'd agree—but they're not at their best right now." All three of them heaved worried sighs. Then she shook her head. "He's already there; there's nothing any of us can do about it—unless a dead body were to show up somewhere and distract him." She gave a weak laugh.

"Don't say that!" hissed Nadine, looking around worriedly. "That's all we need."

"Unless it's Egala," muttered Suzette, then immediately clapped a hand over her mouth. "Sorry. I didn't mean that," she said, her dark eyes wide over her hand. "I really didn't." She looked sincerely pained, and her eyes even glistened with tears. "I don't know what's wrong with me."

"I know," said Jacqueline—and to her surprise, she

meant it. She did know, instinctively and deeply, that neither Nadine nor Suzette were the kind of people who would wish ill on anyone... even if it meant helping or saving someone they cared about.

The question was... was she?

Crusilla Stone obviously thought so.

19

By midafternoon Monday, when the storm clouds were gathering both literally and figuratively, Jacqueline decided it was time to take even more decisive action. Time was running short, and the three old ladies could only stave off the curse for so long. Besides, tomorrow the bookshop was open again, and there would be customers coming in and out, and presumably, Mrs. Danvers and Mrs. Hudson would return from wherever they went when they weren't in the store.

Nothing obvious as far as spell books had leaped out at Jacqueline or her friends when they looked through the vintage tomes in the bookshop. Jacqueline had given the many shelves of titles in the upstairs flat a cursory glance, but again, nothing seemed to grab her attention. She paused for a long time, thumbing through an old children's book she remembered devouring on a borrow from the library when she was nine or ten—*What the Witch Left* by Ruth Chew—before she replaced it on the shelf next to *The Phantom Tollbooth* and other vintage editions of books from her youth.

She glared at the rows and rows of silent and still books, then sighed.

Why couldn't a book randomly fall off the shelf in a *helpful* manner for once?

Determined to take specific action, Jacqueline locked up the bookshop and started her walk back to Chance's Inn. She glanced over at Camellia House as she did so, but it looked quiet and subdued. The eagle was not in sight, but that was no surprise, as the clouds were dark and ominous.

Her chest tightened and she almost made a detour to check on the old ladies, but decided to continue with her plan to talk to the innkeeper at her bed-and-breakfast. If Egala Stone had stayed there, maybe Laura still had contact information for her so Jacqueline could track her down. If she could talk to Egala and tell her about Crusilla, maybe she could get some straight answers from the woman.

Jacqueline knew it was a long shot that Laura would give her Egala's contact information if she still had it, but it was worth a try.

The bed-and-breakfast was quiet. Jacqueline found Laura in the parlor where the bar was set up, washing glasses and refilling decanters.

Jacqueline didn't waste any time beating around the bush. "I need to contact Egala Stone," she said as she slid onto the stool in front of the bar. "Do you have any way to get in touch with her, since she was a guest here?"

Laura, who wore her raven-black hair in a long, straight ponytail today, gave her a wary look. "I can't really give out that information," she replied.

"I figured you couldn't—at least under normal circumstances. But it's really urgent that I get in touch with her," Jacqueline said. "It's a matter of life and death—literally. And I don't use that word lightly."

Laura hesitated, then shook her head. "I'm sorry— I could get into a lot of trouble giving out people's personal information. I'd like to help you—I can see that you're upset about something—but I just can't."

Jacqueline sighed. Real life just wasn't like books, was it? "Well... how about this: I think she's still in town here. Or at least, she was last night. Obviously she's not staying here. Is there any way you can talk to some of your colleagues and see if you can find out where she's been staying?"

Laura pressed her lips together and shrugged. "I don't know about that... I could try. It's all about the privacy thing, though. Look, Miss Finch, I'd really like to help you..."

"Well, couldn't you just, I don't know, be chatty with them and mention what a terrible guest you had once and describe what happened and see what they say? Or find some other way to bring up the topic? Please?" Jacqueline said. "It has to do with the safety of three old ladies who live over on Camellia by the bookshop—"

"You mean the ZAP Ladies?" Now Jacqueline had Laura's attention. She set down the funnel she'd been using to pour Makers Mark into a decanter.

"The ZAP Ladies?" Jacqueline said, but she already understood.

"That's what we call them around here—Z-A-P, for Zwyla, Andromeda, and Pietra. That's who you mean, right?"

Jacqueline nodded. She had to admit that "zap" was a pretty accurate way to describe the three crones and their effect on people. "Yes. And right now, the ZAP Ladies are... Well, let me put it this way: if you

experienced any of Egala's strange and powerful...
shall we call them *reactions*... to things when she was
staying here, then you understand that she's not exactly an average Jane. The ZAP Ladies have been the
recipient of one of Egala's most severe *reactions*, and if
something isn't done, they might not make it." She
looked pointedly at Laura, hoping the young woman
would get the message.

The innkeeper's dark eyes widened. "I see." She bit
her lip. "I get the impression this isn't hyperbole."

"No."

Laura nodded. "All right. Let me see what I can
find out from some of my fellow innkeepers. There are
only a few taking guests during the week right now
because it's too early for tourists."

"I appreciate it."

While Laura used her mobile phone to call her
friends, Jacqueline decided to turn to a librarian's least
favorite choice for research: Google and—ugh
—Wikipedia.

She settled in a comfy armchair in the parlor and
used her phone to search for "frozen heart curse." She
got a lot of results related to Disney's *Frozen*, which
weren't at all helpful. Then she reworded the search to
"curse where heart gets frozen" and was rewarded with
pages of results related to the *Once Upon a Time* television show.

This was exactly why she always started with
books and the Dewey system for research instead of
the Internet. Maybe she should go to the library here
in Button Cove and see what she could find. If not
there, then maybe a trip to a nearby university city—
East Lansing, Grand Rapids, or Chicago—to delve
through their electronic card catalogs. That could be
done online, but since she was no longer a CPL em-

ployee, she didn't have access to the system any
longer.

But she was running out of time. Those libraries
were hours away!

"I found her," Laura said, disconnecting a call as
she walked over to where Jacqueline was sitting. "I
didn't even have to beat around the bush and ask—my
friend Bernie started ranting about her. He's the pro-
prietor of Regal House, just over on Magnolia Street."

"Thank you so much. Do you know if she's there
right now?" Jacqueline replied.

"Oh, yes. Hence the ranting. Apparently, the afternoon tea Bernie put out wasn't to her satisfaction."
Laura bared her teeth in a grim smile.

"Great. Thank you. I'm heading over there now."
Jacqueline got specific directions from Laura, then
started off.

It wasn't until she turned onto Magnolia Street
and saw the sign for Regal House that her firm, no-
nonsense steps faltered.

What on earth was she thinking, confronting Egala
Stone? The woman was a literal *witch*. And she'd already demonstrated her power and ability several times
—which was far more than anything Jacqueline had.

What exactly did she think she was going to do?
Storm into the inn, find Egala, and... do what?

Her heart was pounding from both the fast pace
she'd taken and nerves. Maybe this wasn't such a good
idea.

By now, Regal House was right in front of her. She
stopped by its gate, eyeing the cube-like brick man-
sion that had probably been built in the 1930s. A huge
oak shaded the front yard, giving the stately inn a
shadowy vibe—which didn't help Jacqueline's nerves.

You have to do something.

Yes. She had to do something. But her insides were filled with butterflies, and her palms were seriously sweaty.

She gritted her teeth and walked through the gate, up the straight sidewalk to the covered porch. To the right was a small parking lot and area for guests to unload their luggage. A ramp, flanked by boxwoods on the building side and a small strip of garden on the lawn side, would make it convenient to wheel up suitcases or wheelchairs. Daffodils, crocus, and hellebore bloomed in small clumps along the front walkway as well as the side ramp.

She took note of all of these details in order to *not* think about the fact that she was about to confront an angry witch.

The front door of the inn was unlocked, and Jacqueline pushed it open. A little bell tinkled above, announcing her presence, and a tall, slender man wearing a bow tie emerged from what she suspected was a parlor. Bernie, she assumed.

"Are you Miss Finch?" he said in a low voice, then glanced worriedly over his shoulder. "Laura told me you were coming."

"Yes. Is—"

"She's in there," he said in a rush, pointing to the room from which he'd just emerged. "Feel free to enjoy our highly rated afternoon tea if you like. The clotted cream is from a dairy farm over in Antrim County, and the cherry tea blend is from Orbra's down in Wicks Hollow."

Jacqueline got the distinct impression that this generous offer was nothing more than a bribe for her to attend to Egala Stone and her nastiness.

Great. Now even the innkeepers had expectations of her.

Jacqueline didn't *like* it when people had expectations of her. That just made life complicated and filled with drama—because if you didn't meet people's expectations, they got annoyed with you. Expectations at her job were different, of course, for Jacqueline had been stellar in her position. Not to mention the fact that she totally and completely understood her role, and didn't have to fumble around trying to decide what needed to be done.

It still burned her butt that they'd fired *her* after twenty-five years of high performance and excellent reviews, and not someone else lower on the totem pole.

"Thank you," she replied, briefly wondering if there was coffee along with the tea. Not that she expected she was going to sit and have a friendly little chat with Egala Stone and be able to partake of it.

Bernie gave her a nervous smile, then opened the lace-curtained French doors into the parlor. "A friend of yours, Ms. Stone," he said. "I've told her she's welcome to join you for tea—and of course it's on the house for both of you."

When Jacqueline walked in, Egala's expression turned so shocked it was comical. "What are you doing here?" She half rose from her seat on a low Depression-era sofa upholstered in gold brocade. Today, her eyebrows had been drawn on in pencil-thin arcs reminiscent of silent screen actress Clara Bow.

Jacqueline felt the rush of air as Bernie swept the French doors closed behind her. Clearly he was hoping to contain the two of them.

"I thought it was time we had a chat," Jacqueline

said. Her voice was firm and steady, though her knees were shaking.

"Hmm," Egala replied, sinking back into her seat. Her burnt-orange lipstick was gone except for around the edges. "I'm not interested in chatting with you unless you're here to give me my house."

She was holding a small china teacup that was filled with either coffee or tea that had been liberally mixed with milk. In front of her on a long, glass-topped table was a gorgeous spread for afternoon tea —the English meal, not necessarily the beverage. But Jacqueline's discerning nose had identified the scent of coffee, and she gave a silent "hooray!" inside.

She took a seat on a side chair across the table from Egala. "I'm not here to give you *my* house," Jacqueline said. "But I have information you probably would like to know. Where's the coffee?"

"Here," said Egala, pointing to a tall, smooth teapot made from stoneware. It was the only thing that looked out of place on a table otherwise filled with delicate painted china cups, pots, and plates. A three-tier rack held an assortment of finger sandwiches, and a smaller rack offered mini scones, tiny tarts, and cookies.

"Thank you," Jacqueline said with a gusty sigh, and proceeded to pour herself a cup. Her hand was surprisingly steady as she did so, adding one sugar cube then stirring.

When she looked up, she noticed that Egala was eyeing her closely with narrowed eyes. She leaned rudely over the table as if to get a better look, then, giving a small gasp, heaved back into her seat. Her eyes were wide and she appeared almost afraid. "When did that happen?" she demanded.

"What are you talking about?" Jacqueline asked,

then took a bracing sip of coffee. Ahh. Then she realized. "Oh, my hair?" She touched the curls, still mildly shocked to find them instead of sleek, contained tresses. "That was from you."

"Not that," replied Egala, still eyeing her with what could only be described as wariness. "The mark. You've got the Stone mark now."

Jacqueline reached up and touched her cheek where the six tiny beauty marks had appeared. She was a little surprised to feel their subtle bumps—originally they'd been more like freckles staining the skin, rather than little moles. But now they were tactile. Good grief, she hoped they weren't going to keep *growing*. "This? Well, I've always had the freckles, but *you* made them worse last night when you zinged lightning at me!"

Egala was shaking her head. "No, I didn't do that. The lightning, yes, of course—and the curly hair—but not that. Not that mark." She seemed far more subdued than Jacqueline had ever seen her.

"What is it?" she asked, still gently fingering the little marks.

"You don't know?" Egala replied with a little bit of a whine. "How can this be? Cuddy leaves the damned shop to you, Henbert dies, and you don't even know about the Stone family mark?"

"No." Jacqueline decided not to ask any further questions about the six beauty marks. Not right now.

Besides, the way Egala was acting, she got the impression any questions would just elicit a lot more demurring: "What? You don't know? How can you not know?" and so on.

"Look, I don't really care about this mark on my face," Jacqueline said, for the first time feeling like she actually had the upper hand. (But at the same time, she kept her eyes on *Egala's* hands in case the witch tried something. Said hands were currently gripping a teacup as their owner continued to watch Jacqueline from across the coffee table.) "What I need to know is what happened to Andromeda last night—and how to save her."

"Why should I tell you—" Egala seemed to think better of her strident retort when she glanced at Jacqueline's face again. "What will you do in return if I tell you?"

"I'll tell you about Crusilla," Jacqueline replied. And, no longer able to resist—for she hadn't eaten lunch—she snagged one of the tiny, crustless sandwiches. Cucumber and cream cheese—oh, and chives too, she discovered when she took a bite. Yum.

Egala stared at her. "Crusilla? You've been talking to Crusilla? She's here?" She winced, then looked around as if afraid Crusilla had appeared.

Jacqueline nodded as she swiped another finger sandwich—this time egg salad on wheat, with paper-thin slices of radish. "Yes," she said, wiping her fingers on a cloth napkin, "I've been talking to Crusilla. So, tell me about Andromeda."

Egala looked at her for a long moment, clearly weighing her options. But she was clearly worried. Her indecision gave Jacqueline the opportunity to try some clotted cream on a lemon scone and then a tiny pecan tart. Heaven.

"Are you aware that Henbert died from a frozen heart curse?" Jacqueline asked, choosing another of the cucumber sandwiches.

"I suspected," Egala responded. Her eyes flashed for a moment, and Jacqueline felt a shiver of nerves, but didn't duck. "How did you do it?"

"I didn't do it," Jacqueline replied. "I didn't do *anything*."

Egala snorted. "You expect me to believe that, especially now that you're wearing that mark on your face? I know you killed my brother in order to get the shop."

Again, shades of *The Wizard of Oz*. Far too close for comfort—and strange because Egala was clearly not playing the role of the Wicked Witch of the West, since Almira Gulch had shown up on the scene. Which made Jacqueline Dorothy, right?

So by the way, where was Glinda when Jacqueline needed her? Surely the Good Witch would be able to help her figure this out.

The Good Witch—no, the Good Witches*—are currently succumbing to a curse, Jacqueline. So buck up.*

"Believe what you want to believe," Jacqueline replied. "Do you want to know about Crusilla or not? Tell me how to save Andromeda, or I'm leaving."

Egala heaved a pained sigh. "It's not the frozen heart curse," she admitted. "Even though I told you it was the same thing that happened to Henbert. I was *angry*. And I figured sending you down the wrong path would just make things worse."

"Well whatever it is, it's leaking into the other ZAP Ladies. Affecting them," Jacqueline said. "And I want it stopped."

Egala's eyes widened a little. "That's not possible. Hexes don't do that—leak or spread."

"Stop lying and prevaricating and tell me how to save them. Or I won't tell you about Crusilla." Jacqueline automatically touched the star markings on her cheek and saw Egala flinch as she did so. Very interesting.

"All right. All *right*. I put a life-leeching hex on her —one of my specialties," Egala said.

"Your specialty is life-leeching?" Jacqueline replied. "You know you can go to jail for that. Or worse," she added, and, as an experiment, she turned her face so that her beauty-marked cheekbone was aimed at Egala, who flinched again.

"I hardly ever use it," the witch replied, the whine back in her voice. "It's really just for protectio—"

"I don't want to hear your excuses. I just want to know how to fix it."

"The cure has butcher's-broom, hellebore, and foxglove," said Egala. "But you have to gather it under the full moon—"

"Which is when?" Jacqueline demanded.

Egala frowned. "How can you not know the moon cycles? They're instrumenta—"

"*When is the full moon?*"

Egala jumped a little, leaving Jacqueline feeling kind of giddy. Obviously, something about that beauty mark had changed the balance of power between the two of them.

"It's not for another two weeks," Egala told her quickly.

"Not acceptable," Jacqueline said, her heart sinking. The little bit of headiness she'd been feeling evaporated. "That's *not* acceptable," she repeated in a tense voice. "So you'd better give me another cure—and one that can be done now."

Egala's mouth moved but no words came out, and for a moment, Jacqueline was afraid the witch was hexing her. But then Egala's voice became audible, and she eyed the star mark on Jacqueline's face as she spoke. "There is one other option, but it's highly dangerous."

Jacqueline rolled her eyes. "Of course it's danger-ous. This is a hero's journey story, right? If I'm going to be a hero, I've got to face danger and confront my own issues, and..."

Jacqueline stopped herself. Panic shot through her. *Was* she becoming a character in her own book?

If so, she wanted to talk to the author about all these crazy plot twists.

She shivered and shoved the thought away. No, she was not a character in a book.

Egala was looking at her warily. "I can tell you what the other cure is, but I promise you'd be better off waiting until the full moon."

"I can't wait until the full moon because the ZAP Ladies can't wait that long," Jacqueline replied in a voice that spiraled up a little. "So tell me what to do so I can fix them."

"And then you'll tell me what Crusilla said? You have to tell me before you try to make the antidote, because..."

"Because I might not live through whatever it is?" Jacqueline said bitterly. "Of course." She snatched up the last two cucumber sandwiches and an egg salad one. Might as well eat them—and as much clotted cream as she wanted on as many scones as she freaking wanted—if she might die in the next few hours.

Dammit. Now she *really* wanted to go back to Chicago.

20

"You have to do *what*?" Nadine said.

"That's insane," Suzette added needlessly.

Jacqueline already knew how crazy, insane, and dangerous the task she had to do was.

What was insane wasn't so much what she had to do, but that she was actually *planning* to do it.

Suzette looked up from the notes Jacqueline had made during her talk with Egala. "What in the heck is an athame, anyway?"

"A ceremonial dagger—lots of times it has a curved blade and handle," Jacqueline said. "I'll borrow one from the ZAP Ladies."

"Are you seriously, truly, honestly going to do this?" Nadine asked in a marginally calmer voice. "I mean..."

Jacqueline had asked herself the same question countless times in the last couple of hours since leaving Regal House. It was now nearly four o'clock Monday afternoon, and she and her friends were sitting on the green tweed sofa in the tea room once more. She made a visit to Camellia House before coming back here, and it had been terribly frightening. Zwyla had been unconscious like Andromeda, and Pietra could hardly stand on her own two feet. Jacqueline's insides were a writhing mess when she left the old ladies.

Time wasn't only running out, it was pretty much gone.

She had intended to show the ZAP Ladies the information Egala gave her, but she simply couldn't bring herself to add to Pietra's stress and anxiety. Instead, she merely told her that Egala had agreed to help.

"I have to at least try," she told Nadine and Suzette, who were still staring at her. "Otherwise the ZAP Ladies aren't going to be very zappy any longer."

Her attempt at a joke went over like the proverbial lead balloon. Nadine reached over and gently squeezed her wrist. "It's an awful position to be in, Jacqueline. I mean, you hardly even know them... and now you're going to do something very risky in order to only *maybe* save their lives. That's pretty amazing of you."

"I can't just stand by..." Jacqueline replied, even though her insides were in knots.

"Neither can I," Nadine said. "I'll do whatever you want to help you through this. I might look big, but I'm flexible... I can slip through lots of small places. And I'm pretty strong—I can hold Crow for five minutes."

"Count me in too," Suzette said. "None of this is your fault, so you're not doing any of it alone. We'll figure this out."

Jacqueline's throat dried up and she could only nod. Her eyes stung. Not from fear or worry, but from emotion. "Thank you," she managed to say in a low, rough voice. "You don't have to, but... thank you."

At that moment, her phone gave a quiet alert.

Grateful for the distraction from the anxious at-
mosphere, she looked at the screen and was surprised
to see a text message from Wendy, back in Chicago.

Can we talk? I was wrong. I'm so sorry.

Jacqueline stared at the words and another rush of
emotion flooded her: righteous anger at her so-called
friend, followed by relief that Wendy had reached out.
She considered responding right then, but decided to
wait. The last thing she needed was to be dragged into
a distraction.

Nonetheless, the thought settled in her mind:
maybe she still had a chance back in Chicago. She
could give the bookshop to Egala if the woman wanted
it so badly. At least it would stay in the family—and
for some reason, she'd rather life-leeching Egala have
it than the cranky, murderous Crusilla.

Hmmm. That realization made Jacqueline think.
Why was her instinct to side with Egala instead of
Crusilla?

"Did Egala say *you* had to do it?" asked Nadine.
"The antidote or spell or whatever it is? Maybe Pietra
could help."

"I have to do it," Jacqueline said.

Suzette frowned. "Are you sure you trust her?
What if this spell"—she winced as if even saying the
word bothered her—"really does something else, like
puts the curse on *you*? Or—or somehow gives the
bookshop to *her*? Maybe that's why *you* have to do it."

Jacqueline blinked. "I hadn't thought of that." Now,
along with the hard thudding of her heart, her insides
felt like a writhing mess of snakes. "I wanted to show
the information to Pietra, but I didn't because she was
just too... Well, you know. Not yet, but I will... after I
get all the things we need. She'll know if it isn't a
healing spell or a banishment of the curse—"

"Banishment? What if it *banishes* you from here?" Nadine asked. "I don't think you can trust Egala."

Jacqueline stilled. What was she going to do? What *could* she do? She had to take the risk to save the old crones—and so what if she lost the bookshop in the process? She could just go back to Chicago like none of this ever happened, and that would be the end of this little adventure.

Maybe this *was* her hero's journey, and all this was just supposed to jar her into a new kind of life—but back home in Chicago. Not here in this crazy town.

"Did you tell Egala about Nema-slash-Crusilla?" asked Suzette.

"Sort of. I told her that Crusilla wanted her out of the way so she could have the bookshop, but I didn't tell Egala that she's in the mirror and had watched her from it." Jacqueline's head was spinning. This was complicated, confusing, and more than a little scary. "I wanted to keep a little bit of information back in case I need another bargaining chip."

"All right. Good thinking. What happens if you make Egala be there when you're doing the spell? Or why can't *she* do it?" Nadine asked. "She's the one who set the curse anyway."

"That reminds me," Jacqueline said. "Egala was shocked when I told her that the curse was spreading to the other ZAP Ladies. She said that wasn't possible."

"Maybe Crusilla of the Mirror had something to do with that," said Nadine. "She was probably there, lurking about while all of this was going on. She probably put the curse on Henbert herself."

"I hadn't thought of that," Jacqueline replied, irritated with herself. Usually she was good at picking out plot twists. "Maybe Crusilla did *all* of it—both Henbert and Andromeda."

"But Egala seemed to take responsibility for cursing Andromeda," said Nadine.

"But she was shocked when I told her the curse was spreading to Pietra and Zwyla," replied Jacqueline.

"So maybe Crusilla extended the curse, making it worse or something."

Jacqueline shook her head. "I don't know what to think. I just know I have to do something, and I don't trust Crusilla."

"What happens if you remove the mirror?" asked Suzette. "Take it all the way out of the house."

"I don't know, but I should try it. Having Crusilla there breathing down my neck—figuratively—while I'm trying to create a—a whatever it is, an infusion, doesn't sound like a good idea," Jacqueline said. She sighed. There were so many things to think about, and this was a completely strange and unfamiliar world to her. "I mean, I could try breaking the mirror—"

"And have seven years of bad luck on top of everything else?" cried Nadine. "Why would you do that?"

"Good point."

Jacqueline heaved a sigh, then looked down at her notes, which included the list of ingredients for the curse-banishment spell as well as the steps involved in making the antidote. Most of the items she needed were simple to obtain, and she felt certain the crones would have them at Camellia House—wormwood shavings, elderberry tincture, butcher's-broom. She could get cedar from the tree in Three Tomes' courtyard. And then there was "sacred earth"... whatever that meant. Dirt from a churchyard?

But it was the last item on the list that was scary

and dangerous, and was probably going to kill her. Now she understood why Egala wanted her to wait for the full moon.

As if reading her mind, Nadine said, "When are you—we—going to try to get *that*?" She stabbed her finger at the last item on the list of ingredients. Jacqueline noticed that her friend's hand shook, and she realized her own insides were a squirrelly, writhing mess.

Yep. She was probably going to die today.

But she straightened her shoulders and said, "There's no time like the present."

Nadine sighed. "I was afraid you'd say that."

THE WIND WAS WHIPPING in from Lake Michigan, churning the water into dark, frothy waves. The puffy clouds were ominous in their different shades of gray, clearly carrying plenty of rain to be released at any moment.

Jacqueline saw a flash of lighting way out over the lake, and the resulting rumble of thunder was closer than the ones she'd been hearing.

Button Cove Zoo was located right on the bay, tucked between the scoop-shaped shoreline and the parallel highway that traced the shape of the grand arc on which the town had been built.

"Lions, and tigers, and bears, oh my!" murmured Nadine as they climbed out of Suzette's car. "Lions, and tigers, and bears—"

"Stop that!" Jacqueline said, barely suppressing a giggle. She was feeling more than a little nervous about what they were going to do, and that made her punchy. "We don't need any flying monkeys dive-bombing us."

All three of them looked up automatically, but the only creatures above were the ever-present screeching seagulls... and a bald eagle.

Jacqueline paused to watch him—surely it was the same one she'd seen by Camellia House—as it soared over the bay, then over them. It swooped and dove and seemed to be circling over them.

Only when the bird took off did Jacqueline return her attention to the task at hand. She adjusted the large tote bag slung over her shoulder and grimaced. "Do you smell meat?"

"Yes," said Nadine. "Nice and bloody and ever so raw. How many steaks do you have in there?"

"Three big rib-eyes."

"What a waste," said Suzette sadly.

"So, uh... since we're here... have you figured out how in the hell we're going to get the tooth of a crocodile?" Nadine's pixie cut was ruffled from her agitated hands, and little wings of hair curled all over, buffeted by the gusting wind. Her eyes bulged wide and her voice was high and squeaky. "Without dying?"

Jacqueline gave a weak laugh. "I don't know. But are two crocodiles currently in residence here at Button Cove Zoo." She shrugged, tamping down her nerves as she looked through the zoo's massive iron entrance gates, which were wide open. "The good news, I guess, is that crocodiles lose teeth all the time, and regrow them. A single croc can grow as many as eight thousand teeth in a lifetime, which means it's very common for them to shed their teeth."

"How do you know all that?" asked Suzette. She sounded only marginally less anxious than Nadine.

"I'm a librarian." Jacqueline shrugged jerkily because of nerves. "I know everything."

"I want her on my team when we do trivia night," Suzette said to Nadine. "We'll kick some serious butt."

"If we're still alive after this," Nadine replied. But she didn't look quite as worried as she had a moment ago. "So you're saying we're probably not going to have to play dentist with Mr. or Mrs. Croc, right? No teeth extraction?"

"I hope not. I hope we can just find a tooth on the ground in their pen," Jacqueline told her. "I'm going to toss these steaks in to distract them."

"Those suckers move *fast*," Suzette said.

"Great," said Nadine under her breath. "I can read the headlines now: The Chubby Yogi Attempts Crocodile Pose with Real Crocs and Dies During Shavasana."

"Stop that, Nadine! You're making me freak out. So are we going, or what?" said Suzette. "The zoo might close any minute now due to the weather, and then what will we do?"

Jacqueline turned her attention from the imposing zoo entrance and the angry dark clouds to her friends. And she made a snap decision.

"*I'm* going. Not we. You—"

"No, no, *no*," said Nadine, as Suzette chimed in, "We're all in this together!"

"No." Jacqueline settled her hands on her hips in order to keep her fingers from shaking. She started speaking quickly in an effort not to puke. "We are not in this together. *I'm* in this, *and* I need you to be here, and safe, in case..." She shook her head, then pushed out the words, hardly thinking about what she was saying. She somehow *knew* what she had to say, and to do. "In case something happens. Then you take the information to the ZAP Ladies—hopefully at least one of them will be awake and aware enough to help— and you get Egala to do the antidote. She can have the house. Tell her that."

"No, no, you *can't* go in there by yourself," said Nadine. "It's crazy, it's madness, it's—"

"I am going by myself. I have to. I think..." Jacqueline reached up automatically and touched the six tiny bumps on her cheek. "I think I have to do this. Alone. It's all about the intention, you know? So just... stay here."

"Let us at least come inside the zoo with you," said Nadine. "We can... um... distract the zookeepers."

Jacqueline hesitated, then nodded. "All right. But you stay *away* from the crocodile pen. Keep everyone away from there. I need to climb in and get out without anyone seeing me. Including the crocs." She gave a weak laugh.

Her hands slick with sweat, her insides churning so violently she had to swallow a gag, she turned and marched toward the gates, tote bag banging heavily against her side. Whether it was real or her imagination, she didn't know, but the smell of raw meat filled her nostrils.

She had no real idea what she was going to do— how she was going to get inside the crocodile pen and get close enough to find a tooth, if indeed there was a tooth available to find.

Good God, she was going to *climb inside a crocodile pen*.

With crocodiles *in it*.

What the hell was wrong with her?

"Sorry," called someone as the three of them approached the gates. A figure dressed in a Button Cove Zoo uniform was pushing one of the heavy doors closed. "We're closing early—a bad storm's coming, and we have to get the animals inside."

Jacqueline hesitated, but kept walking. "Oh, please —I just need to get inside for a second. I have to get over by the—uh—the crocodiles," she said, figuring the closer to the truth the better. "I think I dropped my phone over there, and I'm expecting a call from my parents—they live in Florida, and they're elderly, and my father just had his second hip replaced, and I *can't* miss a call in case the hospital tries to get ahold of me." She babbled partly from nerves and partly as a sort of verbal ambush to the zoo employee. Keep talking, keep walking, and don't give them too much time to think...

The female employee paused, but only momentarily and kept pushing one side of the heavy gate closed. "Oh, well, I don't know if I can—"

"Amanda Massermey, is that you? How are you doing?" cried Suzette, rushing forward. "Are you working here?"

The young woman looked up from under her cap and smiled. The gate stopped moving. "Yes, I'm here for the summer—"

"It's so great to see you here! When am I going to see you at class?" asked Nadine, joining Suzette as she approached the young woman who could only Detective Massermey's daughter. Amanda, who had a sturdy build, didn't have her father's strawberry-blond hair, but she definitely had his blue eyes and robustly freckled skin. "You're one of everyone's favorite substitute instructors! Do you have any evenings free to sub?"

"Well, I could probably do a Tuesday night," Amanda said, still holding on to the gate as Suzette and Nadine crowded around her in an obvious effort to distract. "Wednesday is my day off, and usually I have to be here by six a.m."

Jacqueline took the opportunity her friends had given her to dart through the gates with a quick "I'll only be a second."

She'd already looked at a map of the zoo, so she knew exactly where to go to find the crocodiles. Her palms were sweating and her heart was thudding as she rushed into the zoo, hoping that none of the other employees would stop her.

It was no surprise that the zoo was closing early—Jacqueline didn't see any other patrons as she hurried down a paved pathway that curved leisurely around different exhibits. As she passed the tiger's enclosure, she instinctively hugged the meat-filled tote closer to her body. The tiger was watching her with far too much interest for comfort. She threw up a prayer of thanks that the antidote hadn't required the tooth of a large feline. Jacqueline didn't think she'd have considered trying to get a tiger incisor, even for the ZAP Ladies.

Luck was on her side, for the only zoo employees she passed were busy ushering a peacock and two of his peahens to their homes. It appeared the birds had free rein to walk around the zoo's pathways, and that they had no concerns about what appeared to be a thunderstorm of monsoon-like proportions about to be unleashed.

She hurried on, everything she'd read about handling crocodiles running through her head.

If a croc comes at you, run. Don't zigzag. Run straight.
Yes, crocodiles can climb trees. And fences.
Don't splash water; it'll draw attention from a croc.
Move carefully and slowly.
A croc can jump as far as five feet toward its prey.

Grab a croc from behind the head so its jaws can't get you.

Use your second hand to support its torso.

Slip a band over its jaws from behind.

Jacqueline sincerely hoped she wasn't going to actually need any of that information.

She'd watched videos of experts feeding the crocodiles, noting that they threw the meat far away... and had gotten nauseated when she saw how fast those suckers arrived at the meat, and how they downed it so quickly.

Jacqueline was nearly hyperventilating when she arrived at the crocodile pen. An ugly rumble of thunder crashed in the distance as if to punctuate the ominousness of the moment. A glance told her no one was around, but she ducked next to a shade tree in order to keep herself from being noticed just in case an employee walked by.

Then she stared at the site of what would probably become known as Jacqueline Finch's Last Stand.

Barely the size of a baseball diamond, the crocodile's habitat—called a herpetarium—was enclosed by a stone wall that was just about waist-high on Jacqueline. On the other side of the wall was a shallow ditch that presumably kept the crocs from getting close enough to the wall to climb over, though from what she'd learned about crocs, she wasn't sure how that worked.

Behind that was a natural-looking pool large enough for each of the two beasts to sink all the way to the bottom. Reeds grew along the edge of the greenish water. A stony, sandy expanse of ground was the crocs' beachfront, and behind that, at the back of the enclosure, were some natural-looking caves, and several live trees and bushes.

Jacqueline didn't see any crocodiles. Maybe they'd gone into their dens.

Maybe they were sleeping.

Maybe they didn't like thunderstorms.

Shakily, she pulled the binoculars from her tote bag. Her first order of business was to locate a tooth—preferably as close to the stone wall as possible. She wasn't about to climb into that place unless she knew what she needed was there.

Chances were good that there would be a tooth just lying on the ground, considering how often crocs lost them. Jacqueline was basing the entire operation on this presumption.

She trained the binoculars on the ground inside the herpetarium, scanning the area along the edge of the water.

And then she *saw one.*

She actually saw a tooth. It was just lying there on the very edge of the water.

And, thank the Universe, it was on the near side of the pool, not the far sandy shore that backed up to the caves.

Okay. Step one: done.

But now she had to actually *climb over the stone wall.*

Jacqueline's heart was in her throat, choking her, and her knees were shaking. Her fingers were so tight around the tote bag that she wasn't certain she could unclasp them.

But there was still no sign of the crocs.

She trained her binocular-assisted vision on the water, surveying the pool for any sign of amphibian eyes or nostrils. When she saw nothing that broke the surface of the water, which rippled from the wind, she lifted her view to the rocky nooks behind.

Still nothing.

Distant thunder crashed, making her start, and she closed her eyes. *Now or never.*

She took off the binoculars, checked that the meat in her tote was ready to be chucked as needed, and then she placed her hands on the stone wall.

I cannot believe I'm going to do this.

She was nearly hyperventilating, and her knees were so shaky that she didn't think she'd be able to climb over... but the next thing she knew, she was on top of the stone wall.

Heart in her throat, mouth dry, she paused there on top of the wall and looked around again. Now she was slightly higher and had a different view...

No. Still no crocs.

And no one else around.

Okay, okay, she told herself. *Let's do this.*

With shaking knees, she slid over the other side of the wall and basically collapsed on the ground. Her palms were wet, and she wiped them on the front of her jeans.

No movement, no sounds (not that she could hear much over the rising wind and the thunder)... Hopefully the crocs were smart and had taken shelter.

She visually pinpointed where she'd seen the tooth, and then started toward the ditch. How the hell she was going to climb back up once she climbed down into the ditch was a good question.

She paused again, looking at the pool. Still no sign of crocs.

Suddenly she had a horrible thought: would the smell of raw meat draw them out from wherever they were hiding?

Still watching the water and the caves for any sign of movement, she made her way quickly toward the ditch. But her foot caught on something, and she tripped, nearly taking a header into the grass.

And then she realized she'd tripped on a piece of wood.

A plank that would fit across the ditch like a bridge.

She blinked, looking around, feeling like she needed to thank someone for helping her out. What were the chances?

Well, what were the chances a librarian would inherit a bookshop where literary characters came to life?

Jacqueline was past questioning crazy stuff like this. She had no choice but to accept it and move on—and in this case, to move the piece of wood into position over the ditch.

It was exactly the right size, and she wondered whether the zoo kept such an item here, safely between the ditch and the wall, just in case of emergency —for a quick crossing in case a crazy visitor somehow got themselves inside the herpetarium and needed to be rescued. That actually made some sense and was a reasonable explanation for this sort of *deus ex machina*.

She wanted to run across the plank, but she forced herself to go slowly and carefully. Making noise or movement could draw attention from the creatures.

It seemed to take forever to cross that six-foot expanse, and then another eon to make her way to the edge of the pool where the beasts could easily be lurking, waiting to lunge up to five feet at her.

Just as Jacqueline crouched to pick up the tooth, she heard something. And then she saw something move... in the water.

She froze when she saw a pair of eyes rise from the surface.

21

Of course it was going to happen.

There was no way she was going to get in and out of the herpetarium quickly and easily. No one in their right mind would have expected things to work out *that* smoothly.

These thoughts raced through Jacqueline's mind as she stared at the green-yellow cabochon-like eyes of the beast.

He was several feet away, fortunately, but still within that five-foot lunge distance. Some part of Jacqueline wondered whether that five-foot distance would be less if the beast was launching himself from in the water, while another part of her was screaming in terror inside her head.

Fortunately, a third part of her had been prepared for this possibility, and prompted her hand to reach carefully inside the tote bag for rib-eye number one.

As soon as she closed her fingers on the meat—which was wrapped in paper—and began to slowly draw it out, the croc seemed to come to attention... as if he knew what she had and what was about to happen.

That was good, she supposed, pulling it out a little

more quickly now. The sooner she threw it, the safer she'd be. The last thing she wanted was for an impatient croc to lunge for the meat while it was still in her hand.

To her relief, however, though the beast swam quickly to her side of the pool—making Jacqueline feel faint at his proximity—he didn't launch himself at her. Possibly because he was used to being fed by the zookeeper and knew the process?

Jacqueline didn't wait for the creature to get to the shore. She flung the meat as far away as she could (which wasn't nearly far enough for comfort).

The croc went after it so quickly that she gave a horrified gasp. He was in one place, just coming out of the water, and moments later, he was ten feet away. It was as if he'd flown.

Oh my God, I really am going to die, Jacqueline thought as she scrabbled for the stupid crocodile tooth on the ground.

She picked it up and tucked it deep inside her jeans pocket as she began to make her way to the bridge over the ditch, all the while keeping an eye on the croc as well as watching the water for his partner. Once she was assured the tooth was safely deep in her pocket, she dug out the second steak.

The croc wolfed down the first slab of meat, and he was already starting to trundle back in her direction by the time she reached the ditch bridge.

With shaking hands, she threw the second steak in the opposite direction, and again, her terror was renewed when she saw how fast he moved to the treat.

She was just about to step onto the plank bridge when a sleek form lunged from the pool of water. Jacqueline shrieked in surprise and stepped blindly, missing the plank.

Her foot went down onto *nothing*, and she barely stopped herself from tumbling into the ditch.

The second crocodile eyed Jacqueline as she fumbled in her tote bag for the last steak as she edged onto the plank. There was a voice in her head screaming: *Why didn't you get four steaks? Five steaks? Ten steaks?*

Her fingers closed around the crinkling meat paper, and for a moment she couldn't move. It was terrifying to see two crocs only feet away, watching her.

With a whimper, Jacqueline flung the last steak toward the pool. She whirled and darted onto the plank bridge, which bounced and bumped alarmingly beneath her feet as she hurried. As soon as she got to the other side, she yanked that wooden bitch out of position and whipped it to the side, where it tumbled onto the grass nearby.

She collapsed next to it and lay there for a moment trying not to puke. Her breath heaved, her entire body was shaking and cold and hot at the same time, but she was alive! And safe!

Suddenly, she heard a bellow.

"What the hell are you doing?"

She looked toward the stone wall. Four people were just running up to the enclosure, and she recognized all of them: Nadine, Suzette, Amanda Massermey, and—the one who'd shouted—Detective Massermey himself.

Jacqueline dragged herself to her feet on very shaky knees and tottered toward the stone enclosure as Massermey launched himself over the wall. He had her arm in his grip in an instant, and Jacqueline was towed back to the wall and manhandled over it, quickly and efficiently.

"What the hell were you thinking?" He wasn't

shouting at her; he was talking in a very quiet, very scary voice that sounded as if he could hardly believe he was speaking the words. "What... on... earth... possessed... you...?"

"I'm fine," Jacqueline said. "I'm fine. I—uh—I accidentally dropped something in there and had to get it out."

She knew as explanations went that was weaker than a cobweb, but what else was she going to say?

"You *had* to get it out? You *accidentally dropped something*...?" Massermey didn't seem to have any more words, for which Jacqueline was wildly grateful. By all rights, he could probably arrest her if he wanted to...

"Let's get you home," said Nadine, putting an arm around her in an effort to draw her away from Massermey. "That was a horribly traumatic experience, wasn't it, Jacqueline?"

"Ma'am, I'm just going to need to get some more information from you," said Amanda with touching earnestness. "We don't allow visitors to climb inside the animal enclosures, and there has to be an incident report."

Of course there had to be an incident report.

"I'm really sorry," said Jacqueline. It wasn't difficult to sound weak and abashed; her body was so relieved to be safe that she hardly had the strength to stand up, let alone form words. "I-I wasn't thinking."

"What was so bloody important that you had to climb in there?" demanded Massermey.

"M-my cell phone," she said, sticking with the same story she'd given Amanda. Fortunately, the cell phone was still tucked in her back pocket, so she could produce it at will. "I think I must have set it on the wall after taking a picture, and my bag must have knocked it off. I didn't realize until later, and then—"

"And you're waiting for a call from your parents," Suzette said quickly. "Of course you needed it—the hospital was going to call about the results of your father's hip replacement." She added to Massermey, "You know how it is with hospitals—if you don't answer, they won't leave any information. And her parents live in *Florida*, so..."

"You should have asked one of us to retrieve your phone for you," said Amanda.

"I know. I should have. I'm sorry." Jacqueline figured if she kept apologizing, she might not get arrested.

Though the expression on Massermey's face gave her the impression he couldn't wait to slap cuffs on her.

~

SOMEHOW, Jacqueline managed to avoid being arrested while also not being banned from Button Cove Zoo for life. She also got excused from completing an incident report, since she'd emerged from the event unscathed and uninjured (and no one realized how close she'd actually gotten to the beasts).

Part of the reason for all of this might have been that the storm was just about ready to unleash its fury. Even the zoo's street lights were flickering under the assault of the lakefront winds.

By the time Jacqueline and her friends piled into Suzette's small SUV, a beastly, whipping rain had started and they were soaked. The wind was wicked here by the bay, and thunder and lightning filled the air.

"*Did you get it?*" demanded Nadine the minute all the car doors were shut.

"Yes," Jacqueline replied, and was rewarded by loud, relieved exclamations from her companions.

"Sorry about the Massermey thing," said Suzette, navigating the car out of the zoo parking lot. "He stopped by to check on his daughter and the zoo with the impending storm, and she mentioned having to find a customer who came in late. When Massermey saw us, he realized—or suspected—the woman that sneaked past Amanda was you."

"Thank goodness he didn't see me on the far side of the ditch," Jacqueline said. "He would have arrested me for sure."

"Mmhmm. Did you see the way he vaulted over that wall to go in after her?" Nadine said to Suzette, obviously a little giddy now that the threat was behind them. "I bet he'd have loved to put cuffs on you, Jacqueline."

"Oh for pity's sake," Jacqueline replied, feeling her face heat while the rest of her was chilled from the soaking. "He would have done that for anyone."

"Maybe," said Suzette. "But probably not as quickly or smoothly. He did have good form going over the wall there."

"Whatever." Jacqueline shrugged as water dripped liberally onto her shoulders and the back of her shirt. She was cold, but unsure whether it was from the soaking or nerves. "All right, let's get back to the bookshop and see if we can get this antidote made. Thank you again so much for distracting Amanda for as long as you did. And for jumping in with my story. You two were perfect."

"Read the list of ingredients again while Suze drives," said Nadine. "We can split up and get the rest of the items—assuming there's no requirement to interact with deadly animals."

"No, nothing like that," Jacqueline said. It had been an unspoken decision to go for the crocodile tooth first, since if they didn't have that, they didn't need any of the other ingredients. "All right, so: a sprig of cedar branch, black cumin seeds, butcher's-broom, wormwood shavings, elderberry tincture—and sacred earth. Whatever that is. I should have asked Egala, but I was more focused on the crocodile tooth part."

"I'm not digging up anything from a graveyard," said Nadine.

"It could also be from a church or its grounds, I suppose," Suzette said.

"I could get some holy water and pour it on some dirt—would that make it sacred?" Nadine asked. "St. Paul's is right around the corner from the yoga studio."

"It might work. Andromeda said it's all about the intention," replied Jacqueline, suddenly feeling nervous and worried again. What if she didn't find the right stuff?

And how were the crones doing right now?

"I know all about intentions," said Nadine sagely. "Powerful stuff, intentions and affirmations."

"I have to go to Camellia House to get the athame, wormwood, elderberry, and butcher's-broom," said Jacqueline as the car turned onto the court. "And I want to see how the ZAP Ladies are doing."

It was worse than she feared.

No one came to the door when she knocked, and so Jacqueline had to let herself in. Nadine was on her heels, but Suzette had stayed in the car.

"Pietra?" Jacqueline called as she and her friend hurried into the house.

It was silent and still.

"Petey?" cried Nadine, her voice as taut as Jacqueline's body felt. "Zwyla!"

They found Pietra collapsed on the floor of the herbary. Whatever she'd been working on had been in a ceramic bowl. It had shattered, leaving a mess and an unfinished remedy pooling on the floor.

Jacqueline and Nadine managed to drag the older woman to a sofa in the living room, since it was closer, and Jacqueline knew there wasn't a third bed in the infirmary.

Pietra moaned, her eyelids fluttering, but they remained closed. Her pulse was weak and her breathing even weaker.

"What do we do?" Nadine said. Her eyes were wide and makeup was dripping down her face.

Jacqueline told her about the poultices, and they found some still simmering in the cauldron. While Nadine wrapped Pietra's wrists, head, abdomen, and ankles with them, Jacqueline hurried to the infirmary.

The situation there was even worse.

Andromeda felt cool and far too still to the touch. Zwyla's breathing was shallow, and her skin was damp and clammy. Neither of them gave any sort of response or reaction to being poked, prodded, or spoken to.

Tears filling her eyes, Jacqueline rushed from the back and nearly collided with Nadine—who was in no better shape.

"We've got to get the antidote made *now*," they both said.

Back in the car, they didn't need to give Suzette any details. She read the situation in their expressions.

"I'll get the holy water," said Nadine. "We can try to make sacred dirt—hell, I'll dig some up out of one of the flower pots on the altar. If that ain't sacred, or at least blessed, I don't know what is."

"I happen to have black cumin seeds," Suzette replied. "I put them on naan when I make it. But they're at home, so I've got to run there. Ten minutes, tops. I'll drop you at St. Paul's on the way, Nadine."

"I've got the butcher's-broom, wormwood, and the athame," said Jacqueline, who was hugely grateful Pietra had been using butcher's-broom earlier that day and thus helped her identify it. That spike of gratitude was the only flash of emotion she was able to feel other than pure tension and terror. Everything was riding on her. "I'll start to get everything together, so meet me in the apartment upstairs."

As if fear for the crones wasn't enough to terrify Jacqueline, it seemed Mother Nature wanted to make things worse. Her storm was violent and powerful, and even though it wasn't even six p.m., the sky was dark as night. The purplish-black cast over what would normally be well-lit daytime gave the street and its buildings an eerie and forbidding feel.

A huge spear of lightning jolted the sky, and there was a definite *crack* where it struck something. The thunder that crashed immediately following was sharp and loud and terrifying.

Jacqueline dashed into the bookshop, clutching her tote and its contents. She slammed the door behind her. As she did so, she happened to look up at the picture of the Witches Three over the entrance.

It looked different. *They* looked different.

Not healthy. Not at all.

Fear seizing her anew, Jacqueline spun and rushed down the hall toward the back of the house. She had to get a cedar branch from the tree in the back, and had nearly reached the door to outside when someone grabbed her arm, jolting her off balance.

"You're not going *anywhere*!" the figure growled.

It was Miss Gulch.

And she looked terrifying.

22

"Let me go!" cried Jacqueline.

"*No*," replied Miss Gulch, holding on to Jacqueline with a shockingly strong grip. Her face—already not altogether pleasant to look at—was a horrible, frightening sight. "You're coming with me."

Her eyes were wide, her mouth formed a strange shape reminiscent of that from *The Scream*, and her blade-like nose seemed somehow larger and even threatening. She was taller than Jacqueline and thus loomed over her—a dark and unsettling figure with her angular, contorted visage and dramatically flowing skirt. In that moment, Jacqueline shot back to her childhood, when the Wicked Witch of the West terrified her every time she came onscreen.

It was far, far worse in real life.

"No I'm not," said Jacqueline, struggling to shake Miss Gulch loose. *Please, no flying monkeys!*

"We have to get to the cellar!" cried Miss Gulch, dragging Jacqueline away from the stairs. "The storm! There's a horrible storm! We have to get away!"

And that was when Jacqueline realized the expression on Miss Gulch's face wasn't one of evil. It was one of pure, unadulterated terror.

Which made sense, didn't it? Because the last storm Miss Gulch experienced had not only taken her to a strange world, it turned her into a witch... and then she melted.

Still, knowing that didn't change the situation much. Jacqueline wanted—*needed*—to go upstairs to the apartment, and Almira Gulch was just as determined to get them both to safety in the cellar.

Which Jacqueline hadn't even realized existed until now.

Miss Gulch, whether due to fear or physical makeup, was far stronger than Jacqueline, and the next thing she knew, Jacqueline was being thrust toward a dark stairway that led down into even more darkness. The single light bulb at the top of the stairs was little comfort and offered only faint illumination as Miss Gulch pushed her toward the steps.

Deciding it was best to descend on her own rather than fall, Jacqueline hurried down the stairs. On the way, her fingers brushed a light switch and she fumbled it on. Fortunately, its light worked—far better than the single one at the top—and now she could at least see where she was going.

Down, down, down...

Jacqueline wasn't a fan of dark cellars because they usually contained spiders, cobwebs, and sometimes even rodents. They were damp and dark and filled with shadowy corners. But as it was, she had little choice, for Miss Gulch was practically stepping on her heels as she hurried her down the stairs. When a great boom of thunder shook the house, Miss Gulch shrieked and lunged, trying to push past Jacqueline. They collided, lost their respective balances, and tumbled to the bottom of the stairs.

Jacqueline sat up, hurting pretty much everywhere, out of breath, mad, and more than a little frightened. Was Miss Gulch going to keep her down here until the storm was over, or could she slip away and hurry back upstairs?

But before she could stand and find out, Jacqueline actually got a look at the cellar. And... it was not like any other cellar or unfinished basement she'd ever seen.

The floor was concrete and the walls were brick—that was normal, yes—but in the center of the space was a small, shallow pile of dirt. It took Jacqueline only a moment to realize it wasn't just dirt, it was the actual *earth*, exposed in the center of her basement.

And it was no accident, for the area was a perfect circle of about two feet in diameter. The opening to the ground was edged with smooth rocks set into the earth in a deliberate cobblestone sort of enclosure. When Jacqueline looked closer, she realized all of them were Petoskey stones, native to this area of Michigan due to a coral reef that had been displaced millions of years ago.

Beyond the frame of Petoskey stones was another edging created by bricks set into the concrete floor. But it wasn't only this open area of soil that caught Jacqueline's attention, for there was also a soft gurgling sound.

At first she thought the storm had caused her basement to leak or flood, but then she saw the small... well, "creek" was the only word that came to mind, running alongside the circular area of soil. It was tiny, this quiet river of water—no more than five inches wide—and it snaked its way from one wall to another, perpendicular one, then disappeared under the brick foundation.

As she stared at the very strange aspects of her

basement, Jacqueline was aware of a prickle of something... *a knowing,* or a shimmer of some dream, or memory—

A sudden, violent crash of thunder startled her back to the moment. Miss Gulch stifled a scream and threw herself at Jacqueline, nearly knocking her flat. The poor woman was shaking uncontrollably and very nearly in tears. Despite the desperation of her other problem, Jacqueline simply couldn't ignore Almira's terror, and she did her best to soothe Miss Gulch while continuing to observe her surroundings.

That niggle, that prickle in the back of Jacqueline's mind, became stronger as Miss Gulch calmed and quieted.

I've been here before. The thought exploded in her mind so suddenly that she actually gasped.

But it was true. Somehow, she'd been here, in this strange subterranean... whatever it was. Like in her dream...

The shock of this realization had Jacqueline extricating herself from the clinging hands of Miss Gulch —who was only slightly less desperate now that she was in safety—and rising to her feet.

Yes.

The memories were soft in her mind, but they *were* there.

She walked over to the exposed earth, remembering doing the same ever so long ago... remembering crouching on the Petoskey path around the thick, dark, loamy soil, brushing her fingers over the earth.

Sacred earth.

The words popped into her head and settled there, like a word balloon in a graphic novel, and she lowered herself in the same way she had done years be-

fore, gently touching the earth. A shimmer of
knowing, of memory, of something else became
stronger. She ran her fingertips through the rivulet of
running water and felt another surge of energy.

*Your house sits in a high-energy location on the earth.
Like a focal point, where several ley lines come together,*
Pietra had told her. *The Native Americans who lived here
—Mystera's mother's Anishinaabek tribe—recognized the
power and energy of this location.*

And here, preserved, protected, and made acces-
sible for decades, perhaps even centuries—or millen-
nia!—was the center of that energy: in the soil, the
gently burbling water... and the tree root.

Jacqueline rose, feeling as if she were in a sort of
trance or somnambulant event, and her feet took her
to the wall of the cellar nearest to the patch of soil.

Yes.

There it was: part of a tree trunk, jutting from the
wall as if it had been caught peeking into the room. A
piece of its root erupted from the concrete floor—not
as if it had thrust up and broken through the concrete
on its own, but as if the concrete had been poured re-
spectfully, protectively around it. The opening was
framed with more Petoskey stones.

Dazed, she remembered more...

Jacqueline moved closer to the tree that somehow
grew within her basement, along with a creek and an
open patch of earth.

Yes, she thought again, reaching out to touch the
tree. *I remember this.*

A large swatch of bark had been peeled away from
the trunk, leaving a portion of the wood exposed. It
was difficult to make out the handprints that had been
imposed on that smooth piece of what Jacqueline
knew was a cedar tree... the same ancient cedar that

grew just outside the back of the house, shading the courtyard. The handprints on the cedar were faded and irregular, but she recognized them for what they were *because she remembered*. There were many prints from many women over the decades—at least two dozen. Some were so old they were hardly noticeable.

Jacqueline remembered exactly where she'd made hers... near the ground, so it was easy for a young girl to reach.

Now, she pressed her adult hand over the irregular red print she'd made when she was young—five? four?—and a little zip of energy shot through her, heating the stippled marks on her cheek.

Now I understand.

Now I remember.

The dreams she'd been having were memories from the time she'd been here before... when she pressed her hand into some blood-red dye and then made a print onto the living, breathing cedar tree, joining that of many other hands before hers.

Her handprint was by far the smallest of them; the rest were adult-sized. Hers was obviously made as a child... why was that? Because whoever prompted and helped her to make it—Cuddy Stone?—had feared she'd never return to do it as an adult?

Even now, she didn't remember coming here—how she got here, who brought her, when it happened—but she knew she had.

When she pulled her hand away from where it pressed against her child's print, her palm and fingers were stained red. Just like in her dream.

But more importantly, the child-sized print on the cedar trunk was no longer child-sized, but was now the same size as her adult hand.

I'm home. The words popped into her head.

There's no place like home.

You've always had the power to return home, Dorothy.

With a shiver of comprehension, Jacqueline looked at Miss Gulch, who was still huddled in a corner near the bottom of the stairs. *Thanks,* she thought with a great rush of emotion. For she realized if the spinsterish woman hadn't forced her down to the cellar, it might have been weeks or even months before Jacqueline found it. If ever. She didn't like cellars.

And now that she was here, she knew exactly where to get sacred earth, as well as water for steeping the infusion... both of which she needed for the antidote for the ZAP Ladies.

A little prickle ran over her shoulders. The timing of Miss Gulch's arrival was pretty, well, coincidental.

Or was it?

Feeling suddenly, strangely sympathetic toward Miss Gulch, Jacqueline turned to her. "Are you alright?" she asked Miss Gulch, who seemed to be in pain rather than merely frightened now.

"It's my leg," she replied, and that was when Jacqueline got her first good look at Miss Gulch's leg. "I bumped it when we fell."

Jacqueline recoiled in horror when she saw the scarred, mangled mess of the spinster's left calf, which was visible above her folded-down socks. No wonder she had been favoring her leg! "Oh my goodness! What happened?"

Miss Gulch narrowed her eyes as Jacqueline crouched next to her. "I told you—and everyone—it was that little dog! He chased my cat up the tree and then he attacked me."

"He certainly did," Jacqueline said, horrified at the ugly scars and red gashes on Miss Gulch's leg. The injury wasn't just a little nip, or even a solid bite. It was a *mauling*. Jacqueline could hardly believe Miss Gulch could walk, let alone ride a bike. "Have you seen a doctor?"

"Yes, of course, and the sheriff too," replied Miss Gulch in her staccato manner. "That's why I've been looking for him—that little dog. He's dangerous, and he needs to be destroyed before he does worse to someone else."

Jacqueline's heart gave a little lurch. She hated the thought of destroying any animal, but Miss Gulch had a serious point. What Toto had done to her leg was enough to have any dog euthanized—no matter how cute, or how insistent his owner was that he wasn't dangerous and would change, or how much he was loved. It was a tragedy on all counts. "Did you have stitches?"

"Surgery," replied Miss Gulch, reaching absently to rub her wounds, which appeared to be several weeks old. "Had to pull several layers of skin and muscle back into place. One hundred fifty-three stitches, they were. All because of that ratty little dog."

Jacqueline shook her head. "I'm very sorry that happened to you." She really was, and, to be honest, she was filled with disappointment and anger at the Gale family for being so dismissive of Miss Gulch's complaint.

True, the sheriff should have been the one coming to take away Toto, but the way the story went, no one seemed to care about Miss Gulch's injury or that Toto had been very vicious in his attack. Instead, the Gales didn't even apologize to Miss Gulch, but they did insult her.

"And that little girl—Dorothy," went on Miss Gulch. "Why, she called me a wicked witch! And then do you know what happened?" she said, leaning toward Jacqueline. Her gleaming eyes were wide and tortured. "*I became one.* A witch. That little girl must be the most powerful witch of all if she simply called me a witch—and the next thing I knew, I *was* one. She *made* me a witch. She cursed me, spelled me, did *something* to me!"

For the first time, Almira Gulch sounded tearful, and frightened and *hurt*, instead of mean and accusatory.

And for the first time in her entire life of knowing the story of *The Wizard of Oz*, Jacqueline felt compassion for poor, abused, and misunderstood Miss Gulch.

She'd had every right to report Toto, and the county had every right to remove the dangerous dog.

And even though euthanizing any animal was horrific, sometimes it was the only option. At the very, very least, the Gales should have acknowledged the attack on their neighbor.

And Miss Gulch had another point, too—Dorothy had called her a witch and literally turned her into one.

Intentions. Words. Curses...

Before Jacqueline could follow that train of thought, she heard a commotion from above. It sounded like an army trooping through the house, but she suspected it was only Nadine and Suzette, and possibly Danvers and Hudson.

"Down here!" she called, pulling to her feet to hurry over to the bottom of the stairs. "In the cellar."

Moments later, Nadine and Suzette were clomping down the stairs.

"What are you doing down—*Whoa*." Nadine stopped so suddenly at the bottom of the steps that

Suzette nearly ran into her. Both of them were gawking.

"This is... different," said Suzette. She glanced over at Miss Gulch, who was still rubbing her leg and watching them warily. "All of it."

"Is that a *tree*?" Nadine asked, already walking over to the jutting trunk. "It's going to destroy your foundation."

"No," Jacqueline said. "I don't think it will. The house was built around it—around all of this."

Her friends looked at her curiously, but didn't ask. The only other explanation Jacqueline felt compelled to offer was: "I'm pretty sure this qualifies as sacred earth." She crouched next to the exposed ground and scooped up a little of the loamy soil.

"I'll take your word for it," said Nadine. "But I have holy water and flower pot dirt from St. Paul's if we need that."

"And this is a cedar tree, so we've got that covered," Jacqueline said. "It's time to get to work."

For the first time since she'd arrived at Three Tomes, she felt in control. She felt like she understood.

She *knew*.

The six marks on her face were gently warm, and when Jacqueline reached up to touch them, she felt a tiny blip of energy.

It was time.

23

Jacqueline had already decided she would make the antidote for the curse in the flat upstairs. And if she'd had any concerns about Egala giving her a fake recipe that might somehow transfer the ownership of the bookshop, or banish her from it, they evaporated when she saw her handprint in the cellar.

This was her place. She knew it, and so did the house... so did every entity and powerful spirit that lived here.

Nothing could change that.

Nadine and Suzette accompanied her up from the cellar, and when she realized the storm was nearly over, Miss Gulch decided to emerge as well. Uninvited, she followed them all the way up to the flat. Jacqueline didn't really mind the intrusion, now that she was viewing Miss Gulch in a different way. When the gaunt, grumpy woman was cuddling Sebastian—as she was now—she looked serene and what one might even describe as handsome.

Once they got to the third floor, the former Wicked Witch sank onto one of the chairs at the small dining table and murmured to Sebastian while scratching between his ears.

As she, Nadine, and Suzette gathered in the kitchen area of the flat, Jacqueline glanced into the living room at the mirror where Crusilla had been lurking, but she saw no sign of movement in the glass.

Something had to be done about *her* as well.

But first... the cure for the ZAP Ladies.

Feeling surprisingly calm and assured now, Jacqueline followed the instructions Egala had given her, including smashing the crocodile tooth into a powder—which took a considerable amount of muscle. She had to use the athame to chop sprigs of cedar, wormwood shavings, and butcher's-broom, then steep those ingredients along with the sacred earth in boiling water.

She'd brought some of the water from the tiny creek in the bottom of her cellar and added that to a small pot on the stove, then, following the instructions, stirred in the other ingredients one by one. As she did so, Jacqueline somehow knew to touch the marks on her cheek each time, and thought a strong intention of *healing*. She was rewarded with a subtle sparkle of energy with each step.

The crocodile tooth powder was the last to be added, and again, Jacqueline thought of words and intentions and meanings as she prepared to add the final ingredient.

Words and intentions.

Words and intentions could be very powerful.

Jacqueline stirred the mixture and carefully poured in the ground-up reptile tooth, closing her eyes as she did so. She tried to let her mind go blank of everything other than healing and white light and peace for the ZAP Ladies.

But words and phrases popped into her head.

She called me a witch, and I became one.

Women are basically useless after forty-five.
The wise-woman phase is the most powerful.
It's the most powerful.
You're the most powerful.

Jacqueline opened her eyes, those words ringing in her head: *You're the most powerful.*

And suddenly, an audible little *poof!* of smoke erupted from the mélange she was stirring.

"It's done," she said, opening her eyes.

"Sure looks that way," said Nadine in a hushed voice. "Now what?"

"I guess we take this over to Camellia House and get the ladies to drink it," Jacqueline said, suddenly realizing she didn't actually know what to do next. Egala hadn't told her anything more than how to make the infusion.

She was pouring the concoction into a jar when Nadine suddenly grabbed her arm. Jacqueline looked up to see Egala standing there.

"So you did it," Egala said. She wore a sneer that looked far more victorious than Jacqueline liked. "You actually got the crocodile tooth. Brava."

"How did you get in here?" asked Jacqueline. She shoved the jar quickly at Suzette. "Take it," she muttered, hoping it wasn't too late for the ZAP Ladies, then turned her attention back to Egala.

The intruding witch shrugged. "I just walked up. Back door was open." She looked around. "You did it, but—"

"But nothing," Jacqueline said, seeing from the corner of her eye that Suzette had disappeared toward the stairs near the kitchen. "The cure is going to Camellia House for the ladies, and if they don't recover, I'm going to come after you." She bared her teeth in what she hoped was a threatening smile, though she'd never threatened anyone in her life (except Josh, with castration, after she found out about his cheating). For added emphasis, she touched the marks on her cheek.

Egala's sly smile faded. "Well, you can't blame me if it doesn't work. Whatever is going on with them isn't my fault."

"You put a life-leeching hex on Andromeda," Jacqueline said flatly. "You admitted it."

"Yes, yes, maybe so, but it wasn't... Whatever's happening to them isn't my fault. The h-hex I used wasn't at full strength, and it wouldn't leak from her to anyone else—"

"No, it wouldn't." The calm intonation came from the mirror above the fireplace, and everyone turned to look at it. "I did that. Just like I took care of Henbert."

"Crusilla!" cried Egala, stepping back. "What are you doing in—"

But she never finished her sentence. Something snapped from the looking glass—a whiplike sound that moved the air—and Egala collapsed like a broken tent.

"And there we are," said Crusilla from her mirrored vantage point above the mantel. "At last. All taken care of. With no help from *you*," she said, turning her attention to Jacqueline. She looked angry. "I told you to get rid of her."

"Is she dead?" Jacqueline asked, wondering how the hell she was going to explain another dead body to Detective Massermey.

"Don't worry about her," said Crusilla, waving her hand. "She's weak and ineffectual. Now, you and I... we can work together—"

"That would be a hard pass from me," said Jacqueline. "I'm not going to be working with you or for you or on behalf of you or anything. This is my bookshop, my house, and *my handprint* sealed the contract on the sacred cedar more than forty years ago."

Crusilla's eyes widened. She appeared stunned. "You... How do you know about that?"

Jacqueline glanced over at Miss Gulch, who had just lifted her face, interrupting her ministrations to Sebastian.

"Because of her," Jacqueline said. "And now I want you to leave. Begone!" she said, giving a dramatic flourish. "Begone from my house!"

"I'm not leaving," said Crusilla with an ugly laugh. "You can't make me go."

"Take down the mirror," cried Nadine. "Let's get it out of here, then she can't—"

But when she reached for the mirror, great, shocking sparks flew from the silver frame. Nadine fell away, crying out in shock and pain, rubbing her hands as if they'd been burned.

"No," said Crusilla, her hamburger mole jumping with fury, "you can't remove me. I'm here, and here I'll be forever."

Nadine had darted over toward the kitchen, out of direct range of the mirror—though Jacqueline wasn't certain there was anyplace safe from Crusilla.

Before Jacqueline could speak, she felt movement behind her. She turned to see Miss Gulch standing there, her eyes fixed on the mirror. "Dorothy...?" Her voice had gone high and tight. "*Dorothy Gale?*"

Jacqueline did a double take. What?

Miss Gulch moved closer to the mirror, staring at it. "Why, Dorothy Gale," she said, sounding like the Wicked Witch of the West again...and angry. "Look at you...all grown up...while you left me turned into a puddle of mist."

Was Crusilla actually Dorothy Gale? That was... impossible. She didn't look anything like Judy Garland, even thirty years older.

"What are you talking about?" cried Crusilla. She actually sounded frightened. Maybe she recognized how powerful the Wicked Witch actually was. "My name isn't Dorothy."

But Miss Gulch ignored her, moving closer to the mirror. "I'd never forget you, Dorothy. Never. How could I? You destroyed me." She spoke as if she were in a trance, or deep into her memories. "You and your little dog destroyed me."

"No, I didn't do anything like that!" Crusilla said desperately. "I've never seen you before."

"I had a looking glass once... I could see into it— see what was happening wherever I liked... It was very powerful." Miss Gulch murmured in an eerie voice.

"I want to destroy it," said Jacqueline, suddenly inspired. "Tell me how to destroy the looking glass, Almira. Do you know how?"

The Wicked Witch of the West looked at her and cackled—she laughed so darkly and evilly that, for a moment, Jacqueline thought she'd made a grave mistake.

And then she realized that Miss Gulch was actually looking at Crusilla—that her laughter was directed at the entity in the mirror. "I certainly do," she replied.

"What are you saying?" cried Crusilla, and suddenly sparks and flames began to shoot and sizzle from the mirror. Jacqueline dodged them, vaulting over the couch and huddling behind it as Miss Gulch stood facing the onslaught from the looking glass. But nothing seemed to harm her.

"All you have to do," said Miss Gulch as her hair

began to fly loose from the severe bun at the back of her head, "is to throw salt at it." She cackled again, sending shivers down Jacqueline's spine.

"Noool!" cried Crusilla.

But Jacqueline and Nadine were already stumbling over each other to get into the kitchen.

"Thank heavens," Jacqueline cried as she seized a salt shaker left behind by Cuddy Stone.

What the Witch Left, she thought suddenly, remembering the book that had attracted her earlier today. *Whoa.*

She took off the top of the salt shaker and rushed from the kitchen into a storm of sparks and flames.

"Would you like to do the honors?" she asked Miss Gulch—partly because she wasn't certain *she* could withstand the onslaught from the mirror, and partly because she felt like Miss Gulch should have her revenge.

She snatched the shaker from Jacqueline and, ignoring the cries and threats and pleading from the woman in the mirror, poured a great handful into her palm.

Then she threw it at the mirror with great gusto. The salt grains made quiet pelting sounds as they hit the glass. There was a moment that seemed frozen in time, then a wicked *crack*, worse than any thunder Jacqueline had ever heard, snapped in the room.

The glass shattered so violently that Jacqueline and Nadine had to duck again. Silence reigned, and when Jacqueline rose from behind the sofa, she saw a very calm, very composed Miss Gulch standing there holding Sebastian.

"At last," said Miss Gulch, tears in her eyes. "At last, I have my revenge."

24

Jacqueline and Nadine looked around at the fragments of mirror, glittering on the rug, the sofa, the table, and even the kitchen counter.

"Wow," said Jacqueline. "Thank you, Miss Gulch."

"It was my pleasure," Miss Gulch replied, back to her calm, quiet self. Sebastian had returned to her arms as well, and to Jacqueline's surprise, Max was sitting on a bookshelf. He actually looked approving of the situation.

Just then, she heard footsteps—many of them—approaching from the back hallway.

"Well, now, then, luv," said Mrs. Hudson as she bustled into view. "What's been going on here?"

"Inappropriate disorder and disturbance," replied Mrs. Danvers with a disdainful sniff. "Clearly."

Mrs. Hudson responded with a retort about hoity-toity, judgmental housekeepers, which devolved into a spat about housekeepers and landladies and who did what, but Jacqueline hardly noticed—for behind the two characters were Zwyla, Andromeda, and Pietra, looking hale and hearty and a bit smug.

"You're all right!" Jacqueline cried, and before she

realized what she was doing, she'd flung herself at Pietra for a hug. "Oh, thank heavens!"

She embraced Andromeda as well, but was a little too intimidated to offer a hug to the tall, regal Zwyla. Still, Zwyla patted her on the shoulder and gave her a warm smile. "Thank you," she said with great sincerity. "Thank you for what you did for us."

"I'm so relieved it worked!" Jacqueline replied. And she *was*.

"And so the mirror is gone now," said Andromeda, looking at the empty silver frame. "So no more Crusilla."

"No more Crusilla in the mirror, anyway," said Zwyla. "I'm certain she'll not give up that easily."

The low rumble of a familiar voice coming from the back hallway snatched Jacqueline's attention from that ominous statement.

Crap! Massermey was here, and Egala was...

Gone.

Jacqueline stared at the last place she'd seen the witch, but the body had apparently been alive enough to remove itself during the melee, which was a relief.

Suzette and Massermey appeared, and Jacqueline offered a weak smile. He still looked pissed about the crocodile incident.

"Hello, Detective," she said innocently. "What brings you here?"

"There were reports of fire here," he said. "Someone saw what looked like serious flashing and blazes from the window, and I thought I'd better check it out."

Jacqueline declined to point out that it was hardly the job of a homicide detective to check into such incidents. "That was very kind of you," she replied warmly. "As you can see, everything is just fine here."

As she spoke, she saw his gaze travel over the room, taking in the spread of glass, the singed sofas and burn marks on the rug, the torn pillows and knocked-over chairs.

"As I can see," he replied dryly. Then he looked at her. "Are you certain everything is all right?"

"Yes, yes, of course—and you can see that they're all just fine and healthy now too..." Jacqueline said, prepared to gesture to the ZAP Ladies... but they were all gone.

In fact, she realized she and Detective Massermey were somehow alone in the apartment.

He didn't seem to mind. "If you're certain," he said after a moment of scrutinizing the room, and then her.

"Yes, truly." Jacqueline suddenly felt nervous and yet energetic and alive at the same time. This time, his eyes didn't seem quite so cold and interrogative.

Massermey nodded. "All right, then. I guess there's no reason for me to stay—there are power lines down everywhere and accidents on the highway, and so on." But he didn't seem to be in a hurry to leave.

"It was a bad storm," she said, thinking not only of what happened outside, but what happened here in the flat.

"What did happen in here?" he asked. "Ms. Finch?"

She gave him a bashful smile. "You can call me Jacqueline."

He smiled back, his beard curving slowly. "I will. But I'd still like to know..." He stopped himself and shook his head with a grimace. "Maybe I don't want to know after all."

She looked up at him. "Maybe you don't."

"All right, then," he replied, flashing a smile. "But

will you promise not to climb into anymore crocodile
pens?"

"With great fervor."

He gave her a full-blown grin, which made her
stomach flutter. "All right, then, Jacqueline. And once
again... welcome to Camellia Court. Let's just try to
keep things... quiet here from now on, hmm?"

Jacqueline glanced at the empty mirror. "I fully
intend to."

"She was so completely misunderstood," said
Jacqueline, still incensed about the irresponsible way
the Gales had treated Miss Gulch. She was talking to
herself, but she didn't care.

It was the next morning and she was alone in the
bookshop—at least, as far as she knew.

Mrs. Danvers and Mrs. Hudson had taken it upon
themselves to clean up the apartment, where Jacqueline had decided she was, in fact, going to live. Why
not, now that the mirror was gone?

After Miles (he'd told her to call him that) left last
night, Jacqueline had gone over to Camellia House
and hung out with the fully recovered ZAP Ladies, Nadine, and Suzette. She'd been forced to drink tea, of
course, but this time she rather enjoyed it.

No one had noticed Egala leaving the flat, but the
fact that there wasn't a trace of her indicated that
Crusilla hadn't killed her as well as her brother, for
which Jacqueline was supremely grateful.

Nadine and Suzette had told the crones about
what was in Jacqueline's basement, and all three of
them nodded with approval. Pietra's eyes actually
seemed to be glistening with tears.

"I told you Cuddy knew what she was doing," she said, patting Jacqueline's hand and blinking rapidly.

"Was it she who... who brought me down there originally? To make the handprint?" Jacqueline asked. "I still don't have any really clear memory. But I did call my mother, and she said that when I was four, she and my father went on a trip to the Grand Canyon, and I stayed with a distant cousin of hers while they were gone. Maybe that's when I made the visit here."

"Yes," replied Andromeda.

And Jacqueline realized she needed to ask nothing more.

"Thank you again for your selfless acts," said Zwyla. She was sitting at the head of the herbary table and had wrapped a shiny royal-blue scarf around her head. "It was your willingness to do what you did—to save lives, and not to harm them, as Crusilla encouraged you to do—that solidified your connection to Three Tomes."

"If you hadn't done that, your handprint wouldn't have changed," said Pietra eagerly. "And you wouldn't have seen any of the other handprints on the tree."

Jacqueline nodded. She knew something major had happened in the cellar, but she also recognized that some sort of divine providence had helped her in the herpetarium. That plank bridge had been just a little *too* convenient.

Nonetheless, she was happy to take the information at face value. And to move on.

She hoped now things would settle down and she could concentrate on running Three Tomes, presumably with the assistance of Danvers and Hudson.

Now, the morning after, in her shop and alone, Jacqueline was still mulling over Miss Gulch and her involvement in everything that had happened. Almira had told her she didn't know what she was doing here, but now Jacqueline thought she understood.

Miss Gulch needed her revenge, her closure—and in destroying the mirror where Crusilla lived, she'd not only achieved that but helped Jacqueline as well.

She'd actually helped Jacqueline in other ways, but it was the "she called me a witch and I *became* one" that stuck with her.

Words and intentions had power. Jacqueline had no idea how much power until she came to Three Tomes. And maybe it had to do with being a wise woman—after all, Miss Gulch had to be of an age to be a powerful crone as well, with or without Dorothy's curse.

And sadly, perhaps dear Stacey had ingrained such misconceptions into Jacqueline's psyche that she otherwise never would have broken out of a life she thought she'd loved, but that was actually restrictive and repressed.

You are most powerful now.

Jacqueline had no misconception that she was a witch herself; all she knew was that she was here, in her family's house, where she belonged. And that it was no accident that three elements that the Anishinaabek believed were sacred—earth, water, and cedar —were protected and respected here.

Her telephone dinged with an alert.

She looked down and saw that Wendy had texted again. And, to her surprise, a phone call and voice-mail had come in sometime this morning.

Jacqueline recognized the phone number, and she froze.

The Chicago Public Library administration office.

She stared at the voice-mail notification, and then she smiled... and deleted it without even listening.

Whatever it was, it didn't matter any longer. She didn't work there, and never would again... even if they begged her to come back.

Humming to herself, Jacqueline carried a stack of books to the front counter.

To her surprise, a single tome was sitting there where nothing had been only a short time ago. She recognized it: it was the same book that had randomly fallen off the shelf the other night—the night before Miss Gulch showed up.

This time, the book was closed.

Jacqueline picked it up hesitantly, looking around as if to make certain the character herself wasn't there and wouldn't be offended... and that was when she saw the small print below the title: *The movie adaptation.*

Well that explained *a lot.*

She hadn't seen Miss Gulch since last night, and perhaps this was her way of saying goodbye.

Jacqueline smiled to herself and, leaving the other books on the counter, picked up *The Wizard of Oz* movie adaptation. It would go back on the shelf where it belo—

Thud.

Jacqueline stilled. Being a librarian and bookshop owner, she knew exactly what a book falling to the floor sounded like.

Again? Really?

Jacqueline smothered a pained groan and shook her head.

Across the room, Max and Sebastian each sat on their own windowsills in the front, looking at her with their arrogant cat eyes.

Jacqueline glowered at them and said, "I'm not

going to go look at it. It can stay there all year, but I'm not going to look at it."

And Max lifted his chin and winked.

25

"Am I glad *that's* over," said Andromeda, glancing out the window toward the bookshop. "I was getting tired of playing Sleeping Beauty."

"You did a wonderful job," replied Pietra, patting her friend's hand. "And so did you, Z. If I didn't know any better, I'd have thought you really were about to meet your demise. The sweat and everything was very believable. And you must have done something to give your skin a greenish cast, Andi."

"Of course," said Andromeda. She ran her hands through her hair, and suddenly it was no longer saggy and messy but perky and spiky. This time there was a hint of pink at the tips.

"The whole point was to worry Jacqueline, and it worked," said Zwyla.

"To worry her, and to push her into action," Andromeda added. "She's spent her entire adult life looking up things for people instead of *doing* things—for herself or anyone else."

"And believing that bullshit from her friend," said Pietra sadly. "I sure wish Stacey was still around so we could set her straight. Useless after forty-five? That's the biggest pile of bullshit I've ever heard."

"No kidding," said Andromeda, just as vehemently. "But I actually feel sorry for her for believing that."

"I admit, it didn't take Jacqueline as long as I thought it would," said Zwyla thoughtfully. "Once she had it out with Egala and decided to get the crocodile tooth, things moved along pretty quickly."

"She's a smart cookie, our Jacqueline," said Pietra, feeling as proud as if she were Jacqueline's mother. In a way, she supposed, she was. All three of them were.

"Should we tell her?" said Andromeda.

"Certainly not," replied Zwyla, looking even more intimidating than usual.

"I think we should," said Pietra.

"You think we should tell Jacqueline that it was all a test? That she risked her life trying to save us when we really didn't need to be saved at all?" Zwyla said, her eyes narrowing. "That won't go over well."

"Let's not call it a test," said Andromeda. "It was more like an... an orientation. You know, like when a company hires a new employee."

Pietra rolled her eyes. "I forgot you had a few years in corporate America."

"I try to forget about that too," said Andromeda. "Worst three years of my life. We had to read *employee manuals*. And *follow* them." She shuddered.

"At least you didn't have to work in a grade school cafeteria," Pietra told her. "Do you know how many times I had to wash mashed potatoes and peas out of my hair?"

"But it was worth it," said Zwyla. "We all did our time—some of us literally," she added with a nod at Pietra, who had in fact done time (but not because of working in a school cafeteria), "in order to become the wise women we are today. Life experience is what makes a crone a crone."

"Yes. You can't be a crone at twenty-five," Andromeda said sagely. "Or even thirty-five. Or forty!"

"It takes life experience *and* determination," Pietra said. "Not to mention a loss of estrogen to make you *really* not give a shit about what anyone else thinks."

"True dat," said Andromeda. She gave them a cat-like smile. "Speaking of hormones... how long do you think it'll be until Detective Massive Hands gets them on our delightful Miss Jacqueline Finch?"

"I don't know, but I can't wait to see it," said Pietra, beaming. "It's going to be epic."

"You're not going to *watch*," Zwyla said, horrified, looking down at the mirror on the table. "Absolutely not!"

Pietra waved off her friend's outrage with a flap of her hand. "He's already smitten with her—oh, I just love that word, smitten. It sounds so incredibly innocent... when Miles Massermey evokes anything *but* innocence," she said in a purr.

"The way he vaulted over the crocodile fence to get to her—even my old lady bits got a bit of a quiver," said Andromeda. "And the way he smiled when she told him to call her Jacqueline... swoony-McSwoon!"

"I know! If it had been anyone else on the other side of that fence, I doubt he would have been so—so John Wayne-ish," said Pietra. "Speaking of which, I had a dream last night about Lionel Richie riding the range à la John Wayne. And he swept me up in his saddle—poor guy, but at least he didn't break his back—and rode me off into the sunset with him. Talk about a quiver... and I don't mean for arrows!"

Zwyla had lost her composure by now and was chuckling in her low, husky way. "You two... all talk and no action. Your lady bits don't shrivel up at eighty. I oughta know," she added, lifting one slender brow.

"TMI, TMI!" cried Pietra, then collapsed into squeaking giggles.

"Sheesh, Petey, you really need to lay off smoking my herbs," Andromeda said, shaking her head.

"But you make such a good blend," replied Pietra.

"*Anyway*," said Zwyla. "We are not going to tell Jacqueline about our little... deception, all right?"

"But what if Massermey mentions it to her? He did come over here after all, to check on us," Pietra said. "And none of us were at death's door when he was here."

"That was a risk, but we couldn't have him calling an ambulance or something," Andromeda said. "Which he'd probably think he needed to do, being a cop and all."

"And an all-around good guy," added Pietra. "I told you he'd go for Jacqueline instead of Suzette. She's so much more his type. But what about Egala? Eventually, Jacqueline's going to realize she's not strictly the Professor Umbrage type she pretended to be."

"We'll deal with that when we have to. And it's not as if Egala is a saint either," Andromeda said. "After all, she *did* hex me—just not as seriously as Jacqueline believed."

"Well, we certainly can't trust her," said Zwyla. "She still thinks she should have had the bookshop."

"Is her handprint on the sacred cedar? *No*," said Pietra. "So the shop isn't going to be Egala's, and it never was. Cuddy—and Mystera—chose Jacqueline a long time ago, and Egala is just going to have to deal with it."

"All right, well, now that that's all taken care of, we can get along with our regular lives," said Zwyla.

"Ooh, it's going to be so great having Jacqueline

here, and the bookshop open again," said Pietra, her eyes glinting. "Such fun."

"I can't wait to see how it all goes now that Jacqueline has settled in." Andromeda gave Zwyla a catlike grin. "Do you know which book it's going to be?"

"No," replied Zwyla with a roll of her eyes. "That's up to the Fates to decide. You know that."

"But can't we help influence them just a little?" asked Pietra. "I vote for *The Scarlet Pimpernel*. He's just so *dashing*! And clever!"

"What about someone from *Dracula*?" said Andromeda. "It could be very interesting if Dr. van Helsing shows up—or better yet, Count Dracula himself."

"There's an idea... maybe he'd chase Danvers away," said Zwyla.

"Dracula would be a little too dark for my taste," said Pietra with a little shudder. "Why do you always go for the dark ones, Andi? Remember when you were trying to get Dr. Jekyll to visit?"

"Well *he'd* be far more interesting than your pick —*Almanzo Wilder*," retorted Andromeda. "I mean, Almanzo was a nice guy, but *booooring*. What's he gonna do if he shows up—teach us how to store ice in a sawdust-filled icehouse? How to break a horse?"

Zwyla shook her head, chuckling. "It's not up to us. You know that. It's about who comes to the bookshop and needs to be saved or helped or guided."

"One thing we know," Pietra said, "we've got the right person in Three Tomes. Whoever shows up, Jacqueline's the one who'll 'get' it."

"Thank the stars—and Cuddy Stone—for that," said Andromeda.

BEFORE YOU GO...

~

Don't miss any news from Colleen, plus get a *free* short novel,
exclusive only to newsletter subscribers.

Subscribe to her monthly newsletter for sneak peeks, news, freebies, and behind-the-scenes looks at her projects.

Click here: cgbks.com/news

Prefer not to get messages in your email?
Sign up for SMS/Text messages and help keep your
inbox clear!

Just type in 38470 for the phone number,
and then type COLLEEN in the message space!

ABOUT THE AUTHOR

 **Colleen Gleason** is an award-winning, New York Times and USA Today best-selling author. She's written more than forty novels in a variety of genres—truly, something for everyone!

She loves to hear from readers, so feel free to find her online.

~

Get SMS/Text alerts for any
New Releases or **Promotions!**

Text: **COLLEEN** to **38470**

(You will only receive a single message when Colleen has a new release or title on sale. *We promise.*)

~

If you would like SMS/Text alerts for any **Events** or book signings Colleen is attending,
Text: **MEET** to **38470**

~

Subscribe to Colleen's non-spam newsletter for other updates, news, sneak peeks, and special offers!
http://cgbks.com/news

Connect with Colleen online:
www.colleengleason.com
books@colleengleason.com

ALSO BY COLLEEN GLEASON

The Gardella Vampire Hunters

Victoria

The Rest Falls Away
Rises the Night
The Bleeding Dusk
When Twilight Burns
As Shadows Fade

Macey/Max Denton

Roaring Midnight
Raging Dawn
Roaring Shadows
Raging Winter
Roaring Dawn

The Draculia Vampires

Dark Rogue: The Vampire Voss
Dark Saint: The Vampire Dimitri
Dark Vixen: The Vampire Narcise
Vampire at Sea: Tales from the Draculia Vampires

Wicks Hollow Series
Ghost Story Romance & Mystery

Sinister Summer

Sinister Secrets

Sinister Shadows

Sinister Sanctuary

Sinister Stage

Sinister Lang Syne

Three Tomes Bookshop

Paranormal Women's Fiction

Tomes, Scones & Crones

Hearses, Verses & Curses (2022)

~

Stoker & Holmes Books

(for ages 12-adult)

The Clockwork Scarab

The Spiritglass Charade

The Chess Queen Enigma

The Carnelian Crow

The Zeppelin Deception

The Castle Garden Series

Lavender Vows

A Whisper of Rosemary

Sanctuary of Roses

A Lily on the Heath

The Envy Chronicles

Beyond the Night

Embrace the Night

Abandon the Night

Night Beckons

Night Forbidden

Night Resurrected

Tempted by the Night (only available to newsletter subscribers; sign up here: http://cgbks.com/news)

～

The Lincoln's White House Mystery Series

(writing as C. M. Gleason)

Murder in the Lincoln White House

Murder in the Oval Library

Murder at the Capitol

The Marina Alexander Adventure Novels

(writing as C. M. Gleason)

Siberian Treasure

Amazon Roulette

Sanskrit Cipher

～

The Phyllida Bright Mysteries

(writing as Colleen Cambridge)

Murder at Mallowan Hall (Oct 2021)

CPSIA information can be obtained
at www.ICGtesting.com
Printed in the USA
LVHW050906121021
700211LV00010B/1009